PRUSSIAN COUNTERPOINT

A Joseph Haydn Mystery

NUPUR TUSTIN

Foiled Plots Press

Prussian Counterpoint
A Joseph Haydn Mystery
Foiled Plots Press

ISBN 978-0-9982430-4-7

Typesetting services by BOOKOW.COM

Acknowledgments

In the writing of this, the third Haydn Mystery, I've relied upon a number of people whose generous support made my work far easier than I expected it to be.

Solveigh Rumpf-Dorner of the Österreichische Nationalbibliothek never fails to be available when I have a question about Haydn and his times. She is a resource I can count on.

Marlies Sell of the Stadt-und Landesbibliothek in Potsdam helped to clarify questions about the city in the time of Frederick the Great.

Mark Brownlow, who hosts the Visiting Vienna website, shared innumerable resources on sleigh rides in Vienna and the races that both the nobility and commoners held in Haydn's time.

Miriam Posner helped me access articles on espionage, in particular Nadine Akkerman's research on the subject, from the UCLA library.

Fellow writer Jane Gorman helped with a crucial decision on the manuscript when I was at a crossroads.

Historians Tim Blanning and Giles MacDonogh were kind enough to provide detailed answers to questions I had about Frederick the Great. Their biographies of the King were an invaluable resource for this novel.

Richard Gibson of Ted Gibson Frames Inc. in Los Angeles generously spent hours with my husband and me, showing us eighteenth-century frames and explaining the way they were manufactured.

Last but most certainly not least, Professor Gerhard Strasser of Penn State University was infinitely generous with both his time and his expertise. Our prolonged correspondence over the summer of 2018 facilitated my understanding of espionage techniques, in particular of steganography.

Without that understanding, a large part of this novel simply could not have been written.

But research is not the only area where a novelist needs help. I'd also like to thank friend and author K.B. Inglee for introducing my novels to her local radio station, WRTI. Radio host Bliss Michelson was kind enough to mention the Haydn Mysteries to his listeners. I am grateful for that.

But it is to my husband, Matt, that I owe the biggest debt of gratitude. Your support and strength have made my life as a mystery writer possible. I love you deeply and forever.

Overture

THE letter filled her with more foreboding than she cared to admit. It had been months since she had recovered from the smallpox that had nearly killed her, but she still felt its effects. Unable to walk more than a few paces before falling into a chair in fatigue. So short of breath, the windows of her apartment were kept open even in the winter.

The thought of facing another intrigue made her chest constrict, as though an iron fist had closed around her lungs, preventing her from taking another breath. She fell back against her pillows and closed her eyes.

What did Frederick want from her now? Most of Silesia was his. It had been by the skin of her teeth that she had saved the Empire for her Francis. And now, Joseph, her son, was Holy Roman Emperor; his brother Leopold's son to follow after him, God be willing.

She had at least thwarted Frederick in that ambition. The thought made her smile. A gust of the icy Vienna air blew in through the open window, wrapping itself around her neck. It was deathly chill and oddly pleasant against her skin.

What did Frederick want? She would be a fool to think he was content with possessing Silesia. He had set his sights on Poland, but would that be enough to sate his monstrous appetite?

He will never rest until Austria is destroyed. Or the Empire his.

She opened her eyes, glancing down at the letter again. It appeared to be a friendly overture to bury the hatchet.

"Together Austria and Prussia can lead the world," the King had written. "England squabbles with France, bringing havoc to Europe. Russia is grown drunken with her might. What hope of peace unless we Germans stand together?"

And that peace, she supposed, would come from dividing Poland. He must think her as greedy as himself if he thought she would agree to such a despicable scheme.

"If it will avoid war, my dear," she heard her dead Francis whisper in her ear.

"But sometimes war cannot be avoided, Franz," she argued. "If I had turned away from it all those years ago, the Empire would have been lost. Frederick wanted Silesia—"

"He owns the better part of it now, my sweet. The war brought us little enough."

"It kept the Empire in our hands, Franz." The Empress brought her fist fiercely down upon her bedside table. "We would have lost it all, had I acquiesced to Frederick's demands then." It was what Franz had counseled. She had disregarded his words, unwilling to yield even an inch of the lands she had so recently inherited.

But her appetite for war was long gone. She had been a young woman in 1740—a mother, barely twenty-three, ready and willing to take on the reins of power. She longed to relinquish them now.

It was her un-womanly interest in affairs of state that had, she was certain, driven Francis to other women. She had sent Charles, her brother-in-law, to the field while his wife—her sister— awaited his firstborn child. Neither mother nor child had survived, and guilt inextricably coupled with grief had pushed Charles into the grave.

All of this, she had survived, suppressing her grief. It had been one thing to lose a sister and a brother-in-law. One thing to see her beloved Franz dally with other women. A war now would send all her sons to the battlefield. It was not a gamble she could afford.

She perused the letter again. There could, she supposed, be no harm in traveling to Potsdam. The cold north air might bring her lungs some relief.

"And you may be able to talk him out of his devilish scheme to carve up Poland as though it were little more than a leg of lamb," her husband's spirit reminded her.

This time she nodded. There was only so much letters and envoys could achieve. Who knew, but a meeting in person might not serve her purpose better. "Not that I will mention it to either Joseph or Kaunitz. Joseph is as keen to ride into the battlefield as Frederick himself. And the chancellor does little to discourage him."

A more innocuous explanation for her decision to go would have to be supplied. Easily enough accomplished since the King himself had furnished a plausible reason.

Yet her sense of foreboding remained. The King's second request was so unaccountable, it puzzled her no end. What could he mean by it?

Chapter One

"CARL Philipp Emanuel Bach," the Empress said, her eyes riveted upon the gold-embossed letter in her hand. "You are acquainted with him?"

Her voice recalled Kapellmeister Joseph Haydn's attention from the gardens outside, blanketed in snow, to the small study where he sat opposite Her Majesty, Empress Maria Theresa. The lush bounty of leaves, melons, and pomegranates painted on the walls by Johann Wenzel Bergl's hands formed a startling contrast to the bleakness without.

Carl Philipp Emanuel Bach—C.P.E. Bach? The name had dropped like a bolt of lightning from Her Majesty's mouth. What could she possibly want with Herr Bach? Had Her Majesty received a letter from the great Bach himself?

Haydn straightened up in his chair, waiting for the explanation that must surely follow.

But none was forthcoming. The Empress raised her head and glanced across the table at him. Her blue eyes, still sharp despite her age and her recent bout with illness, regarded the Kapellmeister closely, awaiting his reply.

"Only with his music," he replied, unable to conceal his surprise. Surely an enquiry into his associations was not so pressing as to require his presence in Her Majesty's apartment.

The coachman she had sent to the Esterházy Palace on Wallnerstrasse had urged such haste, Haydn had hurried out without so much as a word to his employer, His Serene Highness, Prince Nikolaus Esterházy.

That task was left to Luigi Tomasini, Haydn's Konzertmeister. Haydn had only just remembered his wool coat, his gloves remaining forgotten on the hallway table at the Esterházy Palace.

The Empress nodded, dipping the edge of her toast into her soft-cooked egg. "I did not think you were, but it is such a small matter, I would not have thought it worth the lie." She returned her gaze to the letter.

"We have corresponded," Haydn hastened to add, unwilling to allow Her Majesty to think so ill of a composer he himself held in such great esteem. The letter in her hands must be from Herr Bach. If only the composer had apprised Haydn of his application to the Empress.

Haydn dipped his own spoon reluctantly into his silver egg cup. He had never seen the point of soft-cooked eggs.

Why trouble with cooking an egg at all if one were going to leave it almost entirely uncooked? But the Empress had insisted on serving it to him. The white, at least, was set firm. He sprinkled some salt on it and brought the spoon to his mouth.

"I have not, however, had the fortune of meeting him in person," he continued once he had swallowed the morsel.

Why had Herr Bach lied about such a trivial detail? It was a fact easily put to the test and was hardly likely to win him a position at the Habsburg Court. Haydn rubbed his frozen hands together. The long drive to Schönbrunn had chilled his fingers to the bone. And although he sat by the fire, they still felt numb.

"If Your Majesty wishes to hire him, I can recommend no one more suited for the position or more capable. As a performer, he is incomparable. As an educator, few could be more gifted or learned— "

"He has apparently expressed a strong desire to meet you, Haydn." The Empress raised her eyes again, her pale blue irises fastening themselves upon the Kapellmeister.

"He will be visiting Vienna?" Why had Herr Bach not mentioned the matter to him?

"No, Haydn, it is the King of Prussia who requests your presence in his court."

Ach so! The letter was from the King, then. Haydn's eyes followed the movement of the thick, creamy sheet of paper as the imperial hand that held it swept the air.

"At the urging apparently," the Empress went on, "of a keyboardist he thinks so little of, the poor man receives barely three hundred thalers a year."

Haydn's eyes widened despite himself. Few musicians cared to seek a position in Prussia, it was so well known the King thought little of anyone other than Friedrich Agricola and Joachim Quantz. But Haydn had not thought Her Majesty was privy to these details.

"I have my sources," she explained, her pale lips stretching into a smile. "It is unlikely, I suppose, that Bach would have made such an appeal."

Haydn considered the question. "Not quite as unlikely as the fact that the King heeded it," he replied. "I cannot think what His Majesty could want with me. It can hardly be for my music. He thinks it is just so much noise."

It was not an opinion that offended him. A man who failed to appreciate Herr Bach could hardly be expected to enjoy his work.

But why should Herr Bach need the King's permission to meet him? Haydn could have traveled to Potsdam, if His Serene Highness allowed it. Such a thing was not altogether unlikely. Was Herr Bach himself unable to leave Prussia?

The question filled Haydn with misgiving. If that were the case, it could only mean one thing. Herr Bach was in trouble.

"The request comes, you said, from Herr Bach, Your Majesty?"

"It is what the King says, Haydn." The Empress waved the letter through the air again. "But he habitually weaves such a web of deceit, one can never be sure of anything." She sighed. "Perhaps, he merely means to be polite. Although I am inclined to think there is a more sinister motive behind his request."

"Polite?" Haydn enquired. What need did the King have to be polite to a mere musician?

"He has invited me to Potsdam—a gesture of friendship, he says—in order that the Prince of Condé and I may bring our marriage negotiations to a conclusion on neutral grounds."

Haydn nodded, well aware of Her Majesty's efforts to wed Archduchess Maria Antonia to the French Dauphin. The Empress went on.

"He would, of course, profit from seeming to facilitate the alliance.

"But," Her Majesty paused, suddenly breathless. She gripped her chair, chest expanding, as she drew several deep drafts of air. "I very much fear, the gauntlet is being thrown at us, Haydn. I only wish I knew why King Frederick seeks to involve you."

Rosalie Szabó allowed Gerhard to sweep her roughly into his arms. "Take care of yourself, lass," he said, clasping her so close to his chest, she could hardly breathe. "And do not forget you are now an engaged woman."

"I won't," Rosalie promised. How could she, when he never gave her an opportunity to do so?

She watched him climb onto his rack-wagon and maneuver it out of the Haarhof, the narrow alley on which the wine cellar for the Esterházy Palace, where she worked, was located. There had been no wine deliveries to make. Gerhard had simply come to see her.

To check on her, the palace maid corrected herself. If only he could bring himself to trust her a little more. But Gerhard Heindl, the tavern-keeper from Kleinhöflein, seemed perpetually afraid Rosalie would betray him the way Marlene, his first fiancée, had done.

If Rosalie so much as glanced at another man, Gerhard read her a lecture on the impropriety of her behavior. At first she had secretly reveled in the jealousy he betrayed, seeing it as a sign he was over his infatuation with Marlene. But now. . .

She sighed. It was more than any woman could be expected to bear. She fidgeted with the gold band on her finger. Sometimes the urge to take it off was simply irresistible.

And unaccountable. Gerhard was a good man. And she, the most fortunate woman in Austria, as Mama never failed to remind her.

"Not ready to be tied to one man, are you?" A low, throaty voice jogged Rosalie out of her thoughts.

A woman clad in muted tones, almost entirely covered in a deep indigo cloak, stood by her side. Her lips wore an amused smile; her dark blue eyes had an air of knowing that seemed out of place in one so humbly dressed. She tipped her chin at Rosalie's ring.

"A little soap will ease it off, and for a few hours you may be free of him."

"I don't wish to be free of him," Rosalie said, resenting the woman's too-ready assumptions about her feelings.

"No?" The woman's smile widened. "I must have been mistaken, then."

Her gesture and tone infuriated Rosalie. "Yes, you were." she swiveled around.

"Wait!" The woman's fingers gently touched Rosalie's arm. "I did not mean to offend you—"

"What is it you want?" Rosalie snapped. "If it is a position at the palace, there is none to be had at the moment."

"I merely wish to speak with Herr Haydn. Is he within?" The wind, icy in the gray morning, swept the hood off her head, revealing a broad forehead and lustrous, corn-colored hair. She pulled it back up with a quick glance around the alley.

"Then you should go around to the front." Rosalie gestured toward Wallnerstrasse at the end of the alley.

The woman took a deep breath. "It is a matter of some sensitivity, and I do not wish anyone to know I have been here. Please, I beg of you."

"Oh, very well," Rosalie relented. "Follow me. But I shall have to leave you with Master Luigi, Herr Haydn's Konzertmeister. Herr Haydn was called out early this morning and has not returned."

Rosalie glanced curiously at her companion as they walked together to the palace. Who was this strange woman? And why had she come calling on the Kapellmeister?

8

One of Joseph's women, no doubt, Konzertmeister Luigi Tomasini thought, as he gazed with open curiosity at the stranger Rosalie had ushered into the Music Room.

Ever since the court newspaper had hailed the Kapellmeister as the foremost composer of the Empire, hinting at some of the valuable services he had performed for Her Majesty, women of all kinds had flocked to Haydn's side. Back in Eisenstadt, the alderman's wife, Frau Bruck, had sought every opportunity of seducing poor Haydn.

The dismay Haydn betrayed every time she appeared would have been amusing were it not for the sympathy his predicament evoked in Luigi. Frau Bruck had once set her sights on him. He shuddered. Fortunately that madness had passed.

But this woman, whoever she was, was most breathtakingly lovely. A few years past thirty, Luigi surmised, but the features in her oval face were perfection itself. The lips, the color and shape of a rosebud; the nose, noble; her eyes, wide and lustrous. A woman any man would be tempted by.

"You are acquainted with Kapellmeister Haydn?" he asked, not knowing how else to ask who she was. She had not offered to identify herself. She had the air of a noblewoman, but was so ordinarily dressed, Luigi was unsure how to address her.

The woman smiled. "I have known him since he was a boy," she said.

Luigi nodded, although the explanation failed to enlighten him in the least. An acquaintance from Rohrau, perhaps? Or was she the wife of one of the many musicians who had come to Haydn's aid when Chormeister Reutter had turned him out on the streets with only the shirt on his back?

"And you wish to see him about. . .?" Luigi prompted.

"A matter that I can only discuss with him." The woman was firm.

"Perhaps, you would care to wait in the parlor." Luigi was about to ring for Rosalie, but the woman blocked his path.

"I will wait in the Music Room, if you have no objection."

Luigi hesitated, not at all sure that Haydn would care to have a strange woman let loose into his workroom. For one thing, it seemed too much like the kind of secret assignation His Serene Highness was likely to frown upon. For another, what Frau Haydn would say when she heard of the matter, he did not know.

But the determined expression in the woman's large blue eyes suggested she would brook no opposition.

"Then I will wait with you," he said.

Chapter Two

HAYDN allowed the Empress's butler to usher him into the Hall of Ceremonies. Were it not for their heavy blanket of snow, he would have preferred to depart by the gardens. A walk through the grounds of the imperial summer palace, Schönbrunn, would have done much to calm his unease.

Her Majesty's words echoed through his mind as loud as a voice raised in an empty, cavernous room. What strange motive had impelled the Prussian King to send for him? That it was not for his music was evident.

The King had enquired whether Haydn was indeed the son of a Mark-trichter. Why should that trivial detail be of any interest? Mathias Haydn had been in his grave for over four years. As for his service as a market-judge, Rohrau was as small and insignificant as Eisenstadt. In the eyes of the world, the position must count for very little.

He crossed the vast room, his footsteps heavy on the parquet floor.

Why had Herr Bach even thought to mention the fact? To empha-size Haydn's lack of advantages, and the advances he had made despite them? Or to press the King into enlisting his hand to solve a crime?

Haydn had been of some service to the Empress on two prior occa-sions and cleared up a few small matters in Eisenstadt. Word of this had reached Herr Bach's ears in Potsdam. But the great man could hardly expect him to be of any use in Prussia. He knew so little of the country.

Surely the King had access to men far more capable than he.

The gauntlet has been thrown at us.

He heard Her Majesty's softly uttered words in his ears. Did King Frederick mean to put Haydn's abilities to the test? It was a plausible assumption, given his unaccountable interest in Haydn's background.

Was it possible a crime was expected to befall? Some act of villainy, occurring during Haydn's tenure in Potsdam, that would enable King Frederick to place before him a conundrum—

But if that were the case, that could only mean. . .

That the King himself was about to commit it!

Haydn stopped, his feet jolted out of the steady rhythm of their pace by the thought. The coils of discomfort within the pit of his stomach strengthened into a gut-wrenching anxiety.

To accuse a king of a misdeed was no small matter. Were Haydn compelled to do it, he would be hauled off to Spandau. The King of Prussia had confined men for far less.

He stepped slowly forward, consumed by the overwhelming impression he was walking into a trap. To say or do nothing in such a case was impossible. He could not watch while an innocent man was condemned for a crime he had not committed. But to say anything at all would certainly put him in harm's way.

"Her Majesty intends to travel to Prussia, then?"

The question uttered in a deep, agitated voice propelled Haydn's head up. His gaze collided with the troubled eyes of the Empress's personal physician, Baron Gerard van Swieten. When had His Lordship entered the room?

The Kapellmeister gathered his scattered thoughts and pondered the query. Whether they were to go or not had not even been discussed.

"She has said nothing about declining the King's invitation," he said at last. Not that Her Majesty had said anything about accepting it, either. But then, she would hardly have summoned him had she intended to ignore the offer.

The imperial physician sighed. "Then we may regard it as a fait accompli. She means to go and will not be deterred." Lines of worry creased the broad expanse of forehead beneath his wig.

"You would prefer that she stayed?" Haydn enquired, wondering if the Baron's concern was due to the Empress's recent bout of sickness. A visit to the late Crown Princess's poorly sealed crypt had brought on such a fatal attack of smallpox, Her Majesty had nearly died. The disease had taken the Archduchess Maria Josepha as well.

"As would Chancellor Kaunitz." The Baron led Haydn back across the room toward the benches covered in soft crimson that stood beneath the Empress's portrait. "He thinks no good can come of her going." The imperial physician sank heavily down on one of the benches, gesturing to Haydn to be seated as well.

"I wondered at her agreeing to allow King Frederick to have a hand in the marriage negotiations," Haydn began cautiously, sitting gingerly at the very edge of the bench. "Surely it cannot be in the King's interest to facilitate an alliance between his two greatest enemies—the Habsburgs and the Bourbons."

"Perhaps not," The imperial physician agreed. "Although he should be reconciled to it. The Archduchess Amalia is promised to Duke Ferdinand of Parma and his cousin, Ferdinand of Naples, is soon to wed the Archduchess Carolina. Even if Prussia had any rival candidates to put forward, who would prefer a niece of a king to the sister of the Holy Roman Emperor?"

"But, I suppose, an alliance with the future King of France would be the biggest prize of all," Haydn said. He had detected more than a hint of impatience in the Empress's manner when she referred to the matter. The death of the Dauphin's mother, a woman from Saxony, should have hastened the proposed match.

But despite the care the Empress took to charm the French ambassador, Duc de Durfort, no formal offer had yet been made.

"The King may want nothing more than the pleasure of simultaneously thwarting both his enemies," Haydn continued. He wondered if those were the machinations the Prussian King meant to set into motion. But what role had he intended for Haydn himself? That of a hapless bystander?

Baron van Swieten frowned. "The negotiations progress very slowly, it is true. But I doubt the French would be so easily swayed. The French minister Choiseul is working intensely on our behalf and King Louis himself is so keen on the match, he dexterously avoided committing to his late daughter-in-law's plans."

"But what harm could it do if the Empress were to meet the Prince of Condé in Potsdam? His Highness may have greater freedom to act than the Duc de Durfort." Not to mention, Haydn thought, that the possibility of another scourge taking the Archduchess Maria Antonia as it had her older sister was one that had to be reckoned with.

Were that unfortunate event to take place, there would be no Archduchesses left to take her place as Maria Carolina had that of the deceased Maria Josepha.

"Patience, Chancellor Kaunitz feels, might better win the day," the imperial physician replied. "The French stand to benefit as much or more from the match as we. Being overhasty might spoil the plans or result in the French demanding greater concessions than the alliance is worth."

His frown deepened, the skin between his brow gathering into a series of furrows. "It is something the Empress usually understands. I cannot understand this strange restlessness that afflicts her."

"Who was that woman you were trying to sneak in?"

The words whispered into Rosalie's ear as she stepped into the quiet kitchen nearly made her jump. She clutched the door jamb for support.

Who was that? The kitchen should have been empty. The musicians had long been served breakfast and the midday meal was several hours away.

"Oh, it's you!" she gasped as her gaze stumbled upon the buxom figure of a maid stationed behind the door. "You gave me such a fright, Greta."

"Well, who is she?" Greta drew Rosalie toward the large kitchen table in the middle of the room. "I don't know if you should have brought her through the servants' entrance. She didn't look anything at all like a maid. That cloak covering her from head to toe was made of the finest wool."

Rosalie sank into the chair Greta pulled out for her. "She insisted upon it. She doesn't want anyone to know she's here to see Herr Haydn. She wouldn't tell me her name either. And she evaded the question quite adroitly when Master Luigi tried to pry it out of her."

"Oh!" Greta sat down next to Rosalie. "What could she possibly want with Herr Haydn?"

"She wouldn't say. All she would say is that she is an old friend of his."

"Hmmm. . ." Greta bit her lip, her eyes narrowing into a pensive squint. "I'm not sure I believe that. Do you think she comes from the Hofburg?"

"The Hofburg? After what she suggested to me, I'd be more inclined to believe she was a creature of the night."

"What did she suggest?" Greta gaped at Rosalie, mouth open.

"That I take off Gerhard's ring so I could be free to give myself to other men!"

"Good heavens!" Greta's blue eyes nearly popped out of their sockets. "Why would she say a thing like that?"

Rosalie sighed. Truth to tell, she had brought the stranger's remark upon herself. If she hadn't been chafing at wearing Gerhard's ring. . . She sighed again. "Gerhard is sometimes a bit. . ." she broke off, writhing under Greta's blank stare.

"It is only because he loves you, Rosalie, and doesn't want to lose you. Would you rather he didn't care at all?"

"No, of course not. But if only he could trust me a little. I would never betray him."

Greta squeezed her hand. "I know you wouldn't. But try not to be in too much of a temper over it. It won't make things any better." She puffed her cheeks out. "Still, it was very wrong of that woman to say what she did."

"What made you think she was from the Hofburg?" Rosalie asked.

Greta's eyes brightened as though she'd remembered a bit of gossip she wanted to share. She leaned forward. "Well, because that carriage that came for Herr Haydn this morning." She paused to take breath. "It was from the Empress."

"What! How do you know that?"

They had all seen the coachman who had waited impatiently in the hallway by the entrance. He had not been in the imperial livery. The coach itself, waiting on Wallnerstrasse, had been an ordinary black conveyance like the ones reserved for the musicians' use at the Esterházy Palace.

Greta smiled. "I got it out of the new footman, Stephan. He was standing nearby when Herr Haydn met the coachman and he distinctly heard Her Majesty's name mentioned. 'Schönbrunn?' Herr Haydn asked. I doubt he was happy to undertake such a long journey. 'Ja!' the coachman said, vigorously nodding his head.

"There must be something important going on, if the Empress needs Herr Haydn's help. And now this mysterious woman pretending to be a servant even though she looks nothing like it. I wish Stephan had heard more, but the coachman was mumbling so, he said it was as much as he could do to hear anything at all."

It was nearly an hour later that Haydn returned to Wallnerstrasse to find his Music Room occupied by his Konzertmeister and a cloaked female who insisted upon seeing him in private.

"An acquaintance of yours, Joseph." Luigi sprang to his feet. "From childhood, apparently." Receiving no answer from the astonished Kapellmeister, he went on with a glance at the woman: "I will leave you to it since I see I am not wanted." Giving the lady a gracious bow, he made his way toward the door.

But as he walked past Haydn, the Konzertmeister whispered: "I see no good coming of this, Joseph? Who in the name of heaven is she?"

But if Haydn had ever met the woman before, the incident had failed to consign itself to his memory. He directed a searching glance at her as he walked toward the white-and-gold chairs in the middle of the room.

Despite her modest garb, something about her manner and the air of assurance with which she regarded him suggested she was a person of high birth. Not a woman one could easily forget. He was quite sure he had never laid eyes on her.

He heard the door click shut behind him.

"You claim to have known me since my boyhood, Madame, but—"

"A mere ruse, Herr Kapellmeister," she replied with a low, musical laugh. "Although since we have moved in the same circles, it is quite possible we have met."

"The same circles?" Haydn allowed his eyebrows to arch upward.

"You have studied with Nicola Porpora, have you not? And worked for the Count Morzin?"

Haydn nodded, mystified. What was she getting at? Porpora had never given the lady a lesson that he could recall. And he would certainly have remembered had she numbered among Count Morzin's guests in the years he had served as Kapellmeister to that gentleman.

"These are men my husband and I are well acquainted with."

"I see." His assumption about her had been true, then. She was a woman of noble birth. He took the seat Luigi had vacated. "I am greatly indebted to both the Count and Herr Porpora," he said slowly. "How could I fail to be of assistance to any friend of theirs?"

He left it at that, not wanting to say more. Whether he could indeed be of assistance remained to be seen. And he would offer nothing else until she was more forthcoming.

She tilted her head, her deep blue eyes searching his features. "You are remarkably incurious about my identity," she remarked finally. "Your Konzertmeister tried a thousand different ways to ascertain it."

"Since you have come to me," Haydn said, "I trust you will let me know—in good time. Although I imagine I would not be far off the mark were I to guess that you are in some way attached to the imperial court." Or connected with the Prussian ambassador, he thought privately.

It would have to be one or the other, given the way his morning had begun. Even so, he was surprised to see the other's eyes widen and to hear her sharp intake of breath.

"I see Her Majesty's faith in you is not misplaced. There is little point concealing the truth from you, you have penetrated my subterfuge so easily. I am Maria Wilhelmina von Auersperg."

"The late Emperor Francis's—"

Mistress, Haydn had been about to say but caught himself just in time.

"Intimate friend," the Princess completed his sentence with a smile.

Chapter Three

"THE Emperor Joseph is most anxious about his mother," Maria Wilhelmina von Auersperg began. She leaned forward, lips slightly parted. The eyes that must have dazzled a thousand men gazed candidly into Haydn's own.

"You have come at His Imperial Majesty's behest, then?" What could the Emperor be so anxious about that he was compelled to make his enquiries by such a roundabout means?

The Princess drew back. Why the question should have made her recoil so, Haydn failed to understand.

"No, it was not Joseph who sent me. I doubt he knows I am here. But —" She squinted a little, her lips pushed out into a worried pout. Then leaning forward again, she said: "It is a matter of some concern in the highest quarters that Her Majesty should consider going to Prussia."

"Because the marriage negotiations between Austria and France might flounder," Haydn ventured. What other reason could there be? The imperial physician had already expressed his disquietude on the matter.

"Is it only for that reason that she intends to grasp the olive branch the King of Prussia extends?" The Princess seemed taken aback. "She has said nothing of Poland?"

"What has Poland to do with anything, Your Highness?" The question burst out of the Kapellmeister's mouth before he could stop himself. Now seeing the Princess's reaction, he wished he had restrained himself.

His words seemed to recall Princess Auersperg to herself. A bland expression descended upon her features. "There is unrest in Poland, as you may have heard, Herr Haydn. A civil war is on the verge of erupt-ing. The Emperor fears it may make travel difficult—even dangerous."

"Dangerous," Haydn repeated, careful not to inflect the word in any way. He had said too much already, he feared. There was trouble in Poland, it was true. But the Empress would encounter none of it. They would no doubt be traveling north via Bohemia and Saxony.

Why had the Princess uttered such an obvious falsehood?

He looked up to see her watching him closely. "There are Hungarian territories mortgaged to Poland, Herr Haydn. If the trouble extended to those regions, war would be imminent."

"I imagine Her Majesty knows that," he said lightly. "She keeps her-self well informed."

The Princess appeared to pale at his words. Her fingers clenched her armrest.

"Then for your own sake, Herr Haydn, let me urge you not to meddle in affairs that do not concern you. Nothing good can come of it. The Emperor has matters well in hand."

"I see," Haydn replied. "But in that case, his concerns for Her Majesty's safety seem. . . superfluous. Would you not agree?"

The Princess's eyes flashed. "His anxiety on her account is quite gen-uine, I assure you. The Archduchess Christina herself is in—"

Haydn edged forward, willing her to continue. But the Princess cut herself short, whatever imprudent revelation she had been about to make smothered in the cold light of circumspection.

"She finds herself in agreement with her brother, the Emperor," she finished calmly.

———◆———

"I had the distinct impression of being pumped for information," Haydn confided to Luigi once the Princess had left. He had waited by the window until he had seen her walk out onto the street before sending for his Konzertmeister.

"To what end?" Luigi asked, peering out the window as though he expected to see Her Highness again. But her cloaked form had long since gone.

"That I could not determine," Haydn admitted ruefully. He tried to make sense of the small snippets he had gleaned. The unrest in Poland. The Emperor and his sister Archduchess Christina being for once in agreement with each other. But the fragments were too few to form a complete picture.

"She claimed to speak for the Emperor," he said.

Luigi snorted. "An unlikely story, if you want my opinion. Since when has the Emperor ever needed a spokesperson? He speaks his mind so bluntly and with such blatant disregard for the feelings of whomever he is speaking with, I doubt he would hesitate to approach Her Majesty with his views on the subject of her departure."

"The reason the Princess cited for His Imperial Majesty's concern surprised me as well," Haydn said. "That the marriage negotiations for Archduchess Maria Antonia might be jeopardized by a visit to Prussia seemed not to trouble her at all. But a Catholic uprising in Poland, which surely cannot affect us at all, would be reason enough to avoid Prussia?"

"I would not put it past the Prussian King to have started the trouble." The Konzertmeister turned toward Haydn, a grave expression on his lean, chiseled features.

"I suppose not," Haydn agreed. For all that the King denigrated all religions equally, he seemed to reserve an especial contempt for Catholics. His attitude had disgusted devout Protestants and Catholics alike. Herr Bach himself had complained of it in more than one letter to Haydn.

"His Serene Highness must be apprised of Princess Auersperg's visit, Joseph." Luigi's voice interrupted Haydn's thoughts. "These are matters beyond our ken."

Haydn nodded mutely. What web of intrigue had he got caught up in?

———

The sky was a crisp blue when Rosalie and Greta emerged from the palace that afternoon. The strong winds of the morning had abated.

And the sun, high in the sky, engulfed the glistening snow-covered streets in a warm glow.

"What a perfect day for an afternoon off!" Greta glanced around her, her cheeks flushed a bright carmine from the cold. "Where shall we go?" She rubbed her hands together and turned to look at Rosalie.

"To the Michaelerplatz, of course," Rosalie said at once, linking arms with her friend. "For a sleigh ride around the square." She had wanted to share a ride with Greta ever since Gerhard had introduced her to the pleasure of being pulled swiftly through the snow by a horse-drawn sleigh.

"You'll love it. The wind whistling in your ears as the horse turns sharply around the corners. The seat so close to the ground, you can touch the snow. There's nothing like it. Even though Gerhard says you can go much faster in the open fields or down a slope than in the crowded square."

Greta giggled happily. "It does sound like fun!"

They were almost at the Kohlmarkt when a voice behind them called out.

"Rosalie?"

They spun around to see a cloaked figure regarding them. "It is Rosalie, is it not?" The woman Rosalie had sneaked in through the servants' door peered at the maids.

Rosalie felt herself stiffen. "What do you want?"

"Merely to apologize for giving you any cause for offense this morning." She reached out, lightly placing her fingers upon Rosalie's arm. "Let me make it up to you. Shall we go to a coffeehouse—"

"A coffeehouse?" Rosalie was aghast. Whatever would Gerhard say if she were to frequent one of those sordid places? "But only the worst sort of men go to such places."

Greta drew herself up. "What kind of person are you?" She jabbed a finger in Rosalie's direction. "Advising her to take her ring off. Trying to drag her into a coffeehouse. Go away! We don't want anything to do with the likes of you."

"You misunderstand." The woman's fingers tightened around Rosalie's wrist. "There is a perfectly respectable establishment on the Kohlmarkt. A café in the French style with a salon for women."

"Well, in that case," Greta began when Rosalie interrupted her: "But it may be more than we can afford."

The woman smiled. "It will be my treat. I am only a governess, but I do well enough. You will come, then?" Her blue eyes flickered hesitantly back and forth between Rosalie and Greta.

The maids nodded.

The woman's smile deepened. "I am called Elma," she said as they turned left on the Kohlmarkt, away from the Michaelerplatz.

———————

Prince Nikolaus Esterházy was about to step into his carriage when the Kapellmeister hailed him. His Serene Highness stopped, one foot still on the ground, and glanced over his shoulder, his ample form bristling with impatience.

"What is it, Haydn?"

The Kapellmeister hurried forward. "A most pressing matter, Your Serene Highness—"

"Can it not wait?"

Haydn took a deep breath. "Unfortunately not, Your Serene Highness."

The Prince harrumphed, the sound resembling the irate trumpeting of an elephant. "Very well, then. Enter the carriage."

Haydn had barely taken his seat when the vehicle jolted into motion. "Your Serene Highness is no doubt aware that Her Majesty, the Empress, sent for me this morning."

"Yes, yes, Haydn. And I am aware of the reason for it as well." He gazed squarely into the Kapellmeister's eyes. "If Her Majesty wishes you to travel to Prussia, I am afraid there is nothing I can do to forbid it. If it is any consolation, she would have me accompany her as well."

The Prince gazed out the window at the snow-covered streets. "A den of vipers would be safer, in my opinion, than Potsdam with His Majesty, King Frederick. But that is neither here nor there."

"I have no objection to going," Haydn replied. In truth, he had none. He had his misgivings about the journey, but the opportunity to meet Herr Bach in person was not one any composer could easily refuse. "It was about another matter entirely that I wished to speak with Your Serene Highness. The visit I received this morning from Princess Maria Wilhelmina von Auersperg."

The name caught the Prince's attention. "And what did she require of you, Haydn?" His Serene Highness barely moved as he asked the question.

"Poland?" he repeated when Haydn finished recounting the details. "She wanted to know if the Empress's visit had anything to do with Poland?"

"Not in so many words," Haydn clarified. The Princess had merely asked if the Empress had mentioned Poland. Yet why would Her Majesty mention an uprising in Poland in connection with a forthcoming journey to Prussia? "But it seemed as such to me."

The Prince leaned forward, resting his hand on his right knee. "And she claimed to be speaking for the Emperor Joseph?"

Haydn nodded. "Although she did say she had not been sent by His Imperial Majesty."

"You are sure it was the Princess Auersperg?"

The question startled Haydn. It had never occurred to him to question the lady's identity. She had made such a to-do about giving it, he had not stopped to think she could have been lying when she finally had revealed it.

"It was what she said," he began apologetically. "I have never met the lady and. . ."

The Prince waved his objections aside. "I doubt it was an imposter," he said. "I am merely surprised that she still concerns herself with politics. That she can presume to have any influence at all now that Emperor Francis is no more."

The carriage pulled up outside a jeweler's store housed on the first floor of a coffee-colored building. The coachman opened the door, but the Prince made no move to climb out. Instead, he handed a card to the coachman and said: "Let Herr Boehmer know that I am here, Hans. The Kapellmeister and I still have some things to discuss."

When the coachman left, the Prince turned toward Haydn. "The ornaments for the Archduchess Carolina's upcoming nuptials must be made to perfection. They necessitate an almost daily visit to Herr Boehmer's establishment."

The remark was so strikingly irrelevant to the matter at hand, it was all Haydn could do not to stare at his employer.

"Fortunately, Herr Boehmer's establishment is most conveniently placed." His Serene Highness tapped the window with his walking stick, indicating a gray building across the street. "The apartment on the second floor is occupied by Count von Rohde, the Prussian ambassador.

"I have never observed anything untoward. But perhaps this afternoon will be different."

It took Haydn a moment to understand. "Does Your Serene Highness suppose the Princess Auersperg is in the employ of the Prussian ambassador?"

An amused smile lit up the Prince's countenance. "We shall find out soon enough, I imagine. By reminding the lady that the Empress keeps herself well informed, you appear to have inadvertently stirred up a hornet's nest, Haydn."

Not for the first time that day, the Kapellmeister found himself floundering. He was in waters so deep, he could barely keep afloat. What significance did Poland have? Why should an innocuous remark about the Empress have called forth such agitation in her late husband's mistress? It was all so unfathomable, he felt as though he were walking blindfolded through a thick fog.

Before he could marshal his thoughts sufficiently to frame a question or two, the door to the gray building opened and a cloaked figure stepped out onto the snow. The wind whipped the hood off her hair, revealing a mass of straw-hued hair framing an oval face.

"That is the lady, Your Serene Highness," Haydn said at once, recognizing his visitor from earlier that afternoon.

The Prince nodded, but his eyes were riveted on the carriage that skidded to a halt beside the Princess and the slender, fashionably dressed woman wrapped in furs who drew her inside.

"I am afraid it is much worse than we thought," he said with a sharp intake of breath.

Chapter Four

"How do you know Herr Haydn, Elma?" Greta asked when a young serving girl at the coffeehouse had taken their order.

Elma's gaze dropped to her lap. "He was most attentive to me when I was a young girl."

"Attentive?" Rosalie repeated. "You mean he wanted to marry you?"

Elma's cheeks turned red. "He might have asked the question had I encouraged him. I thought myself too good for the likes of him—a poor, ill-fed, ill-clothed boy barely able to make ends meet. My father was a silversmith. I thought I could easily attract a better man."

The serving girl returned with their coffee and a plate of spiced kuchen.

"That didn't happen, I suppose." Greta dipped a spoon into the dollop of cream topping her coffee.

Elma shook her head. "My father was greatly in debt. What little fortune he had was lost trying to pay off his creditors. I never thought I would be compelled to work." She shrugged. "It is not so bad."

"You would have done well to accept Herr Haydn," Rosalie said, unable to keep a sanctimonious tone out of her voice. At least she had not been stupid enough to give herself airs above her station. "He has done well for himself. His Serene Highness esteems him highly."

"As does the Empress herself," Greta put in.

Elma leaned forward. "I have read of his many services to Her Majesty. He has apprehended an assassin and he singlehandedly brought down a ring of thieves last summer."

Greta nodded. "And now she wishes him to look into Poland."

"What!" Elma looked startled.

"There is unrest in Poland," Rosalie said, although she was not sure of the wisdom of discussing the Kapellmeister's affairs with a woman they barely knew. If only Greta had not mentioned it at all.

"But what does that have to do with Haydn?"

"I imagine one of Her Majesty's enemies is behind the trouble," Greta said. "And she wants him to discover which one it is."

"Indeed!"

Rosalie sent her friend a warning glance. But Greta, relishing her role as possessor of confidential information, was oblivious to every hint.

"We put two and two together, Rosalie and I," she leaned across the table to whisper. "Her Majesty sent for Herr Haydn this morning. And no sooner had he returned, he sent for maps of Poland and asked us to find every newspaper that had written anything at all about that country.

"What else could it mean?"

"What else, indeed?" Elma's features were solemn. The color appeared to have completely drained from them.

That a trip to the Prussian kingdom was imminent could no longer be denied. Even the palace servants had been informed of the matter.

"It is more a question of when rather than whether," Haydn told his youngest brother as they drove to his father-in-law's house on 51 Raabgasse. His Serene Highness had made that much very clear to his Kapellmeister.

"Sister-in-law will not be pleased to leave Vienna so shortly after our arrival here," Johann remarked.

"No, she will not," Haydn agreed. Although Maria Anna would have been just as displeased had His Serene Highness commanded she be left at home.

Johann must have seen him wince. "Wait until Papa Keller is in bed, then," he counseled, "before broaching the subject. His remonstrances on the subject will make the news even harder to bear."

Haydn nodded. It would be the best way to break the news.

But that night as he watched Maria Anna brushing her hair, in better humor than usual, his misgivings returned. He approached the subject with the greatest trepidation.

For a single moment Maria Anna, usually never at a loss for words, sat as though struck dumb. "Potsdam?" she said, her voice rising sharply from the tonic.

"It is a small town situated on the River Havel," Haydn informed her. "About fifteen miles southwest of Berlin." That much he had been able to ascertain from the maps he and Luigi had pored over earlier that afternoon.

"I am well aware of its existence, husband. And not quite so ignorant as you imagine of its situation," she countered with no little asperity in her voice. "But why must we go there? So that you can visit Herr Bach? Can he not come here?"

Haydn sighed. Of course his wife must think he had concocted the whole plan! "It is the King of Prussia himself who requests my presence, Maria Anna."

"You owe him nothing. Can you not send a polite refusal? Tell him His Serene Highness will not allow it."

Haydn sighed again. "His Serene Highness and the Empress herself have asked me to go. There is some trouble, and I suppose Her Majesty thinks I may be of some use to her in. . ." The Kapellmeister's voice faded away. What precisely Her Majesty wished him to achieve he did not understand.

Maria Anna harrumphed. "It will be uncommonly cold there."

"So, it will," Haydn agreed, unable to offer any rebuttal to this.

It was cold in Vienna. The city had seen one of its coldest winters. How could Potsdam, lying as it did far to the North, not be any colder? It would certainly not be warmer than Vienna.

Seeing his wife approach the bed, he pulled the covers back for her. Then, when she had settled herself, he snuffed out the candle. To his surprise, she turned toward him. After the tidings he had given her, he had not expected to be made happy that night. But his hopes plummeted as soon as she spoke.

"Who was the woman who came to see you at the Esterházy Palace this afternoon?"

Haydn swallowed. How had his wife learned of that particular incident? Not that she could take him to task for having received Princess Auersperg. But if news of her visit had already reached Maria Anna, then all the world must be aware of it by now. Could that be a good thing?

He cleared his throat, about to speak, but Maria Anna went on: "Niklas said she was covered from head to toe in a thick, dark cloak. That she would not so much as give her name to Luigi."

Haydn exhaled, letting out the breath he had unconsciously been holding. So it was from his principal cellist that Maria Anna had learned the news. "Niklas was at home, then, when you went to see our godson?"

In the dimness, Haydn saw her nod. "Yes, but who was she? Another one of those women, so taken up with the services you have provided Her Majesty that she felt the need to win your undying love?"

The remark made him cringe. It was true, a swarm of women had been drawn to him of late. More than a man quite as ordinary as himself —not above the medium in stature, pockmarked to boot—could expect. Yet no honey pot could have been more surrounded by bees than he by women professing to admire him.

The state of affairs was embarrassing enough as it stood. But being compelled to prove his innocence to his wife at every encounter was even more painful. What man could safely hope to extricate himself in such a situation?

"No, it was the late Emperor's mis—"

"Princess Auersperg came to see you?" Maria Anna propped herself up on her elbow and stared down at Haydn. "What did she want? A mass in memory of the departed Emperor Francis?"

"No." Haydn pushed his nightcap back from his forehead. "She wanted to know whether Her Majesty intended to undertake the journey to Prussia. Apparently to put the Emperor Joseph at ease, although she claimed not to have been sent by him."

He turned to his wife. "It seems such an unlikely story. Do you suppose it could be true? What reason could the Emperor have for consorting with his dead father's mistress? Surely no son would tolerate such a woman."

"Most sons would not." Maria Anna's head sank back onto her pillow. "But His Imperial Majesty seems to go out of his way to spite his mother. He resents her for retaining the reins of power. So much so that when Papa went to receive his pension the other day, His Imperial Majesty complained—in Papa's presence, would you believe it?— of being no more than the fifth wheel on a coach."

She propped herself up on her elbow again and turned toward Haydn.

But the Kapellmeister merely mumbled, oblivious to the effect of his apparent disinterest on his wife. More serious considerations had entered his mind. He could well believe the Emperor resented the constraints of his position as co-regent. That he complained long and loud to anyone who cared to hear was not surprising either.

But did His Majesty resent his mother so much that he would reach out to her sworn enemy, the King of Prussia? To what end?

No, no. He shook his head, prevented from the softness of the pillow from doing more than rubbing his skull into it. Not even His Majesty would go that far. Most likely, the Princess had flattered him into revealing indiscretions that she then took to the Prussian Ambassador.

Yes, that must be it.

He turned toward Maria Anna only to encounter her back. *Was she really asleep? When had that happened?*

With a sigh he let his head fall back on the pillow and resigned himself to slumber.

Chapter Five

"Potsdam?" Greta wailed as she trotted behind Rosalie to the wine cellar. "Where in the name of heaven is Potsdam? And why must we go there?"

Rosalie shrugged. "Because His Serene Highness says we must." But she was as curious as Greta about the sudden change in the Prince's winter plans. Every winter from November until April, the entire Esterházy household removed from Eisenstadt to Vienna.

Why should this winter be any different? She glanced up, throwing her head back. It was a cold morning, the sky an ominous grey.

Greta's sharp yelp startled her. "You don't suppose it's in Poland, do you?" Her voice rose, ending on a gasp.

Rosalie swiveled around. "Why should it be—? *Oh!*"

Where else would Potsdam be? If the Kapellmeister had been entrusted with the task of looking into the trouble in Poland, he could hardly conduct his investigations from Vienna.

The girls stared at each other, horrified. "I don't want to go to Poland," Greta said at the same time as Rosalie gave voice to the one thought in her mind: "Whatever will Gerhard say when he hears."

"I know what I would say," a low, unfamiliar voice broke into their conversation.

A slight young lad, not much taller than either of the two maids, stood behind them. He withdrew the clay pipe dangling from his mouth and leered at them.

"Don't go. There is trouble in Poland."

"You think we don't know that?" Greta demanded, coming forward to confront the lad. There was something so very cheeky about him.

"Then why are you going? What business can two such pretty girls as yourselves have in that country?" He looked from Greta to Rosalie. His gaze dropped languidly onto Rosalie's bosom and lingered so openly there, she could feel the color rushing into her cheeks.

"It is not like we have a choice in the matter," she retorted. "His Serene Highness wishes us to go."

"I cannot think why," Greta chimed in. "It's not as though the entire household will be leaving Vienna."

"No?" The boy's eyes met Rosalie's, the faint glimmer of a sly grin appearing on his face. "His Serene Highness must think very highly of you, if he insists upon taking the two of you."

Rosalie sighed. It wouldn't have been so bad if everyone were expected to go. But to be singled out like this. "Herr Haydn must have asked for us. Some of the musicians are accompanying His Serene Highness as well."

"Herr Haydn is going to Poland?" The boy's tone was light, but his pupils widened for a single moment before resuming their normal size. "I would not have thought the country was in need of music."

"Herr Haydn—" Greta began indignantly, but Rosalie dug her elbow into her friend's ribs and she subsided into silence. There was no need to defend the Kapellmeister to this good-for-nothing, conceited young rapscallion.

She stared down her nose at his shabby, ill-fitting garb: the olive-green coat, several sizes too large for his slim form, and the brown breeches, rather too snug. But if she thought to faze the boy, she was mistaken. His lips spread into a slow, sly grin; he tucked his thumbs into his pockets and widened his chest.

Rosalie found herself infuriated by his attitude.

"Whatever Potsdam is in need of," she said, her head held high, "I am sure Herr Haydn and His Serene Highness can provide it."

"Potsdam?" The boy's grin faded. "You are going to Potsdam?"

"Yes," Greta said. "Isn't that what we said?"

"No, you said you were traveling to Poland. Potsdam, my dear girl, is in Prussia." With that the boy swept past them down the alley to Wallnerstrasse.

"Prussia?" the maids cried in unison, looking at each other. "What does Prussia have to do with Poland?" Greta demanded.

But it was not a question Rosalie had a response to.

———•••———

"Prussia has much to gain from the current unrest in Poland, Your Majesty," Esterházy said as though he were bringing some fresh insight to her notice.

"I am aware of that," the Empress replied. It took every ounce of effort to remain civil. Esterházy had the most trying tendency of stating the obvious. But the Prince was one of the most loyal Hungarian magnates and one of the few men in whom she had no hesitation in putting her entire faith.

"You are sure it was the Archduchess Christina you saw yesterday with the Princess?" she asked again. Was it possible that Mimi could have betrayed her? Mimi, the daughter most like her? Mimi, who never went against her mother's wishes? Who had even risked her siblings' wrath in bringing to the Empress's notice tidings of their misdoings?

"There was no mistaking her carriage or her figure as she bent down to receive the Princess, Your Majesty." Esterházy hesitated. "I have no doubt the Archduchess means well. Perhaps, she is merely concerned about the prospect of war. . ."

His voice faltered as the Empress turned her gaze toward him, unable to prevent her eyes from blazing.

"There would be no question of war if Russia did not insist upon meddling in Poland's affairs. The civil unrest in Poland and Russia's determination to crush it—" she broke off as a thought occurred to her.

"What is it, Your Majesty?" Esterházy enquired after a few minutes had elapsed in utter silence.

Maria Theresa's gaze slowly made its way back to the portly form of the Prince sitting before her. "Why should Russia be in favor of partition, Esterházy?"

He seemed taken aback by the question. "I imagine she is not, Your Majesty. After all, despite the Turks entering the fray, Russia has so crushed Poland, it will not be long before she can claim the entire country as her own."

"Yet King Frederick insists Russia is amenable to a partition of Poland, an event which would greatly reduce the territory she can claim. Why would Catherine of Russia agree to so disadvantageous a prospect?"

Esterházy coughed. "Perhaps, she has not, Your Majesty. The King may be attempting to force our hand."

"You mean he is lying." The Empress considered this. "It is certainly a possibility." The man was a monster, it was true. Yet there had been such a ring of sincerity about that remark. Her instincts were rarely wrong.

But if Catherine of Russia had already agreed to the proposition, that could only mean—

"Has Your Majesty received any tidings of interest from Potsdam?" Esterházy's voice interrupted her thoughts.

Tidings of interest? He was referring no doubt to the secret despatches that kept them informed of the King's thoughts on every matter.

"There should have been one with the official despatch, but the papers contained nothing." The Empress frowned, troubled at the thought. Had the ambassador failed to send any message or had, God forbid, his messages been intercepted?

A wave of unease gripped her stomach, making it roil. Mimi had been sifting through her papers a few weeks ago. She had thought nothing of it at the time, but had her daughter found something she should not have? Read papers not meant for her eyes?

Conveyed information to—

The Empress resolutely refused to finish the thought.

But she would have to be more careful in the future. And there was no question of allowing Mimi to accompany her to Potsdam. Far better to take Amalia instead.

The girl had been sullen at the prospect of marrying beneath her younger sister, of being a mere Duchess instead of Queen of Naples. A little show of confidence in her might not go amiss in reconciling her to her fate.

———◆◆◆———

The butler had just served the coffee and a plate of warm, buttery butterkekse when Amalia presented herself. The Empress glanced up and forced herself to smile. Her efforts were wasted on the girl.

She entered sullenly and thrust herself down into the chair her mother proffered.

The Empress suppressed a sigh. It had ever been thus with Amalia. The girl had nothing to recommend her. She had not her older sister Mimi's beauty nor her youngest sister Antoine's charms. Where Carolina had strength of character and fortitude, Amalia was merely hardheaded and uncompromising.

"I hear you are to travel to Prussia, Mother." Amalia helped herself to a butterkekse and unceremoniously bit off a large piece. A few crumbs flew from her mouth, dusting her chin.

The Empress hesitated. She had made up her mind to go, but no official announcement had as yet been made. "It may come to that," she said eventually, pouring a cup of coffee for her daughter.

"Mimi will accompany you, I suppose."

The Empress took a sip of her coffee. "I hesitate to separate her from her husband. You know my thoughts on the subject. A wife's place is beside the man she has married."

Amalia gazed at her, the corners of her mouth twitching in a sardonic smile. The pale green gown she wore did nothing for her complexion and was most unbecoming.

"Carolina, then. Who better than the future Queen of Naples to accompany the Empress of Austria? Or would you rather take our lightheaded Antoine and display her charms to the Prince of Condé? If she is to be Queen of France, the sooner she meets the most important of her subjects the better."

The Empress set down her cup, determined not to be bested by her own daughter. "I was hoping to take the future Duchess of Parma," she said, her tone even. "An opportunity to hone your skills in diplomacy and win some favors for the Duchy that is soon to be yours."

Amalia raised an eyebrow, but said nothing.

The Empress fought the urge to look away from her daughter's shrewd and watchful gaze. "It is not what we have or what we inherit, my child. It is what we make of the resources at our disposal. I had an empty treasury, aged, frightened advisers, and enemies at my doorstep when I ascended the throne. My will and my determination to preserve my father's heritage were all I had.

"You may have no more than a Duchy to contend with. But with the right decisions and strategic alliances, what can it not become? A weak queen may be wrested from her throne. A duchess strong in mind can multiply her advantages."

She was pleased to see a smile stretching across her daughter's unpleasant features. The girl was made almost radiant by it.

Relief coursed through the Empress's veins. She had made the right decision.

———

It was dawn when the train of carriages set out from Vienna. Rosalie swallowed her apprehension and stared out the window. Gerhard was standing stone-faced at the corner of Haarhof and Wallnerstrasse. He hadn't uttered a word of protest when she had told him she was to travel over four hundred miles to Prussia.

If he had, leaving him might have been easier.

But the way he had held her in his arms, squeezing her ribs as he pressed her against himself, had told her just how he felt. The carriage turned the corner, and a yellowing wall obliterated him from her view.

Rosalie pivoted slowly around to face Greta. "I wish we didn't have to go. It is such a long journey."

Greta's blue eyes slid slyly up toward her. "Would it get any shorter if Gerhard were traveling with us?"

The question made Rosalie smile. "No, of course not." But it would make her feel safer, she thought as she brought out the note Elma had given her. It had the address of a Count Botta in Dresden.

"He is the Prussian Ambassador in Saxony," Elma had said, urgently pressing the information into Rosalie's hand. "A friend of my father's and a man with a great deal of influence on the King."

Greta glanced at the paper. "Why should the King of Prussia wish Herr Haydn any harm?" she said, her tone skeptical. "Besides, how could he do anything with the Empress and His Serene Highness present?"

"Elma says His Majesty is a wily man. And I can well believe it."

After all, the Prince had insinuated much the same thing. They were to be extremely circumspect, His Serene Highness had advised, and to trust no one. The King had his spies everywhere and was remarkably well-informed.

Unwilling to brook any meddling in his affairs, Elma had said about King Frederick. And it was quite clear to all of them that the Kapellmeister had been tasked with meddling in the King's affairs. Why else was he accompanying the Empress to the lands of a man who had such disregard for the Kapellmeister's music that he bluntly termed it "so much noise?"

Elma had shown them the Prussian newspapers that had faithfully recorded the King's misguided remarks.

"Why couldn't Elma have given those details to Herr Haydn?" Greta grumbled, shaking her flaxen curls. "As though Count Botta would ever listen to a couple of maids like us."

"I know." Rosalie folded the piece of paper and tucked it into her coat pocket. Elma had said her efforts to persuade the Kapellmeister had been in vain.

"Not that it is like Herr Haydn to be so pigheaded," Rosalie went on, turning to face Greta. "But he must think exactly as His Serene Highness and Her Majesty do. That no Prussian can be trusted."

"Small wonder," Greta snorted, "when their king himself is such a devious man. Still Elma could have tried a little harder instead of foisting the matter onto us."

Chapter Six

"IT is the Brandenburger Tor, Johann!" Haydn peered through the carriage window into the evening gloom. Their destination lay on the other side of the triumphal arch that the Prussian King had erected at the end of the last war with Austria.

"A day early, too! Who would have thought it?" Maria Anna interjected before her brother-in-law could respond.

God be thanked for that, Haydn sighed in relief. In a few minutes more he would be able to stretch his legs. His joints cracked as he extended his limbs out in anticipation of the moment. The warmth and comfort of the carriage notwithstanding, it had been a difficult journey.

Twelve days ago they had set out from Vienna, traveling through Bohemia and Saxony on bleak, wintry roads covered in snow. The Empress had insisted on a retinue of light carriages, each to be drawn by only two horses instead of the usual six. His Serene Highness had initially carped at this stricture.

But after twelve days on potholed, rutted, treacherously icy roads, Haydn was grateful Her Majesty had not given in.

"Twelve days would have turned to twenty-four," Johann said, responding with the effortlessness born of long acquaintance to the thought in his older brother's mind, "had His Serene Highness prevailed."

Haydn nodded, too intent on the scene outside to turn toward his brother. The first carriage was rolling through the triumphal arch into the city, waved on by the customs official at the gate. Slowly the entire retinue followed suit.

A few minutes later, the long line of carriages turned left onto Lindenstrasse, entering the gates of the imposing residence of the imperial ambassador to Prussia, Count Ludwig von Seckendorff.

The ambassador, a tall man with the erect bearing of a man who had distinguished himself on the battlefield, was waiting on the marble steps that ascended in a graceful curve to his front door. Two servants in imperial livery stood bearing torches on either side of him.

The ambassador hurried down the stairs. "Your Imperial Majesty," Haydn heard him greet the Empress as His Lordship helped her out of the carriage. Some urgent whisperings followed.

"What can the matter be?" Maria Anna hissed into Haydn's ear. "How long are we to be kept waiting out in the cold? Has the ambassador not room enough for us all?"

"His Lordship would not have opened his house to us if that were the case, sister-in-law," Johann gently reminded her. "He must have news of a more urgent nature to communicate to the Empress. Is that not so, brother?"

Haydn was about to agree when a small, wizened creature in a faded blue military uniform appeared at the gates. "The Queen of Hungary has arrived, I hear!" he bellowed, making his way to the imperial carriage. "Welcome to Prussia, Your Majesty. Welcome to Potsdam.

"Seckendorff, where are your manners? Must I convey your mistress to Sanssouci myself? Supper awaits and grows cold, I fear!"

"What odd manners these Prussians have to be sure." Maria Anna sniffed. "Who sends out soldiers to greet visitors to the city?"

The Kapellmeister turned from the window.

"That is no ordinary soldier, Maria Anna. It is the King of Prussia." Who else but the King would persist in referring to the Empress as the *Queen of Hungary*?

But how, he wondered, had the King heard of their arrival? They had but entered the city.

———

"You had a pleasant journey, I hope, Your Majesty." Frederick of Prussia bent his head graciously toward the Empress as he made the enquiry.

His smile—benign, friendly—should have put her at ease. A long time ago, it had won her Francis over.

But there was nothing benign about the pale blue eyes that held hers in an unflinching stare.

"It was pleasant enough." Her response was deliberately curt. She turned her gaze toward the dark, desolate streets of Potsdam. The steady clip-clop of the horses' hooves beat a relentless rhythm in her brain. Her chest heaved, feeling more constricted than usual.

A friendlier man would have allowed her the courtesy of resting a day after an arduous journey through wintry roads. Instead, the King had barged into Seckendorff's courtyard, demanding her presence at a supper that her ambassador had clearly known nothing about.

Seckendorff's eyes had visibly widened and he had started as violently as a gun-shy horse at the unexpected sound of the King's voice.

"The entire court is so desirous to make Your Majesty's acquaintance, I had not the heart to keep them waiting a moment longer. I trust Your Majesty is not put out at the inconvenience."

The air in the carriage was close, suffocating. The Empress pursed her lips, determined not to give her host the satisfaction of knowing how she felt. As always, Frederick had taken her by surprise. There had barely been time for any of her retinue to change out of their travel garb.

"The men and women who accompany me are more inconvenienced than I am." She turned to face her longtime adversary. "That is my only regret."

Frederick inclined his head. "Your concern becomes you, Your Majesty. But this is a small affair. A gathering of a few likeminded individuals. No one need stand on ceremony."

The carriage climbed up the hill and swept into a semi-circular court of honor flanked by Corinthian columns. Snow glistened on the boughs of the trees, but the cobblestones had been swept clean.

"Here we are, Your Majesty. Sanssouci, my private abode, where we may be without care."

"I pray that we may indeed be that," the Empress replied as she stepped out of the carriage. Not that prayers could achieve any such thing. Not until they were out of Potsdam, at any event. Nothing but constant vigilance could prevent them from being caught off guard again.

The chandelier dangling from the vaulted roof cast a warm glow over the white linen-covered table. But for the presence of the Prussian King and the Empress, Haydn might have fancied himself at a private supper party.

Judging by the seating arrangements around the oval table, rank seemed to count for nothing at this court. Count Seckendorff sat on the other side of the enormous dining table, flanked by Maria Anna on his left and the Archduchess Maria Amalia on his right. Haydn himself was seated between Johann and C.P.E. Bach, the King's harpsichordist.

The Grand Master of France was only a few seats away from where the musicians sat.

"My master is not a man to stand on ceremony, Herr Haydn." Herr Bach, sitting on his left, leaned in toward him to make the remark in a low voice. "Not when the occasion demands it, at any rate."

"It would seem not," Haydn replied, piercing a steamed Brussels sprout with his fork. Butter dripped from the vegetable as he brought it to his mouth. He had never tasted anything so succulent. The chicken spiced with cinnamon would have been to more to his taste had it not been so inflamed with ginger.

"Is it ever, thus?" Johann wanted to know.

Herr Bach shook his head, a sardonic smile on his round features. "No. Only when His Majesty has company and desires to show himself an old soldier with no pretensions. It is an image he assiduously cultivates."

Haydn exchanged a glance with his brother. Herr Bach had no reason to like the King. He had long been unappreciated in Potsdam. His talents wasted in accompanying the King and his flute on the keyboard.

But how deep-seated must his dissatisfaction go, if he concealed it so ill?

The gold-and-cream image of the letter that had summoned him from Vienna entered his mind. Was Herr Bach in need of his help? He cast around for a way to elicit the information from the other.

"The war has affected His Majesty's taste for music, I hear," he remarked as he swallowed another slice of chicken.

"He spends far less on it, it is true," Herr Bach replied. "Keeping the army supplied and the men prepared for another war is more important, I suppose."

"Another war?" Johann glanced up from his plate. "Surely His Majesty can have no appetite for war. Not after the costs of the last one." Prussia, from all accounts, had suffered a greater loss of men and money than any other country in the last war.

"And it has only been five years since it ended," Haydn exclaimed. God forbid the specter of war should rear its head again! The last one had lasted seven long years. Could even a man as hardened as the King of Prussia be in a hurry to march into the battlefield again?

The keyboardist shrugged his ample shoulders. "Who can say what the King wants, Herr Haydn? But if Russia's relentless march into Turkey and Poland should bring Austria into the fray, how could Prussia refrain from joining in?"

"On the Russian side?" Haydn frowned. It seemed unlikely that Prussia would join Austria in an effort to curb Russia. But if that were the case, why extend an overture of friendship to Her Majesty?

"On the side most likely to win," Herr Bach responded. "And the musicians will have to march as well. Or sit at home with no money to feed their families."

Haydn turned toward the man he had long regarded as his mentor. Was that the reason Herr Bach had requested his presence in Potsdam? The Kapellmeister could hardly prevent an outbreak of war, but he did have connections. Did Herr Bach wish to avail himself of them? Or was there some other reason for Herr Bach's petition to the King?

"If it came to that, would the King not release you?" he asked. "There is not a single composer in Europe not indebted to you. How could doors fail to open, should you need them?"

But the King's principal keyboardist ignored the opening. He simply shrugged again. "That is not a bridge to be crossed until we come to it." He smiled and raised his glass of wine. "But for the time being, there is peace between our two countries. And your presence here does us honor."

"It was your recommendation, was it not," Johann enquired, "that brought us here, Herr Bach?"

Herr Bach looked up. "Oh, I had little enough to do with it, Master Johann. Herr Quantz"—he indicated the flutist seated across the table from them—"suggested His Majesty invite a few of the imperial musicians. But His Majesty was against anyone attached to the imperial court. When Herr Quantz enquired whether I knew of anyone more suitable, I could only think of your brother."

"*Ach so,*" Haydn said, although his question had still not been answered. A more pressing matter preoccupied his mind now.

Why had Herr Bach spoken so openly of the King's desire to go to war? Was there any truth to his assertions? Or were they merely the disaffected remarks of a virtuoso gone unappreciated for too long?

———

"I had hoped to meet the Archduchess Maria Antonia." Louis Joseph de Bourbon, Prince of Condé and Grand Maître de France, turned toward the Empress. "The fame of her beauty has reached France." He indicated Maria Amalia seated across the table. "The sisters resemble each other, I take it."

Not for the first time since they had left Vienna, the Empress felt a twinge of regret for allowing Amalia to accompany her. With her long, horsy face and her coarse manners, she gave her sisters a bad name.

"My little Antoine has a beauty and grace that far surpasses anything her older sisters possess." The Empress smiled. "It has not gone to her head, and for that, I am eternally grateful." She tipped her chin at Amalia, who burst into a loud, raucous laugh at some remark the Crown Prince of Prussia had made.

"What poor Amalia lacks in beauty, she makes up for in liveliness of spirits." The Empress winced at the look of utter disgust the King threw his heir and her daughter. The Crown Prince was known to have no morals as far as women were concerned, but her daughter would have only herself to blame if her honor were compromised.

"She is a little too loud and a little too bold, perhaps," the Empress went on, her lips pursed. She must have a word with the child tonight. If she intended to lose her virginity with a man other than her husband, it had best be after her marriage to Ferdinand of Parma. Not before.

Maria Theresa's gaze returned to the Prince of Condé. "We have never stood on ceremony in Vienna. And Amalia's plain features make men forget she is a woman."

She threw her daughter another glance, but Amalia forbore to look her way. The Crown Prince, red-faced and drunk, was clearly lost to all propriety. If only Seckendorff would intervene. But from the look of utter misery on his face, it was clear the richly spiced dishes of the Prussian table had brought on his gout.

The Empress sighed, but the Prince of Condé had gone on to other matters.

"Well, what is Your Majesty's opinion of it?" his voice interjected into her thoughts. "Is it not beautiful?"

She brought her attention back to her companion. What was the man talking about? It took a moment for her to notice the enormous stone of a deep violet hue sitting beside her plate.

"It is the diamond from the Order of the Golden Fleece," she said, startled. But it was out of its setting, the pendant created for the Order.

The Prince smiled. "No, Your Majesty. It is its twin. The stone from which both gems were cut was a gift from India. When His Late Majesty, Louis Roi-Soleil, had the stone cut, he gave this one to my grandfather, Louis de Bourbon. A gift for his numerous services to the King. It has been in the family since."

The Empress stared at the seven-sided, glittering gem, an intense blue on one side, luminescent on the other where the light from the chandelier glanced off it. "It is. . .quite breathtaking."

"Does Your Majesty think it should be made into a pendant? Or be cut into smaller pieces to be set into a necklace?"

"It would depend upon the intended recipient, I suppose," the Empress responded, quite at a loss to understand the reason for the question. Did the Prince mean to present the diamond to Antoine? A small token to accompany the more formal proposal of marriage that Durfort had assured her time and again would soon be coming?

Her pulse trilled a nervous flutter as the Prince weighed the diamond in his palm. "I suppose it would fetch a higher price were it to remain uncut," he said.

"Your Highness means to sell it? A family heirloom?" The Empress's voice rose. Surely she had misheard.

The Prince lived well beyond his means, she knew. A flaw all too French and one that her Antoine would have to curb once she was crowned Queen. But how great could his debts be that he should hawk his wares like a common huckster?

"Your Majesty finds herself interested, then?" An expression of eager hopefulness flitted across the Prince's unlined features.

"No," the Empress cried sharply, determined to put a stop to this unseemly peddling. "My coffers do not permit of such frivolous purchases."

The Prince sighed. "Ah, the thrifty soul of the Germans! Nothing can overcome its prudence, I fear. The King of Prussia has bluntly refused to make me an offer." His head swiveled to take in the other guests seated around the table. "Seckendorff has a soldier's tastes. Would Prince Nikolaus Esterházy be interested, perhaps?"

The Empress felt her mouth harden into a line of disapprobation. "He may well be. It is not for nothing he is called the Magnificent."

"Then, let us pass the diamond down the table. It is a beautiful piece. It would be a shame to deny our companions the joy of reveling in its beauty. And who knows one among them may even wish to make an offer for the damned thing."

Chapter Seven

THE vast kitchen in the imperial ambassador's residence on Linden-strasse was empty. Rosalie had never seen a house so devoid of servants. There had been but a few footmen waiting with His Lordship when they had arrived.

"Where can all the servants be?" she whispered to Greta. There was no one to hear them, but it was so quiet in this vast kitchen—empty save for the copper pots and pans that hung from the pegs—that to speak any louder seemed sacrilegious.

"His Lordship cannot have very many," Greta whispered back. She surveyed the polished stone floors and the gleaming tiles above the stove. "I only wish we knew where they kept their food. I am famished."

"Not at the court?" The deep voice behind them made them both jump.

It belonged to a tall, strikingly handsome man.

"We were instructed to remain here," Rosalie informed him. "Sir," she added after a brief pause not sure whom she was speaking with.

The navy coat and beige breeches were of a far superior quality than the clothing of a mere servant. But no musician or personal secretary, if the Count employed anyone in such a capacity, would casually walk into an area reserved for domestic servants.

"Indeed." The man smiled, but offered no explanation as to who he was. "Yet all the imperial servants have followed Her Majesty to the King's Palace."

"We are not employed by Her Majesty," Greta replied. "We attend to the musicians of the Esterházy Court, and we were told to remain here. Who are you?"

"Boris. The Count's valet." He closed the kitchen door and approached them. "I would have come down sooner had I known anyone was here. The servants of the household are asleep in their beds—"

"Is that not unusual?" Greta interrupted. "How can they be asleep when their master is still abroad?"

"They retire early on most nights." Boris seemed amused by the question. "At His Lordship's orders."

"We don't need anyone to wait with us," Rosalie said hastily. It was a strange household where the servants retired to bed before their master. But if that was the case, there was no reason for them to impose on His Lordship's valet.

"It is no trouble, I assure you," Boris assured her with another smile. "My master will want his poultice of horseradish to ease his gout when he returns. And I must stay awake to prepare it. Besides you will be hungry, I am sure."

His gaze, warm with appreciation, lingered on Rosalie's features.

———

In the Schlosstheater, about a mile to the west of the King's small palace, Sanssouci, Herr Bach's disquieting remarks continued to jostle around in Haydn's mind. The entire party had been conveyed shortly after supper to the theater with its white panels and gilded columns flanking either side of the stage.

"What think you of our opera, my dear Haydn?" The King, who had insisted the Kapellmeister be seated next to him, tapped him on the knee. The Italian greyhound at his feet shifted, flopping itself onto Haydn's feet.

The Kapellmeister stiffened. He had nothing against dogs. On the hunting fields, no animal could be more useful. But what kind of man brought a dog into an opera house? God forbid, the creature should do its business on his shoes!

On the stage, Medea complained of having lost the love of Jason. *A most unsuitable subject for the occasion*, Haydn privately thought. *This opera about a woman who forced her unfaithful husband to devour his children.* But it was not the sort of remark one made to a King.

"It is a most intriguing subject, Your Majesty," was all he could think of saying.

"Indeed." A pair of piercing blue eyes fastened themselves upon Haydn's features. "And why is that?"

Haydn took a deep breath and took the plunge. "One wonders how a man would react under the circumstances, Your Majesty."

"A man would simply cut his losses and move on, Haydn. But women rather than accepting their fate try to interfere, thus spoiling everything."

Haydn's eyes flickered involuntarily to the Empress. Was that the King's assessment of Her Majesty, then?

"My remarks appear to have hit the mark." The King's softly uttered words pulled Haydn's gaze back. His Majesty's well formed lips were curving into an amused smile. "You have the misfortune of being acquainted with such a woman, I suppose, Haydn."

The Kapellmeister felt his cheeks burn at the insinuation. His nostrils flared. "Your Majesty is mistaken," he said as calmly as he could manage. The sound of teeth clicking against metal reached his ears.

The infernal greyhound was chewing on the buckles of his shoes.

"Pepi!" The King called sharply, giving Haydn a start. But it was only the dog that His Majesty was addressing. *So, the hound was christened Joseph, too!* God be thanked, the King had not seen fit to nickname the creature, Sepperl.

A few minutes later, the King leaned closer to the Kapellmeister again. "What would your father, the Marktrichter, think of such a crime, Haydn?"

"Your Majesty!"

"A woman driven to commit a heinous act against her children by her husband's infidelity. Is such a crime deserving of punishment?"

Haydn gripped the arms of his seat. "My father never had occasion to judge such a crime, Your Majesty. The theft of a man's goods, the swindling of an honest housewife, these were the petty crimes he examined."

His Majesty regarded Haydn for a moment. "And such are the crimes you specialize in, I imagine."

What was the King getting at? "I have looked into one or two matters. But it is music that I specialize in, Your Majesty."

"Nevertheless." His Majesty continued to stare at Haydn. "Our guests are to be counted fortunate to have you in their midst. Who among us does not have something valuable that a thief could be tempted by?"

"How could such an incident take place in Your Majesty's presence?"

"What good does my presence do when my guests foolishly flaunt their treasures?"

Haydn frowned. Was His Majesty referring to the enormous, seven-sided violet diamond the Prince of Condé had passed around the table at supper?

"I cannot believe there is a thief in our midst, Your Majesty," he said firmly. "Unless Your Majesty doubts his own footmen and valets." He glanced at the King. Was that the reason for the summons he had received?

But the King merely grunted and turned his attention back to the stage.

———

The loud clanging of a bell shattered the quiet within the imperial ambassador's kitchen and aroused Rosalie from the drowsy stupor into which she had fallen.

"What was that?" Her eyes jolted open in time to see Boris hurrying toward the kitchen door.

"It is His Lordship, no doubt," he replied, glancing over his shoulder at her. "But I thought he had his key." The door swung shut behind him.

Rosalie sat up, rubbing the stiffness out of her neck. Beside her, Greta yawned and moaned and then opened her eyes.

"Has Herr Haydn returned?" she asked.

"Not yet." Rosalie smiled at her friend and then glanced back at the table. It was still littered with the remnants of the meal Boris had warmed up for them—a dish of noodles with spinach and cheese of Parma sent from the King's own kitchen.

"Let us wash the dishes," she suggested, reaching for her friend's plate.

They were just putting the last of the dishes away when Boris returned, agitated.

"The horseradish poultice? Where is it? His Lordship is in great pain."

"Near the stove where you left it." Rosalie pointed, noticing for the first time the stiff left leg that forced the valet to walk with a slight limp. Agitation aggravated it, no doubt.

Boris snatched the poultice up. "I doubt it will suffice," he said, when the bell clanged again.

"God preserve us, who can it be at this hour?" he muttered.

"Herr Haydn, perhaps." Greta briskly wiped her hands on her apron. "You go attend to His Lordship. Rosalie and I will see who is at the door."

Boris bit his lip, hesitating, then shook his head. "No. Let me see who it is. But"—he looked at them—"It would be well if you could get an infusion of horseradish started. It will need some ground elder and meadow saffron as well."

The maids nodded in unison.

"You will find the ingredients in the larder." Boris indicated the larder door with a tip of his head. "Be sure to sweeten it with some honey," he said as he swung open the kitchen door. "It is the only way His Lordship will drink it."

The concoction was simmering nicely and ready to be taken off the fire by the time the valet came back, muttering under his breath.

"Who was it?" Rosalie asked, looking over her shoulder.

"Herr Ritter, the jeweler from the establishment on Gutenbergstrasse. He comes at the oddest of hours and insists upon seeing His Lordship."

The valet shook his head wearily. "I tried to dissuade him tonight, but he said it was urgent and planted himself on a chair in the vestibule." He gestured toward the stove. "Is the infusion ready?"

"What an odd thing to do," Rosalie whispered once Boris had left, horrified that a mere jeweler could barge into the residence of a Count and insist upon a reception.

"His Lordship must be deep in debt," Greta whispered back. "Why else would the jeweler be here at this hour of the night?"

Before they could discuss the matter any further, Boris was back, alarm writ large on his features. "His Lordship is gone!" he said, the infusion of horseradish still in his hands.

"Gone!" the maids echoed. They glanced at each other. "Gone where?"

Boris shook his head. "He is not in his bedchamber, where I left him. I cannot find him anywhere."

"And what of his visitor?" Rosalie asked. "The man you left waiting in the vestibule?"

It was clear from the blank expression on his face that the valet had forgotten all about the jeweler. "I suppose we had best inform him of the fact," he said.

But the vestibule, when they entered it, was empty. The front door stood ajar.

———◆◆◆———

The frozen waters of the Stadtkanal glistened white beneath the gray stone bridge. The Empress brushed a mound of snow from the iron railing onto the white sheet below. Where was Seckendorff?

Beside her, Esterházy shivered in the cold night air, wrapping his fur-lined cloak tighter around his girth.

"Is Your Majesty certain this is the intended meeting place?" Esterházy stamped his feet and looked around him.

The Empress nodded. "Over the bridge near the Katholische Kirche St. Anna." She gestured toward the plain square church with its twin spires rising into the night sky. There was something reassuring about its solidity.

Esterházy stamped his feet again, whether from the cold or impatience, the Empress knew not. "Where can he be then? It is no more than a five-minute walk from Lindenstrasse."

The Empress remained silent, her gaze resting on the church looming above the canal. As they had left the Prussian king's table, Seckendorff had managed to slip a note into her hand. A request to meet her on the bridge near the Katholische Kirche after the opera.

He had important information to communicate. He had sought to give it to her when she had first arrived, but the Prussian king's unexpected presence had prevented him from saying anything.

"What information did Seckendorff have for Your Majesty?" Esterházy's voice, tired and impatient, broke in upon her thoughts.

"We would not be here if I knew what it was, Esterházy," she gently reminded him. He was like a child with his constant questions, but she restrained her own annoyance. Esterházy had after all unhesitatingly accompanied her out.

But where was Seckndorff? Had something untoward occurred?

"It is most likely his gout," she said. Seckendorff had retired soon after supper, returning home instead of accompanying them to the opera house. "The inflammation in his toes makes every step painful."

"Then we should have met indoors. What was wrong with meeting in Your Majesty's apartment?"

"I imagine he preferred not to be overheard by servants," the Empress drily pointed out. "And have everything he said reported to the King."

"A clandestine meeting arouses just as much suspicion," Esterházy argued.

"Ostensibly, it is not a meeting. Merely a walk to relieve my shortness of breath. And you were kind enough to accompany me. And Seckendorff, a gracious host offering us his protection."

"Except he is not here." Esterházy shivered again as he glanced around him. "I doubt he means to come, Your Majesty."

The Empress shook her head. Seckendorff was a man of his word. "What if he is unable to come? For a reason other than his gout?"

Seckendorff was a military man. She had never known him to allow pain or discomfort to rule his life. Mere pain would not have prevented him from coming.

"Then there is nothing we can do until morning." Esterházy handed her the walking stick that rested against the iron railing on the bridge. "Come, Your Majesty. We have waited here over a half hour. We can hardly wait the entire night."

She was reluctant to leave, she knew not why. But what argument could she offer in support of staying? That the Catholic Church of St. Anna beckoned to her?

"Very well." She brushed aside the feeling that she was abandoning Seckendorff. Her ambassador was safe in his bed. Nursing a remedy for his gout, no doubt.

Chapter Eight

THE sun had inched up over the horizon by the time the Kapellmeister and his brother turned onto Yorckstrasse the next morning. Its pale light gleamed on the yellow cobblestones lightly dusted with snow.

The Kapellmeister gazed at his surroundings and sighed. "It is a beautiful little city, is it not, Johann?"

He shifted the basket he was carrying onto his right wrist and slowed down to admire the warm golden patches that brightened the stone bridges spanning the canal on the right.

Johann nodded. "And spacious. The streets are wide; the buildings imposing. Vienna, for all that it is larger, has a cramped, constricted air in comparison."

They stepped to the right—feet meandering in unison—to peer over the low iron railing that separated the street from the city canal. Its frozen waters were bathed in a rosy hue. Behind them, the twin spires of the Katholische Kirche St. Anna towered over the snow-covered, red-roofed houses on the street.

"A plain sandstone structure"— Johann pivoted around to look at it—"but it could hold its own against the more splendid churches of Vienna."

He turned toward his brother. "Are we to meet Herr Bach there or await him here by the canal?"

"He did not say." Haydn peered at his timepiece. "But we may as well make our way there if we are to try the organ. The service begins in an hour."

"Then let us make haste." Johann pushed himself away from the iron railing.

The organ-builder Gottfried Silbermann had supplied the Katholische Kirche St. Anna with its organ—a magnificent piece with three manuals and forty-seven stops. But it was Herr Bach's father, Sebastian Bach, who had overseen its installation.

The meticulous instructions he had left behind for its care had ensured a richness and clarity of tone that surpassed that of any other church organ in Potsdam. Not even the mighty King of Prussia could boast of having an instrument that sounded half so well.

In step with his brother, the Kapellmeister set off at his usual brisk pace, keen to inspect the organ before the congregation gathered for the morning mass. They found the wooden gate leading into the cobblestone churchyard latched and the yard itself devoid of people.

"The pastor is yet to arrive," Haydn noted with satisfaction as he lifted the latch and opened the gate. He let himself in and waited for Johann to follow. "But the church door should be open. Herr Bach says the pastor leaves it unlocked during the night."

"For any chance worshippers who may wish to enter?" Johann smiled. "It is a good thought."

The church door, made of panels of a pale oak matching the yellow sandstone of the walls, was set back within a deep arch that formed a portico over the entrance.

Setting his basket on the stone steps, Haydn reached for the large brass knob and twisted hard. The knob yielded, but the door refused to budge.

"Most peculiar!" Haydn stepped back and stared at the oak panels. "It is unlocked, I can tell." He twisted the knob again and, placing his left palm flat against the wood panels, pushed hard. The door opened a few inches, its edge grating harshly against the stone floor.

Haydn leaned against the panels, breathing hard. "There must be something behind this door that prevents it from opening," he said when he had sufficiently recovered his breath to speak.

"Why would anyone have blocked the door?" His brother wanted to know.

The Kapellmeister shrugged. "It makes little sense. But what other reason could there be for it failing to open?"

"Perhaps the hinges need oiling. Here, let me help you."

Johann braced his shoulder against the wood panels. But even under their combined weight, the door barely yielded a few more inches, scraping against the floor with an unpleasant rasp.

"It will go no farther, Johann," Haydn grunted. "And I fear our attempts to force it back might only scratch the floor."

The elaborate floral mosaic that decorated the entrance had been recovered from a thirteenth-century Venetian church by the Great Elector, the Prussian King's great-grandfather. Any damage to it would not be suffered lightly, the Kapellmeister was sure.

Sucking his belly in, he squeezed himself through the narrow opening. His eyes blinked in the dim interior, barely brightened by the few shafts of light that entered through the stained glass windows set high into the walls on either side.

He heard Johann behind him and took another step forward, his feet squelching into a dark, slippery substance that covered the floor.

"What is that foul odor?" Johann's low voice sounded eerily loud in his ears. Haydn did not know, but he had detected it as well. A strange metallic odor that intermingled with the close, damp air within the church.

His eyes strained to see the floor. What was it they had stepped in? A walking stick lay on the ground, one end wedged under the door, the other lying in a trail of—

"Blood?" The Kapellmeister's voice rose. His head twisted around to meet his brother's startled eyes. "It is blood, Johann."

———◆◆◆———

"You're a fidgety little thing, aren't you?" Frau Göss, wife of the imperial count's Hausmeister, looked over her knitting at Rosalie and smiled.

Rosalie sighed, a heavy, drawn-out breath of boredom. "I am unused to such idleness," she confessed. "There is so little to do here."

She had dressed Frau Haydn's hair, draped her gown, a simple affair of blue silk lined with wool and embroidered with white flowers, around her slim form. But after that, there had been nothing to do.

One of the Count's footmen had directed the Kapellmeister's wife to the white-and-yellow breakfast room overlooking the gardens and orangerie. Frau Göss had prepared the morning meal and her husband along with some of the footmen had overseen the serving of it to the Count's guests.

Frau Göss unwound some more yarn. "I am surprised the Count wasn't at breakfast this morning. It is not like him at all to be late to his meals. Especially when he has guests. And Boris, his valet, is nowhere to be seen either."

"His Lordship was out late last night," Rosalie informed the Hausmeister's wife, recounting the events of the previous night.

"Hmmm. . ." Frau Göss frowned. "It is not like His Lordship to dash out like that either. Without a word to Boris or anyone else for that matter. And you say, he went without his cloak?"

Rosalie nodded, troubled now. What business could have taken the imperial ambassador out on such a cold night? Without his cloak? And when he was so afflicted by the gout?

Something was clearly wrong. She should have heeded her inner promptings to look into the matter. But Greta had so taken her to task that morning for even mentioning Boris—"*I don't care where he is, and neither should you. I saw the way he was looking at you last night!*"— that she had put all thought of the valet and his master out of her mind.

She rose to her feet, determined. "Let me take a tray up to His Lordship, Frau Göss," she said. "And I will look in on Boris as well."

Frau Göss bit her lip, clearly doubtful of the wisdom of disturbing the Count. Then she put down her knitting "It might be the best way." She pushed back her chair. "If anything is amiss, we had best find out what it is and raise the alarm."

They were about to approach the door when it swung open and Boris appeared in the doorway, disheveled and distraught.

"The Count!" he said, his gaze wildly perambulating the room. "Where is he? Have you seen him?

Frau Göss's hand flew to her throat. "Is he not in his bed?" she asked, although the answer to that question was apparent in the valet's features.

"His bed was not slept in," Greta said. She had been standing so quietly at the doorway, Rosalie had not noticed her. Greta followed Boris into the room.

"It seems His Lordship never returned home." She turned to Rosalie. "Boris here was waiting up for him in His Lordship's bedchamber and fell sound asleep there. He only awoke when Ada and I entered the room to clean it."

"But what shall we do?" Frau Göss stood as though petrified. Her eyes sought Rosalie's.

"We must inform Her Majesty," Rosalie said quietly.

It was what His Serene Highness had instructed them to do in the event that something untoward occurred. If neither Herr Haydn nor Master Johann were available, they were to waste no time in seeking out Her Majesty or His Serene Highness.

For what seemed like an eternity, the Kapellmeister and his brother stood by the door, unable to move, their eyes transfixed by the disorderly scene within the church.

"What can have happened here?" Haydn whispered. He stared at the black cane with its ornate gold handle. That must have caused the door to stick. His eyes followed the trail of blood that meandered from the cane to a large cloak-covered figure lying prone at the base of the marble font.

The sight galvanized them to action.

"Good God!" Johann muttered. "Who would do such a thing? Do you suppose the poor man is still alive?" He hurried toward the figure.

Haydn followed, taking care to avoid the rivulet of blood.

"I trust he is not beyond help," he said. But he had his misgivings as he knelt down beside the tall muscular figure lying with his head against the bloodstained base of the marble font.

Very gently, as though touching a sleeping man, the Kapellmeister reached out and placed his palm on the man's broad back. The ribs did not rise and fall. He lifted the man's wrist—it was as cold as ice—and pressed his fingers into it. He could detect no pulse.

The sickening sensation he had managed to keep at bay returned with full force.

"I fear he is already gone."

He glanced up at his brother, still holding the dead man's wrist, loath to let it fall back into the congealing pool of blood it had lain in. Johann nodded, tight-lipped. It had not needed as close an examination as the Kapellmeister had effected to know the man was dead.

Johann's gaze, Haydn noticed, drifted toward the pool of blood spreading out from beneath the man. It made an unsightly stain on the gold-flecked marble floor. "The blood cannot be cleaned until the authorities arrive," he reminded his brother, although the urge to wash the floors clean of the dark, viscous mess that stained them had afflicted him as well.

"I remember," Johann said quietly. It was not the first time they had encountered violent death, and each time Herr Hipfl, the barber-surgeon of Eisenstadt, had taken care to drive home the importance of disturbing the scene as little as possible.

"But he will need to be turned over to be carried out." He knelt down on the other side of the body. "And it would be best for him not to be lying in his own blood."

"True enough," Haydn agreed. Herr Hipfl, the barber-surgeon, might have found some reason to argue against this course of action. The Kapellmeister, for the life of him, could not.

It took an effort to move the body. In life, the man had been considerably taller and heavier than either the Kapellmeister or his frail younger brother. In death, his lifeless body seemed as heavy as a millstone.

With a deep grunt, the brothers lifted the right side and twisted it until the body fell with a thud onto its back. Panting heavily from the exertion, the Kapellmeister stared at the dead man's torso.

Vicious gashes were carved into the chest. A particularly deep slash under the ribs appeared to have caused the most bleeding.

He was overcome by a fresh wave of revulsion. "Who could have done such a thing? In a church, no less?" he demanded. "What foul people live among us?" He had almost said *here*, the ethereal beauty of Potsdam in the dawn besmirched forever in his mind by this awful incident.

But no doubt such things could happen in Vienna as well. *Had indeed happened*, he thought recalling the brutal murder of his friend the previous year.

He turned toward his brother, but Johann—his face frozen into a mask of horror—appeared not to have heard a word.

"What is it, Johann?"

His brother's lips moved, but not a single word came out of his mouth. He swallowed, cleared his throat, and opened his mouth again.

"It is the ambassador, brother." The words came out in a hoarse croak as Johann's forefinger stretched out toward the dead man's face. "It is Count Seckendorff."

Chapter Nine

THE Palace, when Rosalie and Greta arrived in search of the Empress, was in an uproar. The nervous tension could be felt near the stables where the horses whinnied, tossing their manes and stomping their hooves. Grooms snapped at stable boys. Maids hung near the kitchen door, chattering excitedly.

Rosalie came to a halt between the stables and the kitchen. "What can possibly be the matter?" she whispered to Greta.

They had hoped to enter through the kitchen and thence make their way quietly toward the guest rooms. But with the servants swarming around the back door, they would have to fight their way in.

"Let us go—" she began to say when Greta suddenly yelped, "Ow!" and stumbled back against her.

"*Ach*! Don't just stand in the middle of the path." A footman hurrying toward the kitchen tossed the admonition over his shoulder. "Get a move on!"

"Get a move on, indeed!" Greta cried indignantly. "The servants are as rude as their master is known to be." She put her hands on her hips. "That's it. We're not going in through the kitchen. We'll go in through the front and use our seal. That'll teach these thickheaded clods to mind their manners."

The door to the entrance hall was thrown wide open. The maids stepped inside.

"You there!" Greta hailed a footman about to leave the hall.

The man turned sharply. His features arranged into a polite mask rearranged themselves into an expression of fury. "What are you doing here? This is no place for servants." He strode toward them, shaking his fist. It appeared to be the same man who had unceremoniously bumped into Greta.

Rosalie brought out the imperial seal with its double-headed eagle from her pocket and held it in front of her like a shield.

The footman stopped, bewildered.

"We are here to see Her Majesty, Empress Maria Theresa," Greta announced with as much dignity as she could muster. "It is a private matter and rather urgent. You will show us to her rooms immediately."

Rosalie bit her lip, stifling a giggle as much at her friend's stern tone as at the footman's expression as he stared first at Greta and then at herself. It took him a while to recover his composure. Then he gestured toward a hallway leading off from the entrance hall.

"The guest rooms are to your right—Madame," he added, when Greta glared at him.

"Excellent!" Greta said. "Show us the way and get a move on, will you?"

The footman frowned and hesitated.

Seeing his lips set into an obdurate line, Rosalie smiled. "You seem to be extraordinarily busy today. What is all the hubbub about?"

The footman hesitated again. Rosalie forced her lips to stretch into an even wider smile. "Trouble with one of the guests?" She made herself sound sympathetic.

"One of our guests *has* lost a valuable item," the footman conceded." It appears to have been stolen."

———◆◆◆———

"God in Heaven!" Haydn crossed himself a second time as he stared at the imperial ambassador's lifeless body. Innumerable questions crawled through his mind like maggots within a rotting corpse.

Would to God, Herr Bach would arrive soon. Or the pastor. To leave the body unattended while they went in search of help seemed somehow not at all wise. The passerby Johann had accosted outside the churchyard had been frustratingly unhelpful.

"It is the Amtsrichter you need if you wish to report a crime," he had said. "Not the Bürgermeister."

"Very well," Haydn had replied patiently. "And where might we find the Amtsrichter, then?"

The passerby had blinked. "At this hour? At his home, I imagine. Where else would he be?" And with that singularly worthless bit of information, he had walked away, shaking his head.

As though their questions were supremely absurd, Haydn thought, the memory of the encounter still gnawing upon his nerves.

"His Lordship left the palace shortly after supper last night." Johann's voice broke into the Kapellmeister's thoughts. His younger brother looked up at him, his gray eyes wide. "Do you suppose he was killed on his way home?"

"But this was not on his way home. What was he even doing here?" The Kapellmeister closed his eyes, pressed his fingers to his throbbing temple, and forced himself to calm down. He would need to concentrate if he wished to discover anything at all useful.

He opened his eyes again and looked closely at the body.

A shirt of white silk with ruffles peeped out from above the long gold waistcoat, slashed into ribbons and bloodied. The white breeches were soiled with blood.

"These are the garments His Lordship was wearing at supper last night, are they not?" he asked, although he was quite sure they were.

"Yes, but he is without his military coat," Johann said. "It was white with broad cuffs of blue. I recall seeing one of the palace footmen helping His Lordship into it last night."

"He appears to have exchanged it for that cloak." Haydn pointed to it. It was made of fine wool, but its midnight blue hue had faded and it was worn at the edges. The sort of garment that had so clearly seen better days, it would be more likely to be owned by one of the Count's servants.

And yet, here it was on his person.

"A disguise, do you suppose?" Johann had with his usual perspicacity divined the questions in the Kapellmeister's mind.

"Possibly. But that would mean he was at the church on some surreptitious business." The hairs on the nape of Haydn's neck stood up and he gathered his coat about him, suddenly cold.

Was the ambassador, God rest his soul, a spy?

If so, had His Lordship been discovered? By the King? Haydn closed his eyes. But why wait until the arrival of the imperial party to despatch him?

He opened his eyes and stared at his brother. "Does it seem like a coincidence that His Lordship should have been killed on the very night of our arrival?"

Johann frowned, about to ask a question, but Haydn went on: "In the very church we planned to visit this morning."

"But who else other than Herr Bach could have known of our plans?"

"I mentioned it to the King at the opera last night," Haydn said quietly.

Johann sucked in his breath so sharply, the sound echoed through the empty church. He looked down at the Count.

"Then we had best make sure His Lordship is not found with any incriminating evidence upon his person."

———

Working together, Haydn and Johann conducted a quick search of the imperial ambassador's person.

"His Lordship's purse is missing," Johann announced, pausing to look up at his brother.

Haydn surveyed the body and its surroundings. His brother was right. Count Seckendorff's purse, a pouch of fawn-colored calfskin was not on his person or anywhere near him.

"He must have left without it," he said. "His Lordship appears to have returned home only to set out again."

He pointed at the Count's feet. They were encased in leather mules with green satin uppers embroidered in gold thread. Not the kind of footwear a man wore outside his bedchamber.

Haydn pulled them off and immediately averted his face as a pungent whiff of horseradish assailed his nostrils. That it came from the poultice wrapped around the big toe of His Lordship's right foot was plainly evident.

Johann frowned. "The appointment that brought him out must have been unexpected, then."

"Or His Lordship's gout was so painful he preferred to wear loose-fitting bedroom slippers."

Haydn felt the pockets on the long gold waistcoat, torn now and bloodstained. "He appears to have brought no papers with him, but —" His voice broke off abruptly as his fingers closed around a large, faceted object. Smooth and cold to the touch and extremely hard.

He had barely withdrawn it from His Lordship's waistcoat pocket when the church door was flung open, flooding the ghastly scene with bright morning sunlight.

"Herr Haydn! Master Johann!"

Herr Bach's explosion of horrified surprise brought the Kapellmeister's head up with a jerk. He stared, open-mouthed, at the King's harpsichordist until Johann's mild cough recalled him to the object in his hand.

He dropped it hastily into his own pocket. His hands felt sticky and he wiped them on his coat.

"I am afraid I was unaccountably delayed." Herr Bach hurried in. "His Majesty wished to practice on the flute and insisted upon being accompanied on the harpsichord. But"—his gaze rested astonished on the gruesome scene at his feet—"what is all this, Herr Haydn?"

"It is the imperial ambassador, I fear, Herr Bach." Haydn rose, his heart pounding within him. Had Herr Bach seen what he had discovered?

"We found His Lordship when we arrived here," Johann explained, rising as well. "Lying on his stomach in a pool of blood. When we turned him over, it was clear he was beyond hope."

Herr Bach nodded white-faced, his eyes still on the body. He brought out a large white handkerchief and wiped his broad, fleshy features with it. "Dear God!" he whispered.

"Th-the magistrate will have to be informed. And the body removed" —the harpsichordist pressed his handkerchief to his nose and looked behind him at the door—"before the pastor arrives."

"So a passerby informed us," Haydn said. "But could tell us nothing more about the magistrate's whereabouts than to say he could be found at home."

A faint glimmer of a smile twitched at the corners of Herr Bach's lips. "The people here are ever taciturn. Words seem to them as precious as thalers. The Amtsrichter will be at the Rathaus. It is not far from here."

He turned toward Johann. "Would you accompany me, Master Johann, while your brother stands guard over the body?" At Johann's nod, he continued: "We had best hurry, then. The pastor will soon be here."

The Amtsrichter of Potsdam, a tall, broad man with the rigid posture of a soldier, listened to Herr Bach attentively. He stood on the steps of the city hall, his hands behind his back, punctuating Herr Bach's narrative with emphatic nods of his head.

"His Majesty will need to be informed at once," he solemnly declared once Herr Bach had finished. His head bobbed up and down again.

"His Majesty?" Johann hoped the dismay he felt at this news wasn't discernible in his voice. He had hoped to convey the news to the Empress first. "Is this not. . ." His voice faded.

Too trivial a matter, he had been about to say. But what was so trivial about the brutal murder of the imperial ambassador to Prussia?

"His Majesty insists upon being informed of everything that happens within the city walls," the Amtsrichter explained. "He may even wish to oversee the investigation himself."

God in Heaven! Were they to expect constant meddling from the King himself. Johann glanced at Herr Bach.

"I will take it upon myself to inform His Majesty," Herr Bach said briskly. "But the poor gentleman must be removed from the church immediately. Can you imagine the consternation of the pastor when he arrives? Not to mention the alarm of the congregation at the brutal murder of a Catholic visitor to the city?"

Johann frowned, puzzled. What did the religion of the murdered man matter at a time like this? It took him a moment to understand why Herr Bach had underscored the point.

"The murder of a Catholic in a Catholic church." The Amtsrichter's sun-browned cheeks paled. "The unrest and disorder the news will create among the Catholics does not bear thinking of?"

"No," Herr Bach agreed simply. "Potsdam is supposed to be safe for Catholics and Protestants alike. Jews, too. And, God help us, the Turks and heathens whom the King has encouraged to live among us."

"But he cannot have died on account of his religion?" The Amtsrichter wiped his brow unhappily.

"One hopes not," Herr Bach said in a tone of exaggerated fervor. "But it would be best to. . ." He allowed his voice to trail off as he surveyed the market square. Next door, the baker was opening his doors. Behind them, a few maids carrying baskets crossed the cobbled square.

"To call for help. Yes, yes. Of course." The Amtsrichter scratched the short, stubby furze of growth on his scalp. "I will have some men sent to the church directly."

He shook his head. "But what could have brought on such a heinous crime? I cannot understand it."

Creases of worry lined his forehead and his eyes crinkled in perturbation. "Such a thing has never happened before."

Chapter Ten

HAYDN had just emerged into the sunlight when a small, gray-haired man in a black cassock bustled through the gate into the church-yard. The pastor, no doubt. The Kapellmeister drew the church door shut and stood in front of it.

The pastor hurried down the path with his head down. It was only when he had reached the square block of stone that served as a step that he looked up, startled to see his path blocked. For a moment, the two men stared at each other. The pastor with a kindly, enquiring expression on his lined features; Haydn at a complete loss for words.

"It would be best not to go in," he said eventually. "There is. . ." He paused, unsure how to break the news, and scanned the street beyond. Would to God, the magistrate were here! How far could the city hall be?

Seeing no sign of his brother or the personage he had been sent to fetch, Haydn took a deep breath and gazed into the pastor's eyes. "A man has been murdered. The imperial ambassador to the kingdom of Prussia. My brother and I discovered his body within. The Amtsrichter is on his way."

"Murdered!" The pastor's shocked gaze was drawn toward the door. "Within the church?" He made a sign of the cross. "Who would do something so unspeakable? Who would kill a man while he was at prayer?"

"At prayer?" Haydn enquired. The ambassador was no doubt as God-fearing as the next man, but surely it was not prayer that had brought him to the church.

The pastor nodded. "His Lordship often frequented the church at night for that purpose. It was at his request that I kept the church door open. He was a most devout man."

"*Ach so.*" Haydn frowned. It seemed unlikely that a mere desire for communion with the Lord had brought the ambassador out in his bedroom slippers. But the pastor's features were so earnest, the Kapellmeister could not but wonder if there was any truth to the story.

It was clear the pastor had never thought to question it.

A small group of colorfully dressed people approaching the church recalled Haydn to his purpose. He inclined his head in the direction of the gate. "The congregation must be kept away. This is no sight for common folk."

The pastor swung around. "No. No, of course not. I will lead them to the church hall." He hurried back down the path.

Haydn watched as the pastor shepherded his congregation down the street. Had the imperial ambassador really ventured out to pray? Or was there some other reason for his presence at the church?

Haydn touched his pocket, feeling the sharp contours of the diamond he had discovered on the ambassador's person. How had it found its way into His Lordship's waistcoat pocket?

"Seckendorff returned home, you say?" The Empress beckoned Rosalie forward.

The maid nodded and stepped forward. She felt an inexplicable desire to grasp Greta's hand, but it would have been unseemly in the imperial presence.

"His gout prevented His Lordship from attending the opera," she said.

"And then, despite the agony he was under, he left again?" The Empress turned toward His Serene Highness, who stood by the window. "He must have been coming to see us. What think you, Esterházy?"

"It was very likely the case," His Serene Highness agreed. "You did well to come to us." He inclined his head at the maids with a paternal smile, a gesture that went a long way toward putting them at their ease.

"Yet, he never arrived. Unless"—the Empress thrust her lower lip out —"he arrived only to find us gone." Her Majesty directed a reproachful glance at the Prince. "We ought never to have doubted him. We should have stayed longer."

"But His Lordship failed to return home," Greta reminded them. "And he is not here at the King's palace. Where could he be?"

The Empress sighed, her lips compressed into an anxious line, her face chalky under its thick covering of powder. "The girl is right, Esterházy. Even if we are to assume the Count's gout prevented him from returning home, where could he have taken shelter—"

And what of the jeweler who came to see His Lordship? Rosalie thought, but was prevented from voicing the question by the sudden, startled cry Her Majesty emitted.

"The Katholische Kirche St. Anna!" she exclaimed, swiveling around toward the Prince in her excitement. "He must have taken shelter there. I felt strangely drawn to it last night. I only wish we had gone inside. My instincts have never been wrong."

Her Majesty rose. "Ring for a carriage, will you?" she said to Greta who stood closest to the bell. "And after that, find Haydn wherever he is and have him meet us at the church."

Rosalie's gaze fluttered toward Greta. What strange coincidence had directed the Kapellmeister to the selfsame church?

"Herr Haydn and Master Johann are already there, Your Majesty," she said, her voice subdued by a vague sense of unease. Were Elma's fears coming to pass?

———————

The Amtsrichter, when he arrived with Johann and a group of four stalwart men, stared gravely at the scene.

"Such a thing has never occurred in Potsdam," he declared, surveying the immense quantity of blood, still wet in the cold Prussian weather and viscous; the bloodstained marble font; and the lifeless corpse.

How the Amtsrichter could stomach such a sight, Haydn knew not. But the magistrate's uniform studded with medals spoke of long experience in the battlefield. And he had likely seen worse in the numerous wars he had fought.

The magistrate's gaze fell on the imperial ambassador's contorted features, and his lips tightened. "No one in Potsdam has ever defiled a place of worship in this manner."

Was the official blaming the imperial ambassador for his own death? Haydn's eyes sought Johann's, who responded with a sympathetic shake of his head.

"The people of Potsdam have always lived in harmony, no matter what their religion," the magistrate went on. "Until now."

He turned toward Haydn. "What was His Lordship even doing within the church? Had he an appointment with you? It was you who found the body, was it not?"

"We both did as I have already explained," Johann said patiently. "As to why His Lordship came here—"

"It was to pray," Haydn interjected, glad to have a ready response to the question. The magistrate seemed to have taken it into his head that having made the gruesome discovery, he and Johann were somehow responsible for it.

"So the pastor said," he continued when Johann turned sharply to look at him, his eyebrows rising in disbelief. Haydn's gaze returned toward the magistrate. "His Lordship was wont to seek out the church for that purpose. The door was always kept open so he could let himself in."

"Was it nothing more than chance that you and your brother followed His Lordship here?" The magistrate's blue eyes bore into Haydn's with such intensity, the Kapellmeister felt a headache coming on. "Only to find him dead?"

"It would appear so," Haydn replied evenly. To express his own doubts on the subject would only implicate them further.

"And you arrived but yesterday?" The magistrate turned to Johann, seeking corroboration of facts he must already have been supplied with.

Johann sighed. "Our presence here this morning was at Herr Bach's invitation, Herr Amtsrichter. He wished us to try the organ, to hear for ourselves the sonorous notes it produces."

"Besides, it was at night that His Lordship came here to pray." Haydn rubbed his temples. "Not at dawn. The state of the blood and the body speak for themselves."

"Nevertheless, you will allow it is a most suspicious circumstance." The magistrate waved the waiting men forward. "You there! Remove the body and inform the barber-surgeon a corpse awaits his attention."

He glanced around him. "The church floor must be cleansed. Although God knows if that will be enough to appease the Catholics," he grumbled to himself. "If the incident is not contained, there will be civil discord in Potsdam just as in Poland."

Poland! The mention of the country caught Haydn's attention, he knew not why. Princess Auersperg had referred to the state of affairs in Poland as well. A mere coincidence? Or was the situation in Poland in some way entangled with the ambassador's murder?

"I trust you and your brother did no more than turn the body over."

Haydn's thoughts were interrupted by the magistrate's voice.

"His papers and belongings are intact?" The magistrate gazed at the Kapellmeister and his brother, seeking reassurance on the point.

"What His Majesty will say if he discovers any evidence was tampered with, I cannot say. He will not take kindly to it, I know."

"Nothing was taken, I assure you." God forgive him for the lie. In a house of worship, at that. But what else was he do? He resisted the urge to glance at Johann.

"But I would like to keep the Count's cloak. His Lordship's servants may need something of his to accept. . ." Haydn inclined his head at the pallet the men were carrying out, hoping the reason would suffice.

He could think of none better. There was certainly no question of revealing the truth.

The magistrate hesitated. Then, to Haydn's relief, he nodded. "Very well. I don't suppose His Majesty will find any reason to object."

"Let us stop awhile, Esterházy," the Empress huffed, the long walk from the palace having made her breathless.

Prince Nikolaus obediently stopped, allowing her to lean heavily against his arm while she regained her breath.

"We are almost there, Your Majesty," he said, refraining, she noticed, from pointing out that it would have been more comfortable to have driven. But taking one of the King's carriages would only have served to alert Frederick to their whereabouts.

The cold air was refreshing; the snow-covered streets peaceful. The burning in the Empress's lungs gradually dissipated as her gaze came to rest upon the twin spires of the Katholische Kirche St. Anna looming in the distance.

A strange foreboding filled her, quickening her senses as she espied a city official leading a group of men carrying a pallet. She drew Esterházy's attention to the sight.

"What do you suppose that is?" Her fingers tightened around his arm, causing him to wince.

"Nothing that concerns us, I imagine, Your Majesty," the magnate reassured her. She wished she could believe him. But to give in to her fears had never been her way.

"Let us be on our way," she said, determined to confront whatever it was that awaited them.

The church gate stood ajar when they reached their destination a few minutes later. Haydn, carrying a worn blue cloak over his arm, and Johann were hurrying toward it when they became aware of her presence.

"Your Majesty!" Haydn came to an abrupt halt. The color drained from his already ashen features. He stared first at her and then at Esterházy.

"Your Majesty has heard the news, then?" Johann enquired. "We were about to seek your presence. . ." his voice trailed off.

"What news?" the Empress demanded, although she was certain she knew what it was. "Where is Count Seckendorff?" She tipped her chin at the church. "Is he still within?"

"The magistrate has just taken charge of the body," Haydn informed them.

"The body? Whose body?" Esterházy exploded. "Explain yourself, Haydn."

The composer looked stricken. He swallowed, staring at them as though hoping the truth would suggest itself to them.

The Empress sighed. "I believe what Haydn is trying to tell us, Esterházy, is that Seckendorff is no more."

Haydn bowed his head. "We discovered him in the church this morning." The Kapellmeister took a deep breath. "But that is not all, Your Majesty."

"No?" It was more a statement than a question. She watched him closely. Had he divined the truth about Seckendorff?

But she was not prepared for what he brought out of his pocket.

"It is the blue diamond belonging to the Prince of Condé, Haydn!"

Her startled gaze flew to his features. "He reported it missing only this morning. All of Sanssouci is in an uproar as a result. How came it into your possession?"

"We found it on His Lordship's person, Your Majesty," Johann's quiet voice interjected. "It was in his waistcoat pocket. Brother thought it best to retrieve it before the Amtsrichter arrived."

"What could the Count have wanted with the Prince of Condé's diamond, Your Majesty?" Haydn wanted to know. But the Empress had no answer for him.

She was still struggling to frame a response when an unpleasantly familiar voice intruded upon her consciousness.

"What? Is Seckendorff truly dead?" The King of Prussia walked through the gate, leaning on his cane. Stopping beside them, he twisted around to face the Empress and Esterházy. "Your Majesty appears to have been apprised of the fact before even I was."

Haydn's outstretched palm, with the diamond within it, remained frozen in the air.

Chapter Eleven

THE King's gaze fell on the violet-hued gem in Haydn's hand.

"Ah! What have we here?" He plucked the diamond, still covered in a sticky white residue, from Haydn's palm.

"It is the Prince of Condé's diamond, as Your Majesty is well aware," the Empress retorted, her exasperation ill-concealed. His Serene Highness, standing beside Her Majesty, merely nodded, his features deflated.

The King could not have come at a more inopportune moment.

"So, I see." The King continued to stare at the stone. "Covered in custard, I believe." He rubbed some of the sticky residue off the gem and brought his finger to his tongue. "Yes, indeed. Just as I thought."

Custard? Haydn looked at Johann. Why in the name of God had the stone been covered in custard? They had been served iced bowls of it at supper the previous night. Did that mean—?

The King interrupted his thoughts before he could bring them to a conclusion.

"The Prince of Condé will be relieved to learn his precious diamond is not lost." His Majesty raised his eyes toward the Kapellmeister. "But how is one to explain its presence in your palm, Haydn?"

Haydn's breath caught, its passage down his throat interrupted by the King's insinuation. To let it stand was to allow himself to be accused of theft. But what explanation could he provide?

There was no question of revealing the truth. Were the slightest hint of suspicion to fall upon the deceased imperial ambassador, the consequences for his Empress and his country would be disastrous.

But the Empress bristled. "Is Your Majesty accusing Haydn of theft?" she demanded.

The King bowed. "What accusations has Your Majesty heard me level? I am merely satisfying my curiosity."

He turned back to Haydn with an icy glare and drew himself up on his walking stick. "And I demand an answer. I imagine the Prince of Condé will be asking the same questions."

"We found the diamond within the church, Your Majesty," Johann replied. "We had just discovered His Lordship, Count Seckendorff, murdered and—"

"And nevertheless found time to catch sight of this lustrous gem?" The King's eyebrows arched upward. "A likely story."

"It was found near Seckendorff's dead body," the Empress interjected.

"Yes," His Serene Highness nodded. "Is that not what you said, Haydn?"

"Will the Amtsrichter corroborate this?" the King enquired, still staring at Haydn. "If it was found near the body, it is a piece of evidence. Am I to understand that the Amtsrichter granted you permission to remove it from the scene?"

"No, Your Majesty, he did not," Haydn confessed. "He was unaware of its existence."

Why had he not simply concocted some story and sought the magistrate's permission to keep the gem?

"I had already retrieved it before his arrival, and in my confusion omitted to mention the fact to him."

"Indeed." The King turned toward the Empress and Prince Nikolaus. "Then, I have no choice but to order your man's arrest."

<hr />

There was a moment's silence. Even the birds seemed to have stopped chirping. Johann stood stupefied, his features bloodless.

Then the Empress burst into speech.

"Arrest!" Her Majesty expostulated. "On what grounds would you arrest the man?"

The King shrugged. "The disturbance of the scene of a crime is a serious offense. One for which any Prussian, nobleman or peasant, would be forced to serve time.

"I trust you will understand, Your Majesty, that I cannot have one law for my own people and another for visitors. All are treated equally in Prussia."

His gaze returned to Haydn. "Follow me. I will escort you myself to the City Hall."

"No." The King was about to leave when the Empress laid a hand upon his arm.

"Tell him the truth, Haydn," Her Majesty commanded.

"Your Majesty!" His Serene Highness protested, but the Empress shook her head, adamant.

"We have no choice, Esterházy. And I will not let Haydn take the blame for this."

The King turned around, his thin lips stretched into what could only be called a smirk.

"The truth, then. I shall be glad to hear it."

The low buzz of human voices drew Haydn's glance toward the church gate. Passersby had begun thronging it, recognizing their beloved King Frederick, no doubt. The King, Herr Bach had told them, frequently allowed men to approach him in public with their petitions.

"Would it not be best to find a more private place, Your Majesty?" he enquired as Her Majesty's startled gaze veered toward the growing crowd at the church gate.

"It is Herr Haydn and Master Johann!" Rosalie turned eagerly from the window to the other occupants of the servants' hall.

"Along with His Lordship?" Greta's voice mingled with that of Boris, the Count's valet.

For the first time that morning, the valet's pale features brightened. He thrust back his chair, almost falling over himself in his haste to reach the window.

"*Oh!*" A sharp sound of intermingled surprise and disappointment escaped his lips.

"What is it, Boris?" Frau Göss looked up from her knitting. The valet's broad, muscular back obscured much of the width of the window.

But Boris, intent upon the scene outside, appeared not to have heard her. Rosalie glanced at him. Surely it did not bode well that the Kapellmeister and his brother had returned accompanied by Her Majesty and His Serene Highness.

She wondered if Boris recognized the bent, wizened creature in uniform leaning upon a walking stick. The stranger had an air of authority about him for all that he seemed old and insignificant. Even the Empress seemed wary of him.

"I don't see Count Seckendorff." Greta's voice broke in upon Rosalie's musings.

She turned to see her plump friend standing on her heels and craning her neck at the small section of glass visible between her own form and Boris's. Frau Göss peered anxiously over her knitting.

"His Lordship is not with them," Rosalie informed the two women. "Only the Empress and His Serene Highness—"

"And His Majesty, the King." Boris swung around to face the room, a haunted expression upon his handsome features. "What can that mean Frau Göss?"

Overcome with curiosity, Rosalie and Greta huddled near the door that opened onto the entrance hall. Boris had gone out to greet their visitors. The King was the first to enter through the wide wooden double doors.

His penetrating blue eyes surveyed the room as he stood to one side, waiting for Her Majesty to cross the threshold. The Empress's lips were pursed, Rosalie noticed. And her brow furrowed into a perturbed frown.

What could have happened to so distress and annoy Her Majesty?

"Do you suppose the Count has been arrested?" Rosalie felt Greta's warm breath tickling her ear as her friend hissed the question.

"Why would he be arrested?" Rosalie hissed back, rubbing her ear lobe.

"For treason," Greta ventured, but her voice sounded hesitant.

His Serene Highness followed with Herr Haydn, his face set, and Master Johann, his mild features pulled into a worried expression, behind him.

The King took off his hat. "Boris, is it?" he asked, giving the valet a curt nod.

Boris inclined his head wordlessly. It was evident that the visitors had no need to be informed that His Lordship was not within.

"Your master is dead, I fear." For a single moment, the cynical expression on the King's lined, lopsided features receded, replaced by what looked almost like compassion. Then it faded.

"Dead!" Boris's voice echoed the stunned thought in Rosalie's head. She was not sure what she had expected to hear. How was it possible a death should occur so shortly after their arrival in this strange city?

"Dear God!" she heard Greta whisper in a low voice beside her.

Rosalie clapped her hand to her mouth to suppress her own gasp as the valet's head twisted wildly from the King to the Kapellmeister.

"But he was not ill, Your Majesty. He only had the gout."

"His Lordship was murdered, Boris," Herr Haydn now said, his voice warm with understanding for the Count's man, left suddenly bereft. "The King's men, I am sure, will do all they can to find the man who did it. In the meantime—"

"It would be best to keep the information to yourself," His Serene Highness gruffly interjected. He turned from the bewildered valet to the Empress. "No need to distress the servants just yet. What think you, Your Majesty?"

The Empress nodded, then reached out to clasp Boris's hand. "Your master was a man most dear to me. Rest assured his death will not go unavenged." Her Majesty's voice hardened as her eyes shifted toward the King. "And your loyalty and that of your fellow servants will be most liberally rewarded," she went on to reassure the valet.

"I could swear the King looks almost pleased at the news," Greta muttered, horrified. Rosalie's eyes slid toward His Majesty's features in time to detect a small smirk as it disappeared. Inexplicably, it annoyed her.

Nothing she had heard of the King of Prussia had led her to expect he had an excess of warmth in his personality. The Empress had openly referred to him as "that monster."

But was His Majesty so accustomed to death that it affected him not at all? Had he so little awareness of what Boris must feel at a time like this? Could he not feign even the slightest concern for a fellow being?

"We will do our best to find the murderer," the King assured Boris in a matter-of-fact tone. "But for now, direct us to a quiet parlor where we may discuss the matter in peace. You are not required to stand guard at the door. But keep the servants away. Is that understood?"

Poor Boris nodded mutely, his shoulders bowed.

Rosalie eased herself away from the door and turned toward Greta, uneasy. What could the King have to discuss about the matter? And with Herr Haydn and Master Johann, no less?

"What is it?" Greta asked.

"Herr Haydn and Master Johann were at the church this morning," Rosalie replied, her tone tentative.

"What of it?" Greta's perplexed gaze met hers.

Rosalie clasped her hands together. The King had not revealed where His Lordship's body had been discovered. If it had been at the Katholische Kirche St. Anna . . .

She took a deep breath.

"If His Lordship was murdered at the church," she began, "the King might think—"

"That Herr Haydn and Master Johann were responsible?" Greta's voice rose, clearly aghast at the suggestion.

Rosalie nodded. "What else can they have to discuss? They have not asked to speak with the servants—"

"But what could we tell them?" Greta dismissed Rosalie's concerns with an impatient shake of her curls.

"That His Lordship inexplicably left the house shortly after Herr Ritter, the jeweler, entered it," Rosalie reminded her.

"There is that." Greta sucked thoughtfully on her finger, then glanced at Rosalie.

"There is a secret compartment behind a painted panel in His Lordship's music room. It has a peephole that provides a glimpse of the parlor and a listening device through which you can hear everything said.

"Ada showed it to me when I was helping her sweep the rooms this morning," Greta explained when Rosalie stared at her in surprise.

"Should we use it?" Rosalie had never been comfortable with the thought of eavesdropping on her betters. But in this case. . .

"I think the situation calls for it, don't you?" Greta said.

Chapter Twelve

THE cabinet concealed behind the painting of a lute player was small and cramped. Squeezing herself in beside Greta, Rosalie peered through the tiny eyehole. The parlor was plainly visible. Its settees and armchairs upholstered in blue velvet and covered in cushions embroidered with blue and pink primroses.

"Ingenious, isn't it?" Greta whispered, pressing her ear to the listening tube. "This tube goes through the plaster cherub on the parlor wall and flares into the horn at its lips. And the tube from the eyehole connects to the cherub's blue eyes."

"Shhh . . ." Rosalie hissed, straining her ears to hear. "What are they saying?"

Greta listened intently. "Herr Haydn discovered something on His Lordship's person."

"What?" Rosalie wanted to know.

Greta listened again, then shook her head. "I cannot tell."

"In the imperial ambassador's waistcoat pocket, eh?" Frederick the Great, King of Prussia, reclined against the blue velvet cushions of the wide straight-backed armchair within Count Seckendorff's parlor.

Haydn nodded stiffly, annoyed at being asked to confirm the detail. Had he not already confessed to discovering the Prince of Condé's blue diamond on His Lordship's person? That he could not think of a ready explanation for the fact annoyed him even further.

The King uncrossed his legs, stretching them out on the marchepied at his feet, and turned toward the Empress and His Serene Highness seated on the settee on his left. "That puts Your Majesty in a pretty pickle does it not?"

"Yes, yes." He nodded, answering his own question. "I imagine it does. If word were to reach the Grand Master's ears—"

"It does not need to, surely?" the Empress said sharply.

Her Majesty's fingers closed frantically around the folds of her black gown edged with gold lace. Even His Serene Highness's shoulders sagged.

The implication of the situation was not lost on Haydn. Any hope of wresting the long-awaited proposal for Archduchess Maria Antonia's hand from Louis XV's reluctant lips would be destroyed if news of the incident reached French ears.

The Kapellmeister's gaze flickered unhappily toward his brother. But Johann appeared just as helpless as he. The Kapellmeister wished the Empress had simply allowed him to bear the brunt of the blame.

He saw Her Majesty swallow hard, her lips pursed in distaste, before she continued: "I trust Your Majesty will be gracious in allowing Count Seckendorff that much dignity in death."

The King crossed his legs again. "It would take considerable effort to prevent the information reaching the Prince of Condé's ears. Your Majesty will appreciate that. Such unsavory news has a way of coming out, no matter our best efforts."

The King turned his pale blue eyes toward Haydn. "Then, there is the not inconsiderable matter of a piece of evidence being purloined from the scene of the crime."

His Serene Highness turned pale. "Haydn is a mere musician, Your Majesty. He knew not what he was doing. I beg Your Majesty will spare him."

"A Marktrichter's son with no knowledge of the law? That is strange."

Greta withdrew her ear from the listening tube. "I don't understand all of what they're saying, but Herr Haydn is in trouble."

"They must think he stole the Prince of Condé's diamond," Rosalie said, still looking out onto the parlor. She had never seen the Kapellmeister look so pale. Master Johann, sitting quietly in his armchair, gripped his armrests hard as he watched the King.

"It must have been what was reported stolen at the palace this morning," she continued, recalling what the palace footman had told them. She stepped away from the eyehole.

"They wish to arrest him," Greta gasped, pressing her ear to the listening tube again. She turned toward Rosalie. "Elma was right. She said His Majesty would seek to harm Herr Haydn and that neither His Serene Highness nor Her Majesty would be able to do anything about it."

Rosalie nodded. She had not taken their new friend's dire predictions to heart. But Elma had been right to fear for the Kapellmeister's safety.

"What should we do?" Greta whispered, tugging at her arm.

"We write to Count Botta in Dresden," she said. "Just as Elma advised us to. He will be able to prevail upon His Majesty if no one else can."

She reached for the doorknob. "And we had best do it at once while they're still preoccupied with their discussions."

"What of Frau Haydn?" Greta wanted to know, following Rosalie out of the cabinet. "Do we tell her of this development."

Rosalie shook her head. "It will only make her fret. There is nothing she can do."

Within the parlor, the conversation continued.

"Haydn's father may have been a market-judge," the Empress snapped. "He is not. What is it Your Majesty desires? An alliance with Austria? A decision on the Polish question? Such matters cannot be decided so easily."

"Not without the Emperor or the Chancellor," His Serene Highness agreed.

"It is as you wish." The King shrugged and made as if to rise. "But I cannot provide any guarantees without any expectation of return."

He turned toward Haydn. "You will be so good as to accompany me, Haydn—"

"No!" The Empress cried. "What is it Your Majesty wishes? I make no promises. But—"

The King sat back in his armchair and smiled. "You will not find my demands onerous, I promise. All I ask is a guarantee against any Austrian attempts to recover Prussia's holdings in Silesia."

The Empress bit her lip and hesitated. "Very well," she finally said. "Austria will not declare war against Prussia for the purpose of recovering our Silesian lands."

Haydn suppressed a smile. It was a cleverly worded promised. Austria was unlikely to declare war solely for the purpose of recovering its lost Silesian promises. But were the two countries pitted against each other in some other conflict, why there was still hope of recovering the rich lands she had lost.

But the King, unfortunately, was not taken in.

"No, Your Majesty. That will not do. No attempt must ever be made to seek those lands. Even if Austria should prevail against Prussia in any other cause."

The Empress hesitated again. Much longer this time, Haydn noticed. Then, to his relief, she lowered her head in the smallest of nods. Not that he would have baulked at doing his duty if the situation demanded it. But there was little he could do to get to the bottom of the affair from a prison cell in Potsdam.

"I must have those guarantees in writing." The King leaned forward to make his point. "Within three days or Haydn here goes to prison."

"And what of the other matter?" His Serene Highness sputtered. "The Grand Master of France—"

"Yes, that is a delicate matter." The King rubbed his chin thoughtfully. "It necessitates the concoction of an elaborate lie and its subsequent maintenance. The greasing of palms should the truth be discovered by some unsavory character wishing to exploit it. . ."

The Empress folded her hands in her laps. "I will consent to whatever Your Majesty is requesting. But I require a week to confer with my son and co-regent before any guarantees are drawn up. And I shall need written guarantees from Prussia as well."

The King of Prussia looked amused. "Certainly. An agreement on the lines we have already discussed along with the Duchies of Teschen and Troppau to be added to —"

"What?" The Empress's head jerked up sharply.

"Does Your Majesty wish the Dauphin to marry a Saxon princess? There are still parties in France strongly in favor of such an alliance. Not to mention that there are German princesses aplenty who would be equally suitable and less threatening to the French ministers than an Archduchess of the House of Habsburg."

"Her Majesty cannot consent to giving away Teschen and Troppau," His Serene Highness burst out only to be interrupted by the Empress.

"It is a small price, Esterházy. Austria will pay it."

Silence reigned within the parlor for several minutes after the King's departure. It was Esterházy's voice that broke it.

"Neither Teschen nor Troppau are yours to give away, Your Majesty."

The Empress nodded, her heart heavy. The Duchy of Teschen had been granted to Mimi's husband, Albert of Saxony. Troppau belonged to the Princes of Liechtenstein.

Far easier to wrest Teschen from Albert's hands than to persuade the Liechtensteins to give up Troppau. Even so, how was she to tell Mimi, or Albert for that matter, that Teschen was to be given away?

Might have to be given away. She had committed to nothing in writing yet.

"Will three days be sufficient time to resolve this affair, Haydn?" She raised her eyes toward the Kapellmeister who sat in silence before her. The King had bludgeoned her on that point as well.

Haydn let out a deep breath. "I suppose it will have to be, Your Majesty."

He inhaled as though in readiness to speak, but no words emerged from his lips. The Empress watched him carefully. Could the Kapellmeister possibly entertain any doubts about Seckendorff?

She glanced at Esterházy, but he was staring vacantly at an impossibly ugly cherub on the wall. She had never seen eyes so large and blue. They seemed to cover the cherub's entire face. And as for the horn in its lips, it had an opening so enormous, the cherub would be better served employing it on the battlefield than in the heavenly choir.

Her gaze returned to the Kapellmeister. "I have known Seckendorff from the time he was a boy, Haydn." She paused as his eyes met her, finding the necessity of defending Seckendorff from the charge of theft distasteful. "You could not find a more honest man."

The Kapellmeister gave an almost imperceptible nod. "I do not doubt that, Your Majesty."

But the response failed to satisfy the Empress.

"I tell you, Seckendorff had no interest in the diamond. The Prince of Condé said as much himself." Her words caught Haydn's attention. "The Prince has been trying in vain to sell the jewel, and displays it on every occasion he can to interest a buyer. Seckendorff had not the slightest interest in acquiring it."

Rosalie twirled the silver pen from Frau Göss's traveling ink case in her hands, resisting the urge to gnaw on the ornate cap at the top. Resolving to write to Count Botta was one thing. Figuring out how to send a message undetected to the gentleman quite another.

"Write plainly," Greta said. A suggestion so reckless, Rosalie could scarcely believe her ears. She twisted around in her chair to stare at her friend.

Greta lay propped up on her elbows on the thin, hard mattress of one of the two small wooden beds that furnished their sleeping quarters in the imperial ambassador's residence.

She tossed her blond curls and shrugged. "I doubt the King's men will open a letter from one servant to another. Why should they?"

"Hmmm. . ." Rosalie hemmed. That was true enough, she supposed. What reason could the King's men have for opening every maid's letter to her friends? Her message to Count Botta was going to be sent under cover of a letter to Elma, ostensibly the Count's servant.

That had been Elma's idea.

A letter addressed to her, Elma had assured them before they left Vienna, would be sure to gain Count Botta's attention.

Rosalie turned back to face the narrow writing desk at which she sat, dipped her pen in the inkwell, and drew the tablet of paper toward herself.

She was just about to bring the metal nib down upon the paper when her gaze fell on the small desk seal in the tortoiseshell ink case the imperial ambassador's housekeeper had allowed her to borrow.

"I don't think it would be wise to set down our thoughts too plainly." She turned toward Greta, who sat up, puzzled. The movement made her bed, which had evidently previously seen service as a trundle bed, squeak in protest as its castors rolled forward a half-inch from the wall.

"Why not?"

"His Lordship's seal will give us away." She held it out to Greta. The miniature crown topped with six feathers and the tiny flag with a thick leafy vine entwined into a figure eight were unmistakable.

"It will be opened," Greta concluded, her voice flat.

"There will be no preventing it, for all that it is merely one servant writing to another."

The imperial seal on the cover of their letter and its destination to the Prussian ambassador's residence in Saxony made it almost inevitable that the King's men would open it and peruse its contents.

It was from His Serene Highness, Prince Nikolaus, that they had learned of this.

"Be careful what you write," their employer had warned. "The King makes it a point to read any letter that he deems to possess information pertinent to himself."

"Well, what are we to do then?" Greta wanted to know. "Have a basket of eggs delivered to Count Botta's house?" That had been Elma's second suggestion when they had baulked at entrusting anything to paper.

But even then the ruse had seemed preposterous. Now, the girls merely smiled ruefully at each other. If only it were as easy as that.

For one thing, it would take more time than they had to prepare the eggs. "They are to be soaked in vinegar first," Elma had instructed them.

That would sufficiently soften the shells for a slit to be cut into them.

Then, once the message had been inserted, the eggs would have to be soaked for a second time— this time in cold water—to re-harden.

"Then all you must do," Elma had finished, "is to find some farmer's wife and have her carry your eggs across the Prussian border."

But where was such a woman to be found? And what reason could they give her for sending a basket of eggs to Count Botta's residence? It was not as though the Saxons had any dearth of either hens or eggs.

"Artichoke juice," Greta ventured with a shrug. The movement, though slight, made the bed emit yet another squeak of protest as it shifted forward. "God knows, His Lordship has an abundance of them in his greenhouse."

"True enough." Even if the letter were opened, no one would suspect that an invisible message had been inscribed between the harmless scribblings of an ordinary maid.

But was the paper from the tablet Frau Göss had given her thick enough? Very thin paper treated with artichoke juice was all too prone to accidentally reveal its contents to prying eyes.

She tore off a sheet from the tablet and dipped an old quill into the cup of milk at her side.

"Well?" Greta asked as Rosalie held the sheet up to the light.

"It isn't nearly thick enough for the writing to be undetectable. You have only to hold the message up to the sun to see a faint trace of the letters. And under candlelight, I fear. . ." She pursed her lips unhappily. There was only one other way forward, and she was not looking forward to it.

Chapter Thirteen

"WHAT is it, brother?" Johann's voice interrupted Haydn's thoughts. The Kapellmeister looked up. They were on their way to Sanssouci to return the Grand Master's diamond to him, but Haydn's feet had inexplicably stalled beside the Winzerberg, the terraced vineyard at the edges of the Sanssouci palace park. The gate leading into the vineyard rose above them, a mass of stone.

"What is it?" Johann asked again. "Something must be troubling you. It is not like you to drag your heels, but your steps have grown progressively slower. And we have stood like this by the Winzerberg for a minute or more."

Haydn paused, trying to marshal his thoughts, burgeoning in every direction like an overgrown, unruly bush. "If we had found a man dead in that church, as we did His Lordship, with a stolen diamond in his pocket, what would our first thought have been?"

For a moment Johann looked startled, then his gray eyes crinkled as he considered the question.

"I suppose," he said after a while, the skin between his lightly drawn eyebrows beginning to furrow, "I suppose I would think the man a thief unfortunate enough to have had a falling-out with his accomplice."

Haydn nodded and resumed walking. "A natural enough conclusion. And yet, why should the killer then proceed to leave the diamond that had caused all the trouble in his fellow's pocket?"

"If he were interrupted in his task, perhaps. . ." Johann's voice trailed off.

Haydn sighed heavily. "I had not thought of that. It is certainly a possibility. Or perhaps the killer heard a noise, thought he was on the verge of being discovered, and fled."

"Even so, would he not have stayed in the vicinity?" Johann objected. "Looking for an opportunity to return and retrieve the diamond?"

"Unless he was prevented—No." Haydn shook his head. "If that were the case, we should have found another body."

"But surely you do not believe His Lordship stole the diamond?" Johann's eyes searched the Kapellmeister's features, his voice swelling in mingled surprise and disbelief.

"No." Haydn shook his head again, ruefully. "I was hoping to establish he had not."

"If whoever orchestrated His Lordship's death meant us to think it was a falling-out between thieves, then he clearly failed in his task. I think you have established that well enough, brother. Even if the killer were interrupted, what could have prevented him from returning to the scene to retrieve the diamond?"

"True enough." But the Kapellmeister wondered if they had merely succeeded in persuading themselves that was the case? Were they twisting the facts to suit their own interpretation of the event?

"Is it possible His Lordship was killed for some other reason?" he asked. "That the killer had no reason to suppose His Lordship was in possession of a precious diamond?"

"Why kill him, then? In a church, no less? Would that not suggest a murder committed suddenly in the height of passion? What could His Lordship have done to deserve to be so brutally stabbed?"

An affair, perhaps," Haydn surmised. "But could a woman have inflicted such violence?" He paused by the Neptune Grotto. At any other time, he would have marveled at the pink and white marble used in its construction and the corals and shells that adorned the cave room.

Now his eyes passed vacantly over the structure, barely rising to take in the figure of Neptune, with a trident in his hands, that crowned it.

"If not a woman, then a cuckolded husband," Johann suggested. "But that would mean His Lordship had already purloined the diamond from the supper table. How else could it have ended up in his waistcoat pocket?"

"That it was covered in custard would suggest that it was stolen at the supper table," Haydn agreed. "But. . ."

But there was something not quite right about the explanation.

He withdrew the stone from his pocket. It had been wiped clean of the white residue that had covered it. Emboldened by the Prussian King's gesture, Haydn had tasted it as well, and confirmed His Majesty's conclusion.

Haydn stared at the diamond, unable to suppress the feeling he was being led by the nose.

"Someone must have placed it upon His Lordship's person. I am quite certain of it." It was the only premise that made any sense. "But" —he raised his eyes to meet his brother's gaze—"other than my conviction, I have nothing concrete that points to that fact."

The Prince of Condé, Grand Master of France, was leaning disconsolately against his writing desk when a palace footman ushered Haydn and Johann into his bedchamber. His features brightened visibly at the sight of the Kapellmeister and his brother.

"Ah, Haydn! There you are. With your brother, too. The gracious Empress must have sent you to my aid." He gestured magnanimously toward a gilded seat with an ornate back and an embroidered cushion in the middle of the room.

Haydn managed a small smile. "I hear Your Highness has lost a diamond," he began. He would have preferred to stand, but the Grand Master thrust his beringed palm so insistently at the chair that he lowered himself into it.

"Not just any diamond, Haydn." The Grand Master uncrossed his arms and walked over to where Haydn sat, forcing the Kapellmeister to crane his neck back to meet his eyes. "It was the largest, most lustrous, violet-hued stone you ever saw. Sent all the way from India."

"When did Your Highness notice it was gone?" Johann enquired, pausing in his circumnavigation of the room. Haydn hoped his younger brother had succeeded in dropping the stone somewhere on the carpeted floor. "Is it possible it was left behind in the Marble Hall last night?"

The Grand Master shook his head emphatically. "I had it with me when I left the supper table. It was in the pocket of this very coat." He patted the gold lining of his white silk coat. The tail of it reached almost down to his knees, Haydn noticed. But it was the Prince's words that caught his ears.

"Your Highness is quite certain of that?" he asked. "And the diamond was in your pocket at the opera as well?"

"I ought to have returned it to its case when I retired to my bedchamber last night, but. . ." The Grand Master shrugged his narrow shoulders.

"It was still in Your Highness's coat pocket?" Haydn frowned as he asked the question. If that were the case, how had the diamond come to have custard remnants on its polished facets? And when had it been taken from the Grand Master's bedchamber and found its way into the imperial ambassador's waistcoat pocket?

"Yes, of course it was, Haydn. I felt it within my pocket. I recall thinking that I should return it to its case, but I neglected to take that precaution. And now it is gone. But not for long, I hope." He turned expectantly toward Haydn. "You can find it, can you not? It should be a simple enough matter for a man of your abilities.

"The King of Prussia has sung your praises to us for a week or more."

Haydn inclined his head, forcing himself to smile his thanks. But the news did not please him at all. It was clear the King was setting him up for a fall—not an experience any man could relish.

He surveyed the room. "If Your Highness had the diamond last night," he said, "then, no doubt, it is still within the room. Has anyone other than your valet entered it?"

"I have refused to let even the maids come in to clean the room," the Grand Master replied. "But it is not here, I assure you. I have looked everywhere. The coat was hanging upon a hook within the closet there." He pointed to his right.

"It can do no harm to search the room one more time," Johann suggested, continuing to walk around the chamber, peering closely at the carpet.

"Ah!" he cried, a few minutes later. He was between the closet and the writing desk.

"What is it?" Haydn hurtled out of his chair to join his brother.

"A blue stone." Johann handed him the diamond he had pretended to discover. "It looks remarkably like—"

"That is it, gentlemen!" The Grand Master's face was suffused with pleasure. "You have found it. I can hardly believe my valet and I failed to find it. We searched the room most thoroughly."

He raised his eyes, smiling joyfully at Haydn. "But I suppose little evades a man with your capabilities of detection, Haydn. And your brother, I see, is similarly gifted."

The Kapellmeister and his brother re-entered the Entrance Hall of Sanssouci, about to leave when a footman standing by the marble Corinthian columns that edged the room stepped forward.

"Herr Haydn?" At Haydn's nod, the footman continued, "His Majesty wishes to speak with you." He gestured behind him. "If you would be so good as to accompany me. The King is in his study."

Haydn hesitated. Was there a reason plausible enough to deny the request? He glanced at his brother, who shrugged. No, of course there was not. Best get it over with, then.

"Certainly." He turned halfheartedly back to the footman, resigning himself to the encounter.

King Frederick was at his desk, poring over a sheaf of papers when the footman ushered Haydn and Johann into the study. His Majesty scribbled a few lines in the margins of the topmost paper before leaning back in his armchair and twisting his head around to greet his visitors.

"Ah, Haydn!" With a flick of his wrist he dismissed the footman and then beckoned the Kapellmeister and his brother forward.

"The Prince of Condé has regained possession of his diamond, I hear."

"Yes, Your Majesty." News traveled fast in this tiny palace, Haydn thought sourly, if the King had already received word of the gem's restoration to its rightful owner.

"A remarkable feat. How did you manage it?" The King gestured toward the chairs by the window. "Draw up a chair and sit down. I should like a full report."

As though he worked for the King now, Haydn thought, swallowing his resentment at these orders. Silently, he carried the proffered chairs from the window to the King's writing desk, the task giving him the time he needed to consider his words.

To be direct would be foolhardy. Who knew who might be listening at the doors, waiting for some false word that might break the already fragile alliance between the French and the Austrians.

"We were fortunate enough to find the gem in question, Your Majesty," he began when he and Johann had both sat down.

"Find it?" the King replied, looking at Johann as though seeking confirmation of Haydn's words. "Where did you find it?"

"On the carpet by His Highness's closet, Your Majesty," Johann said. "When His Highness confirmed the diamond was in his pocket when he returned to his bedchamber last night and that no one but his valet had entered the room since then, brother surmised that it was still in the room."

"It must have fallen out of his coat sometime this morning," Haydn added.

The King smiled, the corners of his eyes crinkling in amusement. "A good story. I like it. Of course, we all know that is not what happened. And unless your Empress agrees to my terms, the truth shall reach the Prince's ears."

Haydn inclined his head. "I will convey that message to Her Majesty."

He would have left it at that, but a thought occurred to him and he raised his eyes. "The Prince of Condé has himself affirmed the diamond was in his possession last night. That begs the question of how it could have been removed—if indeed it was—by any persons not within the palace."

The King's smile was gone. "What are you suggesting, Haydn?"

"Your Majesty was concerned last night that one of your guests might lose their valuables. I was only wondering if there was any reason for Your Majesty not to trust one of your servants."

"There is not. You may take your leave now."

Chapter Fourteen

IT was late afternoon when a porter dumped a bag of mail onto the
table by the door of a tiny chamber within the Potsdam City Palace.
The soft thump of the cloth bag as it hit the table attracted the attention of Ulrich, a twenty-five-year-old soldier drafted into service in the
King's cabinet noir.

"Diplomatic mail," he announced to Peer, his gray-haired colleague,
as he retrieved the bag and emptied its contents onto two trays.

"Just in time." Peer, who was standing by the stove, glanced over
his shoulder. "The kettles are steaming nicely." He took the tray Ulrich
handed him.

"There are more letters than usual today," Ulrich said as he and Peer
began the laborious work of softening the seals on the topmost letter.
"We shall have to work fast."

Peer grunted. Wasn't that the way of it? Two men expected to do the
work of ten. They had but two hours to read, copy, and re-seal every
letter before the bag had to be returned to the Thurn-und-Taxis postal
chamber.

"No need to open every letter, then," he said.

"No?" The uncertainty in Ulrich's voice chafed Peer.

"Why bother with letters from members of an ambassador's household?" He forced himself to be patient. "Take this one." He picked up a
small packet with the imperial ambassador's seal imprinted on it. "It's
clearly from a servant. Look at the careful, almost childlike printing.

"Now, if it were from the ambassador himself—"

"The imperial ambassador is dead, Peer," Ulrich cut in. "He won't be
writing any more letters."

Peer looked at him, irritated. How had Ulrich come by that news? Not that he had any doubt it was accurate. Ulrich always seemed to know what was going on in the city.

"Very well, we'll open this one. Although, I'll wager all three of the sheep I own it isn't much more than gossip between maids."

Ulrich said nothing. He carefully lifted the seal and unlocked the letter.

"It seems harmless enough," he said a moment later. "But there's an odd reference to artichokes."

"Probably a secret message to a lover," Peer replied. But he took the letter all the same and cast his eye over it.

"*My dearest Elma,*" he murmured, reading aloud. Then he chuckled. "*Under the eaves nest birds.* . . A servant who's learned to read, and she fancies herself a poet."

The lines were too closely written to admit of any secret writing in invisible ink.

And, yes, there was the reference to the imperial ambassador's artichokes. A foolish method for a diplomat to use, but it was carelessness such as this that had earned Ulrich and himself many a bonus.

He handed the sheet back to Ulrich. "If there's any secret writing, it'll be at the bottom. Hold it up to a candle. If you see anything, we'll copy it. If not, re-seal it and return it to the mailbag."

———————

Warmly wrapped in the red serge cloak Gerhard had given her, Rosalie anxiously paced the street in front of the imperial ambassador's residence. When would Herr Haydn and Master Johann return? It was imperative she speak with them.

The letter she had enciphered to Count Botta had provided nothing more than the barest essentials. But then she had understood so little of the matter herself, she would have struggled to put it into words even if it had been possible to write more plainly.

Besides, if she had taken any longer, they would never have gotten the letter out. The mail coach was already rumbling off by the time Greta ran to the door. She had sprinted out, just managing to catch up to it.

"May I never have to run as fast as that," Greta had said when she returned, clutching her belly and panting heavily.

Rosalie smiled at the memory. Her plump friend detested exercise of any kind. A walk might be tolerated. To run anywhere was simply unthinkable.

A gust of icy wind blew open her cloak. With cold, numb fingers, Rosalie pulled the edges back together again, wishing she were enfolded in Gerhard's arms instead. His mere presence would have been comforting.

And he could've reassured her that she'd been right not to tell Frau Haydn anything. Where was her husband, Frau Haydn had asked. At Sanssouci on an errand, Rosalie had replied. Not that there'd been very much more to say at the time.

But the reply had sufficed. Frau Haydn, in a hurry to visit Frau Bach, had simply nodded and climbed into the carriage, taking Greta with her.

It had taken Rosalie some time to figure it all out. All she knew was that the King of Prussia suspected the Kapellmeister of theft. But the more she had considered the facts, the less sense His Majesty's conclusion made.

The Prince of Condé's diamond had disappeared from Sanssouci Palace that morning. At a time when the Kapellmeister and his brother were at the Katholische Kirche St. Anna—making their gruesome discovery, no doubt.

How, then, could anyone say the Kapellmeister had stolen the diamond?

The only conclusion was that he had found it within the church. Not that this explained how it had gotten there to begin with.

Then she had run into Boris staring bewildered at a bloodstained blue cloak. After his first words to her it had all started to make sense.

The afternoon sun felt pleasantly warm on Haydn's face as he wended his way with Johann back to Lindenstrasse. It was time for the midday meal, but he ignored the rumblings of his stomach, too preoccupied with the events of the day to be distracted by hunger.

How had the French Grand Master's blue diamond ferreted its way onto the imperial ambassador's person? That it had not left the supper table was believable. After all, if it had, the alarm would have been immediately sounded. Yet there was the matter of the custard.

"There must have been two diamonds!" The words erupted from his lips almost as soon as they entered his mind.

"What?" Johann visibly flinched at the Kapellmeister's voice, startlingly loud on the quiet path by the wine terrace.

"Two diamonds," Haydn repeated. The more he thought about it, the more sense the explanation made.

"A false gem that was exchanged at some point during supper last night when the Prince of Condé was passing the genuine article around the table."

"Then the diamond returned to His Highness last night—" Johann began.

"Was a cleverly manufactured fake."

"And *that* was stolen as well? But why?"

"Why else but to implicate Count Seckendorff in a despicable, petty crime?" Haydn came to a halt in the middle of the winding path and turned to his brother.

"One that has the potential to erode all possibility of friendship between France and Austria. The marriage alliance itself could be threatened if a single word of this affair were to reach the Grand Master's ears."

"Unless the Empress accedes to the Prussian King's demands," his brother reminded him. "But I see what you mean. It puts Her Majesty in a singularly difficult position."

Johann stared at the shadows flickering at their feet, dancing in and out of the sunlight. "The thief, whoever it was, must have had an accomplice. Someone to carry out the genuine diamond in the bowl of custard."

"One of the footmen waiting upon us, I have no doubt," Haydn agreed. His gaze rested upon the snow-laden boughs of the trees lining the road. The branches gently swayed and bobbed, pushed down by sudden gusts of wind. "The same servant must have lifted the fake diamond from the Prince's coat pocket later."

Haydn sighed. It was one thing to surmise such a possibility. Quite another to establish it beyond the shadow of a doubt. "It will require considerable ingenuity on our part to discover the second diamond," he said as he and Johann continued on their way.

They were almost at Lindenstrasse when Johann spoke again. "Do you suppose the thieves will have found it necessary to deposit the genuine article in His Lordship's pocket?"

"You mean. . ." The question arrested Haydn's movement. He stared at his brother. "You know I think you might be right. The counterfeit stone would have sufficed just as well to implicate His Lordship."

Johann nodded. "And with the theft so easily accomplished, who could resist the temptation to keep the original? His Highness was so glad to have the gem returned to him, no thought of evaluating it entered his mind."

Haydn scratched his chin thoughtfully. "Quite understandable given where it was discovered. But perhaps Her Majesty can persuade His Highness to have it examined. If it proves to be spurious, it will bolster our point. That Count Seckendorff was falsely implicated in the theft."

He rubbed his hands together, a little lighter of mind. They were well on their way to successfully resolving one problem. But there was still another.

"I find it impossible to believe, however, that was the only reason to kill His Lordship. It would have been easy enough to embarrass him without resorting to murder."

<hr />

With her cloak drawn about her, Rosalie had turned around for the tenth time when the Kapellmeister and his brother rounded the corner.

She ran toward them, eager to accost them before they entered the imperial ambassador's residence.

"Herr Haydn! Master Johann!" she panted as she neared them.

The Kapellmeister and his brother drew to a halt, alarmed. "What is it, Rosalie?"

She clutched a hand to her chest and took a few deep breaths. "The gem stolen from the palace, Herr Haydn. I think I know who took it?"

From the look on the Kapellmeister's features, it was clear he had not expected her to know anything at all about the stolen diamond.

"We heard about it from a footman at the palace," Rosalie explained hastily, lest he think she and Greta had been listening in on their conversation.

The Kapellmeister nodded—warily, it seemed to her. "Go on," he said quietly.

"It was—" Rosalie stopped. How was she to explain her suspicions without letting the Kapellmeister know her surmise was founded upon what she had overheard?

"Shortly after Count Seckendorff returned home last night," she began, choosing her words carefully, "he had a visitor. A jeweler by the name of Ritter. But before Boris, His Lordship's valet, could inform the Count of the matter, His Lordship was gone. As was Herr Ritter."

"A jeweler?" Herr Haydn repeated with a glance at Master Johann. The information appeared to cause them more concern than Rosalie had thought possible.

"He visited frequently, Boris says."

The Kapellmeister seemed about to say something, then thought better of it. His agitation was apparent as he turned toward Master Johann again.

"But what does any of this have to do with the stolen diamond?" Master Johann asked, seeming unwilling to believe there could be a connection. Why, Rosalie could not begin to fathom.

She hesitated.

"What if this Ritter had stolen the diamond? What if—" She paused again, unsure how to put her suspicion into words.

"The blue cloak you had with you when you returned, Boris recognized it at once. It is covered in blood. And it belongs to Ritter."

There, let the Kapellmeister figure out for himself what that meant.

Herr Haydn's lips tightened. "Where is Boris?" he demanded.

Chapter Fifteen

THE news Rosalie had brought gave the Kapellmeister no comfort at all. He had been at pains to establish, in his own mind, the imperial ambassador's innocence. He thought he had discovered an excellent means to prove it. But if His Lordship had been entertaining regular visits from a jeweler, it would be no easy task to exonerate him.

What could His Lordship have wanted with a jeweler? Had the Empress not expressly disavowed his interest in all such frivolities?

Haydn cast his mind back to the King's supper table on the previous evening. "I can recollect no one by the name of Ritter at His Majesty's table," he said in a low voice to Johann as they strode behind Rosalie.

"Nor anyone who was a jeweler by trade," Johann replied, as careful as Haydn not to speak loudly. "Although it is possible we are both mistaken."

Haydn nodded. His memory of the supper last evening was hazy. Small wonder, too. He had been so exhausted after their long journey, he had scarcely been able to keep his wits about him.

He wondered now what had taken place in the church last night. Had Count Seckendorff followed Ritter to the church to retrieve the diamond from the jeweler? But who had killed the Count?

Ritter? Or someone else?

"What reason could a killer have for covering the corpse of his own victim?" Johann's voice broke in upon his musings.

"To assuage his own guilt, I suppose," Haydn replied. Had the imperial ambassador's death been an accident? But no, Haydn shook his head. The viciousness with which His Lordship had been stabbed suggested otherwise.

Someone had wanted the imperial ambassador dead. And had made sure of it. But whether the diamond left upon His Lordship's person had anything to do with his death remained to be seen.

———◆◆◆———

The imperial ambassador's valet was in the servants' hall. Sunlight poured into the room making Haydn squint as he opened the door. Boris, sitting at the table with his back to the window, showed no sign of having heard the door scraping gently against the stone floor as it opened. Or the soft echo of their footsteps as they entered the room.

"Boris?" The Kapellmeister tentatively sounded out the valet's name. Every fiber of his being revolted at having to question the man while he was still numb with the shock of his master's death. Yet it had to be done.

"Herr Haydn and Master Johann wish to ask you about Herr Ritter." Rosalie laid a hand on the valet's shoulder as he began to stir, thrusting an untouched plate of food away from him. The sight of the sausages and potatoes made Haydn's mouth water.

But his hunger was soon forgotten, put out of his mind by the valet's first words.

———◆◆◆———

With a quiet click, the door closed behind Rosalie. She had wanted to remain within the servant's hall, but the Kapellmeister, with his dark eyes traveling from her face to the door behind her, had made his wishes quite clear.

She stood there for a minute, hand still on the handle.

Should she stay close? But what was there to hear? There was nothing Boris could tell Herr Haydn that she didn't already know. Besides, it would look odd if any of the Count's servants caught her with her ear pressed close to the door. She stepped away.

At the end of the passage was a door that led out into the courtyard. The sound of carriage wheels scrunching to a halt on the icy cobblestones reached her ears the instant Rosalie opened it.

Greta, she thought, *back with Frau Haydn*.

She quickly stepped out, the wind whipping her cloak behind her and pulling the door shut.

Frau Haydn swept down from the carriage, her expression stormy. "Has my husband returned?" she demanded the minute she espied Rosalie. "Where is he?"

Rosalie's gaze darted toward Greta. What had happened to put Frau Haydn in such ill humor? But Greta looked pale and shaken, too.

"Within," Rosalie replied cautiously. "Speaking with Boris, His Lordship's valet."

If there was anything else to say, surely the Kapellmeister could say it.

"Is it true His Lordship was killed? And that my husband discovered his body?"

Frau Haydn had not taken a single step forward, yet Rosalie found herself taking a step back, impelled back by the furious onslaught of Frau Haydn's questions. She stayed quiet, unsure what to say.

"Why was I not informed of this?" Frau Haydn glared at both maids. Her nostrils flared delicately. Crimson splotches burned in her pale cheeks.

"We learned the news from Frau Bach," Greta said with a desperate glance at Rosalie. Her friend had evidently feigned ignorance as well. "His Lordship was brutally stabbed." Greta's hand flew to her throat and she flinched as though fending off an attack.

Rosalie swallowed. Small wonder her friend looked white-faced and sick. No one had told them the Count had been hacked to death. In fact, no one had told them he was dead, she realized. She turned toward Frau Haydn.

"We have just learned of his demise, Madam." Her voice, even to her own ears, sounded deflated. "His Majesty, the King, wished the news kept quiet." Someone had wished the news to be kept from the servants. Rosalie didn't recall whom. Not that it mattered. Her words had sufficed to curb Frau Haydn's displeasure.

"Well, I wish husband had said something. Frau Bach offered her condolences, and I had nothing to say. I have never felt more foolish, I can tell you that. Not knowing that it was our host who had died."

She lifted her skirts and carefully made her way to the steps. The maids watched her climb the steps, her small, slender form rigid against the icy wind.

Then Greta slid her arm through Rosalie's. "What does Herr Haydn want with Boris?" she asked.

———

"He is dead, too, I suppose." Boris fingered the worn, bloodstained blue cloak spread out on the table before him.

"Why would you suppose that?" The faint echo of Rosalie's departing footsteps reached Haydn's ears as he pulled out a chair and thrust himself into it.

Out of the corner of his eye, he saw Johann lowering himself into a seat on Boris's right.

"What else is one to think?" Boris gestured toward the cloak, smeared with blood.

Haydn's gaze followed the valet's. There were splotches of blood on the cloak, near the top where it had covered the imperial ambassador's chest and a third of the way below that.

From the little he knew of such matters, he doubted Ritter had been killed. He was about to say so when he heard Johann's voice.

"We found the cloak covering your master's body. Are you certain it belonged to this Herr Ritter?"

Boris smiled, a slight twitching of the corners of his mouth. "Herr Ritter seemed to have but the one faded cloak. In all the time he came to visit His Lordship, he never wore anything else. All the servants remarked upon it."

"That he had the one cloak?" Haydn asked. It seemed a poor sort of cloak for a man who was a jeweler and must surely earn enough from his trade to apparel himself in better garments.

Boris shook his head. "That he dressed so shabbily. That his fingers and nails always seemed blackened with ink."

"A jeweler with ink-stained hands?" Johann was incredulous. "He sounds more like a clerk than a jeweler. What could His Lordship have wanted with such a man? I would not have thought him to have any interest in jewels and suchlike frivolities."

"I know not." Boris's handsome face had become strangely expressionless. "It was not my place to ask such questions." He stared down at his hands.

The Kapellmeister's eyes widened and turned to encounter his brother's equally perplexed stare. That the valet knew more than he was willing to reveal about his master's affairs was evident. But why should Johann's remarks have prompted such circumspection?

Were the Count and the jeweler engaged in some illegal activity?

The Kapellmeister drummed his fingers upon the table, uncertain how much of the Count's predicament to reveal to his servant.

"It may help us discover His Lordship's killer if you can tell us what little you know, Boris?"

"I can think of no one who would have wished to harm my master. His Lordship was well loved by all who knew him. Why, even the King himself regarded him as a brother."

And yet His Majesty had shown no signs of grief at the imperial ambassador's brutal murder. Was the valet lying? Or had he simply succeeded in deceiving himself? Haydn bit his lip. He had hoped not to be compelled to reveal all the unsavory facts regarding His Lordship's death to his servants.

"Your master appeared to be a man of integrity," he began.

"That he was," Boris agreed.

"The Empress herself is convinced of the fact," Haydn continued. "But—" he drew a deep breath and glanced at his brother.

"But His Lordship is now suspected of theft," Johann finished in a tone tinged with such regret, his words could cause no offense.

Boris turned sharply toward Johann. "What is he suspected of taking?"

"A large, many-faceted blue diamond belonging to the Grand Master of France," Johann replied. "It was found upon his person."

"Then someone placed it there. My master would never stoop to such petty villainy."

"Why did Herr Ritter visit your master so frequently, Boris?" Haydn was deliberately blunt, but the valet seemed prepared for him.

"Knives," he said at once. "He would bring His Lordship knives with ornate sheaths. They are in his study."

Johann sighed. "Are you certain that was all it was?" He paused. "It is a question of your master's reputation. Would you allow it to be sullied in death?"

Boris was quiet.

"A word from you could clear your master's name," Johann reminded him.

"But I know nothing," Boris protested. "That was how His Lordship wanted it. To keep us all safe."

"Is there truly nothing you know that can shed light on the matter?" Haydn persisted. It was impossible the valet should be as ignorant as he claimed.

The servant wavered, then reached within the waistband of his trousers. "About a month ago, His Lordship asked me to take charge of this notebook. He would meticulously record certain details. The specific days and times Herr Ritter came to visit. The days he himself worshipped at the Katholische Kirche."

Boris extended the notebook to the Kapellmeister. Haydn flipped through the pages. It recorded, as the valet had claimed, such insignificant details. Page after page of it. But to what avail?

"And he entrusted this to you a month ago, you say?" What had happened then, the Kapellmeister wondered.

"He did not want it to fall into the wrong hands." An expression of uncertainty flitted across the valet's features as his eyes fell upon the notebook.

Small wonder, the man had been so wary, Haydn thought. How could he possibly know whom to trust?

"I will keep it safe," he assured the servant. "In the meantime—"

"If I may ask, what has become of Herr Ritter?" the valet interrupted him.

"We know not," Johann replied before the Kapellmeister could. "He may well be alive. Can you lead us to him?"

"I know where his establishment is," Boris said. "It is one of the largest in Potsdam."

"So, Herr Ritter was in the church when His Lordship was killed?" Greta frowned. She lay on her stomach on her bed, elbows on either side of her, chin cupped in her hands.

"He must have been." Rosalie edged closer to the stove. It was cold in their tiny room, despite the flames that crackled within the stove. The window panes rattled, and she could feel the cold tendrils of wind creeping in through the cracks. "How else would his cloak get there?"

She took a candle and held it to the flames. The small window let in little enough light, and it was gloomy inside.

"But why did he steal the diamond?" The bed creaked and a scuffling movement indicated Greta was rolling onto her back. "For His Lordship?"

Rosalie was about to set the candle down, but the question made her pause. She had been quite sure the jeweler had stolen the diamond. How else would it have made its way to the church?

Herr Ritter had arrived, unexpectedly, last night. His Lordship had disappeared shortly after. And then the jeweler's cloak had been discovered alongside His Lordship's dead body.

But why had the jeweler stolen the diamond? Rosalie hadn't stopped to consider that question. And—

"Why would he visit His Lordship right after stealing the diamond?" Greta voiced the question in her mind.

"But he never had an opportunity to meet His Lordship." Rosalie was unwilling to believe the Count had anything to do with the theft of the jewel. One might as well suppose His Serene Highness or Her Majesty had stolen the item. "He left before His Lordship could meet him."

"Perhaps, they left together." Greta rolled over onto her side and looked up at Rosalie.

Rosalie set down the candle and considered this. "Why would they need to go anywhere at all if all Herr Ritter wanted to do was hand over the diamond?" But it was true both men had ended up at the church. But His Lordship had been stabbed and the jeweler—Well, presumably, he was still alive.

"Do you think Herr Ritter was sent to lure His Lordship to his death?" That seemed more plausible, she thought. "The diamond was a reward for his efforts, but in the fray, it fell from his pocket and no one noticed it until Herr Haydn and Master Johann discovered the body."

"Would he have been so foolish as to leave his cloak behind?" Greta sat up and gazed at Rosalie, her head tilted to one side.

Rosalie chewed her lip. "I suppose not."

"Is Boris quite sure, it is his?"

"It was what Herr Ritter wore every time he came to see His Lordship. Boris recognized it the moment he saw it."

"Then perhaps someone wanted to implicate Herr Ritter. After all, no one saw him. The servants were all in bed. You and I were in the kitchen and—" Greta clapped her hand to her mouth as the implication of her words sank in.

"We have only Boris's word that Herr Ritter was here." Rosalie stared at her friend. Had Boris been mistaken? By the time they had gone to the vestibule, the jeweler was gone.

"And Boris sent us up to bed immediately after," Greta recalled.

Rosalie nodded. "Because it was late—and we were tired," she said. *Or had there been some other reason?*

Chapter Sixteen

THE sun was just dipping into the Elbe, bathing the icy river waters in a glow of fiery orange, when a footman delivered a letter to Count Botta and his visitor.

"A letter for Elma, Your Lordship." The footman lowered the silver tray with its contents—a small packet and a silver penknife—to the Count, managing at the same time to execute a bow in the direction of the beautiful lady seated on his master's left.

Maria Wilhelmina von Auersperg smiled—a mischievously radiant smile that caused the tall young footman to falter and stare soft-eyed at her. Wilhelmina's smile widened as she glanced away. She was over thirty. A woman long married. But she could still dazzle men.

And this young footman—she cast another surreptitious glance from under her thick, long eyelashes at his muscular form—was certainly worth dazzling. If she weren't already involved with his master, she could perhaps—

Catching sight of the Count's eyes on her, she reined her imagination in.

"Well?"

The Count dismissed the servant.

"I can make nothing of it." He tossed the letter toward Wilhelmina, who reached up to pluck it out of the air in one fluid movement.

She cast a critical eye over the missive. "She's a clever little one, our Rosalie. With all the makings of a good spy. But too loyal to Haydn and Esterházy to be tempted away, unfortunately."

Count Botta snorted. "I suppose you have deciphered the message already."

Wilhelmina looked up. "My dear Count, she tells us in her own words how to decipher it. Listen." She began reading aloud.

"My dearest Elma, Greetings from Potsdam. We are here at last thanks to Padiel, who skipped two steps all the way. The city is most beautiful.

"Two steps from the left," Wilhelmina repeated. "A reference to Trimethius's tables. I imagine we are to skip the first two words, taking the first letter of every third word. The only question—" She felt her brow beginning to pucker, but restrained the movement.

A woman her age could ill-afford to frown; the expression showed her age. And the danger of it marring the smoothness of her skin was all too real.

"The only question is: where does the coded message begin?"

"Treat it with fire," the Count suggested. He extended a fresh candle to the fire burning in the grate and lit the wick.

"The King's men appear to have done the same thing with little success," Wilhelmina said, turning the letter face-up toward the Count. The lower edge of the paper was burnt a dull brown.

But she held the paper over the candle flame all the same. A minute or two elapsed, the ticking of the Count's gold clock the only sound in the room. Then two words emerged at the end of the words she had just read.

Message below.

Wilhelmina extended a soft white palm. "A pen, if you will. Marking the letters is much the easiest way to proceed, I have always found."

She laid the letter flat upon the low table in front of her as her fingers closed over the gold pen the Count placed upon her palm. "The Catholic church. . ." she began to read softly, marking the first letter of *church*, the third word.

The Catholic church here is over by Yorckstrasse. Under the eaves nest birds, their tail feathers falling down by the entrance. The robins and the thrushes dance. We're in heaven, Greta says.

All is well. Yesterday on a dark and cold night, we arrived in Potsdam. Padiel never failed us.

Post your news, Elma dearest. We return to Rohrau in two weeks.

_Lovingly yours,
Rosalie._

P.S. _His Lordship is uncommonly fond of artichokes and has some very fine specimens in his Orangerie._

"Eliminating the postscript," Wilhelmina murmured to herself, "we have 'countdeadhaydninperil.'"

"Count dead." She raised her head, the color draining from her face. Did the girl mean Seckendorff was dead? "Haydn in peril."

This time she allowed her brow to furrow.

"I thought Seckendorff was to be embarrassed. And recalled. Not done away with." Her voice was sharp. Had Botta, the old fool, known of this?

Botta shrugged, the fleshy folds of his chin bulging as his grizzled head receded into his shoulders. He arranged his carefully tended hands upon a rotund belly.

"What does it matter, my dear Wilhelmina. We are rid of him. Isn't that what we wanted?"

He waved a hand in the direction of the letter. "What peril do you suppose the musician is in? Nothing that will cause him to endanger our plans, I hope."

"I don't know," Wilhelmina said, her frown deepening. She had hoped for news of Haydn's investigation. But Rosalie had provided no information at all. She had instead reached out for help.

Wilhelmina tapped the letter thoughtfully. What was she to do? Ignore the call?

The Count crossed his legs. "Well, if his wings are clipped, I suppose there is nothing to worry about."

"I doubt he's the type whose wings remain clipped for too long," Wilhelmina replied.

"The jeweler Ritter must have been very closely acquainted with His Lordship." Johann set down his glass of wine and looked at the Kapellmeister.

They were sitting in the imperial ambassador's library, a room that appeared to have also served as His Lordship's study. Two wide steps led up to its double doors from the parlor where, hours earlier, they had conducted their talks with King Frederick.

Haydn fingered his wine glass and stared at his surroundings, pondering his brother's question. The candles in the wall sconces had been put out, but the three tapers on His Lordship's desk cast a warm glow around the semi-circular room. Bookcases lined the walls and shelves framed the window seats of the three bay windows.

"He visited often enough," he said finally, seizing upon the only fact available to them. The imperial ambassador's notebook recorded numerous visits paid by the jeweler.

The Kapellmeister supposed that implied a degree of friendship. Boris, the valet, appeared to have taken it as such. It was his sole reason for believing Ritter to be innocent of His Lordship's murder.

It would not have sufficed to convince Haydn, but another more compelling reason had brought him around to the same view. Ritter could not have killed the imperial ambassador.

The jeweler's blood-encrusted cloak lay in a heap upon His Lordship's desk. Haydn pointed to it.

"Do you recall my telling you about Hans, the baker's boy in Vienna?"

"He was condemned for killing his master, was he not?" Johann seemed unsurprised by the Kapellmeister's sudden change of subject, willing as always to wait for his older brother to reveal the significance of this apparently unconnected detail.

Haydn nodded. He had been little more than a boy himself at the time, but the incident had etched itself into his mind. "The guards were convinced he had killed the baker. All because the poor lad had cradled his dying master in his lap, and so gotten himself besmirched with blood."

"*Ach so!*" Johann's gray eyes seemed to grow larger and more luminescent. "I take it the stains on Ritter's cloak are of the same type."

Haydn set his glass down and leaned forward. "Splotches of blood," he said, spreading out the garment. "No rivulets of it dripping down, which would suggest he himself was bleeding. No teardrop-shaped stains and sprays that would indicate he was the one doing the killing. I should have seen it much earlier. On the basis of the cloak alone, we can exonerate him."

Had Porpora, Haydn's own master, not sent him to a butcher, Haydn would never have learned to see the difference.

"It is more than a musician should be expected to know," he now said. "But it saved Hans's life all those years ago. It may save Ritter's now."

Even so, had Boris the valet not drawn his attention to the cloak again that afternoon, he would not have seen it. He had seen the bloodstained cloak and made the common mistake of assuming its owner had killed His Lordship.

"Although the closeness between Ritter and His Lordship," Haydn continued, rubbing his chin uneasily, "only gives further credence to the King's theory. The Count wished to steal the Grand Master's diamond. And had an accomplice."

"A jeweler, no less." Johann reached for his wine glass but made no motion to pick it up. "That does not bode well for our efforts." He stared at the ruby-red contents of his glass for a while.

"There was no jeweler at the supper table that I can recall. Is it possible, there was a third man involved? A footman who passed the diamond to Ritter. Ritter, in turn, then brought it to the Count, but was followed by the footman, who waylaid both men at the church."

"Yes, but that only seals His Lordship's guilt." Haydn stared at his brother, stunned. Why would Johann even contemplate such a possibility?

"Should we not at least consider it?" Johann countered, his fingers still encircling the stem of his wine glass. "We know nothing of His Lordship. Only that he seems to have been a man of strange customs."

"That he was." Haydn pensively cupped his chin in his palm. "Do you know he worshipped at the church on the very nights Ritter visited him? Mere hours after receiving the jeweler on some days."

"And that is where His Lordship went last night," Johann reminded him. "Despite being in such pain from his gout that he returned home shortly after supper."

"Then, something about Ritter's visits always prompted a desire to go to the church." Some nefarious activity, it was clear, but Haydn forbore to mention it.

He glanced up to see his brother watching him.

"But Her Majesty seems to put the utmost faith in him." It was a feeble protest.

And it elicited no response from Johann. The thought entered Haydn's mind that the Empress was deceived in her ambassador. But it was hard to stomach.

"If there is a plausible explanation," Johann said at last with a slight shrug, "perhaps Ritter will be able to provide it."

If he can be persuaded to tell the truth, Haydn thought at the same time as Johann added: "I myself can think of none."

The Kapellmeister heard the words and held himself rigid, unable to say anything. His brother had never questioned his beliefs or his assumptions. Until now.

After an eternity, he shifted in his chair and cleared his throat. "If nothing else, assessing the diamond we returned today should serve to clear His Lordship's name. Of theft, that is to say."

There *were* only two ways the gem could have ended up in His Lordship's waistcoat pocket. Either he had placed it there himself.

Or the killer had.

Chapter Seventeen

THE candles sputtered, the wax burning low. In unison the brothers pushed their chairs back—about to retire for the night—when a loud knock startled them. The double doors to the imperial ambassador's study were flung open to reveal Boris, the ambassador's valet, and the magistrate of Potsdam.

"The Amtsrichter wishes to have a word." Boris stepped into the study. "And to look around." His uneasy glance took in the desk and the cloak spread upon it.

The brothers stumbled to their feet, Haydn gripping the edge of the desk. Were there any incriminating documents concealed within it? The ambassador's notebook was safely in his pocket. The cloak needed no explanation.

"Do sit down." The Amtsrichter strode in, the sound of his voice reverberating off the walls in an ominous echo. He waved Boris away and planted himself on a chair beside Johann.

"What may we do for you, Herr Amtsrichter?" Watching the magistrate closely, Johann lowered himself into his seat. With an indrawn sigh, Haydn sat down as well.

The Amtsrichter steepled his fingers and regarded the Kapellmeister. "I would not ordinarily approach a private citizen, but I hear you have no small ability in such matters."

"You refer, I assume, to the imperial ambassador's murder?" Haydn said. The question was merely a ploy to gather his wits. What the magistrate was referring to was quite clear.

"It is true, brother has some experience," Johann broke in. "Was it His Majesty, the King, who mentioned it."

It must have been, Haydn thought. What better way to monitor his investigation? He studied the magistrate's features. He had seen statues wrought in marble that were more expressive than the stone-faced demeanor of the man before him.

"No, it was Herr Bach." The magistrate glanced away, red-faced, appearing almost bashful. "And it occurred to me that with your assistance, we may discover His Lordship's murderer all the sooner."

Haydn shifted uneasily in his chair. Had Herr Bach really divined their involvement? And been indiscreet enough to mention it to the magistrate? Or was the latter simply clutching at straws?

"We are mere musicians, Herr Amtsrichter," Johann hastily countered the magistrate's assumption. "And we arrived but last night. We know next to nothing about His Lordship. How can we, ordinary men, assist you?"

The magistrate held up his hand. "Do not tell me you are not already involved, Master Johann. I am told your brother's abilities have inspired the confidence of the Empress herself."

He gestured at the bookcases, barely visible beyond the small circle of light cast by the shrinking candles, reduced almost to puddles of wax now.

"And here you sit in the imperial ambassador's study. You have examined his papers, surely. Have you discovered anything that sheds any light on this heinous matter?"

"It is not our place to go through His Lordship's papers." Johann spoke quietly, but the outrage in his tone was unmistakable. He lit a fresh candle and snuffed out the dying flames of the old tapers.

The new flame flared, standing tall between the newcomer and themselves.

"It is true, we have not." Haydn raised his eyes from the flame and stared straight into the magistrate's blue orbs. They had not yet searched the study. That it needed to be done that very evening had not occurred to him.

Although perhaps it should have. Why should the Prussian King waste any time hunting for any shred of evidence that could further incriminate the Count as a thief, or worse?

"Then, why do you sit here?" the magistrate asked.

"We were discussing his funeral music." It was the first thing that entered Haydn's mind. Prompted, no doubt, by the harpsichord that stood on the right of the double doors and the transverse flutes on the desk. "It would be unusual to have a flute concerto, I suppose—"

"But a fitting tribute, nevertheless," Johann joined in. "Given His Lordship's interest in the instrument."

Much to their surprise, the Amtsrichter appeared to agree. "A splendid notion. It will certainly please the King. His Majesty is a flutist of some note, as you are no doubt already aware. And the Count was a good friend."

"Of the *King's*?" Haydn could scarcely keep the astonishment out of his voice.

The magistrate leaned forward and said in a low voice, "They were remarkably close. Perhaps, unnaturally so. But that may be no more than a rumor—inevitable under the circumstances. His Majesty has long been estranged from his wife. And Count Seckendorff appeared to have no—"

"He was widowed," Haydn explained, unwilling to hear any more about the King's unnatural tastes. They might know nothing of the Count, but surely there was no reason to tar His Lordship with the same brush.

"How can you be so sure the imperial ambassador was in His Majesty's favor?" Johann smiled as he asked the question. "What you have told us seems nothing more than the unfounded talk of common folk. Surely it would not be wise to set any store by it."

The magistrate flushed angrily.

"Why should His Lordship not be in the King's favor? He was the nephew of the man who was responsible for saving the King's life. Have you not heard the story? His Majesty's father, Frederick William, was determined to hang him for a traitor. If it were not for the intervention of old Seckendorff, King Frederick would not be among us."

"We were aware of that," Haydn conceded, recalling the details. But General Seckendorff had later been imprisoned by the Empress's father on charges of treason. When the Empress had released him, he had immediately defected over to King Frederick's army.

"However, I did not think His Lordship was so well acquainted with his uncle." The Count had been raised in Vienna, deliberately kept apart from his traitorous relative.

"They exchanged frequent letters. It was always Seckendorff's hope that his nephew should join him in Prussia. It must have been why His Lordship sought this post. Unfortunately, by the time he was assigned it, his uncle had died."

"So it was merely on account of his uncle that His Majesty held Count Seckendorff in such great esteem?" Johann voiced the question in Haydn's mind. He fingered his near-empty wine glass, twirling the dregs that remained.

"Not at all," the Amtsrichter replied. "It would take more than that to win the King's affection. And His Lordship must have won it to earn this." He picked up one of the flutes on the desk. "His Majesty does not give these to just anyone. Look at the inscription."

Haydn and Johann dutifully looked at the ornate gold lettering on the ebony flute. It was dedicated to "my dear Prometheus from your friend, Frederick." They exchanged a glance. What had His Lordship stolen—and from whom—to earn that nickname?

The wide bores of the instrument and the brass tuning slide revealed the exquisite workmanship of Johann Joachim Quantz, the King's favorite flutist. The magistrate was right. To receive such an instrument from the King was indeed a mark of honor.

Clearly, when it came to His Lordship they had taken too much for granted.

Her walk brought her to the Chinese Teahouse just as the rising sun crept above it, peering over the gold parasol of the figure on the copper cupola. Leaning upon her ebony cane, the Empress took in the view. A rosy hue bathed the roof, which flared, like a woman's skirt, over the circular, clover-shaped teahouse.

The rays glancing off the cupola glowed a bright red. The color of blood. *Seckendorff's blood.*

The Empress walked toward the building. Who had killed her ambassador? And to what end?

Not many in Austria had approved his appointment, the nephew of a treasonous general. Joseph, her son, foremost among them. To send such a man into the arms of her enemy was the work of a fool, they had warned.

She tapped her cane impatiently upon the icy cobbles of the path. She had held strong against their urgings. Until the ambassador's communications had abruptly ceased—not to exist, but to be of any significance.

Now, he was dead.

Bracing herself on the cane, she pivoted around. Time to return to the palace. And her daughter.

"The ambassador, I hear, has been killed." Amalia brought a tiny porcelain cup of coffee to her lips and gazed at her mother. The Empress had insisted her daughter join her that morning. A way of preserving the child's reputation.

Seckendorff had not been the only one of the King's guests to miss the opera His Majesty had staged for them on the night of their arrival. Amalia and the Crown Prince had disappeared after supper as well, nowhere to be seen all through the previous day either. God forbid, they should have spent the entire time in each other's company.

Maria Theresa brushed the thought aside and nodded—a terse, curt movement of the head. Her daughter as always was a day late in acknowledging the news.

"On the night of our arrival, within a Catholic church, as you must have heard." It must have been the Crown Prince, Frederick William, who had informed her of the matter.

Amalia's lips twitched. Her face, thought the Empress, seemed paler than usual. "Haydn. I suppose, is on the case?" the girl ventured.

"Potsdam has a magistrate to see to such things," the Empress replied, seeing no need to make any official announcement of Haydn's involvement in the matter. Anything she said would most likely go back to the Crown Prince's ears and thence to his uncle, King Frederick.

"What was the Count doing at the church? A clandestine meeting with someone, do you suppose?" Amalia took another sip from her cup, her pale eyes staring at her mother from over its rim.

"What does anyone do within a church? Other than worship the Lord," the Empress countered. But the selfsame question had preoccupied her as well. Seckendorff had arranged to meet them on the bridge —

To what end? Had there been some information, after all—
Then, how had he come to be at the church?

"Was he killed there? Or simply placed there to create trouble?" Her daughter's voice brought her abruptly out of her musings.

"I imagine whoever murdered Seckendorff did so at the church. The magistrate has said nothing to counter that supposition?"

But despite herself, the Empress leaned forward, intrigued. Amalia's questions were most astute. Could the site of Seckendorff's murder point to the reason for his death? Or the hand that had struck him?

"Who do you suppose would benefit from such trouble?" she asked, genuinely interested in her daughter's views.

But Amalia shrugged, her fingers fluttering up to indicate she had given the matter little thought. "Perhaps the Catholics in Poland, incensed by the new freedoms they have been forced to grant to Lutherans and the Orthodoxy alike, seek to stir up strife in Prussia."

"Perhaps," the Empress agreed.

Had that been the motive for killing her ambassador? The murder of a powerful Catholic man brutally killed within a Catholic church might cause strife even in a country where men of every faith were forced to abide together in peace.

If Prussia were preoccupied in keeping order within its own borders, there would be few men to spare for Catherine of Russia's efforts in

Poland. The treaty Russia had signed with Prussia—shortly after the last war—and the clauses within it were an open secret.

Everyone knew that Russia's efforts in Poland must inevitably bring Prussia into the war. That it had not done so already was no doubt simply due to the fact that Russia needed no one's help to crush Poland.

But if Amalia was right, did that mean Seckendorff had been lured to the Church?

She must have spoken aloud, for Amalia immediately exclaimed: "*Lured*? I thought you said the Count habitually worshipped at the church, Mother. Whoever killed him must have been familiar with his habits."

Chapter Eighteen

Frau Haydn was already dressed by the time Rosalie went up to her bedchamber bearing her morning coffee. She sat before her mirror, lips set into a line of disapproval, hands tightly clasped in her lap.

Rosalie's eyes flitted toward the elaborately fashioned ormolu clock on the dresser. But she had come at the usual hour. She set the tray with its pot of coffee and Frau Göss's almond-flavored biscuits on a table, about to offer an apology, when Frau Haydn spoke.

"Where is my husband? I have seen neither hide nor hair of him since the night of our arrival. When he came to bed last night, I know not. If he came at all. And this morning when I woke up, he was already gone."

"Herr Haydn wished to see His Lordship's jeweler, Herr Ritter," Rosalie explained, glad to have the information. What Frau Haydn would have said had she thought the Kapellmeister had left without any word as to his destination, Rosalie did not know.

To her dismay, Frau Haydn's features brightened. "A jeweler?" She turned around. "Why would husband wish to see a jeweler?"

Rosalie bit her lip, tempted to concoct a lie. But it would only create trouble for the Kapellmeister. She doubted he would have the forethought to purchase a bracelet or necklace for his wife. The Count's inexplicable murder was the only thought in his mind.

"Herr Ritter was here to see His Lordship on the night of his. . ." She paused.

Frau Haydn rolled her eyes. "And husband thinks he will own to murdering the Count, I suppose. As though a jeweler would kill his patron!"

No, he would not, Rosalie thought. All the more reason to believe it was not the jeweler who had come, but someone purporting to be him.

"When is he expected back? Or did he not deign to mention it?"

"He did not, Madam." Rosalie lowered her eyes. Neither she nor Greta had even been downstairs at the time. It was Frau Göss who had attended to the Kapellmeister that morning. Frau Göss who had thought to inform them of his whereabouts, lest his wife should ask. "I only know that he left at dawn with Master Johann and His Lordship's valet."

Frau Haydn sniffed loudly. "Well, since he can never be troubled to come to me, you may give him that yourself." She picked up a rectangular packet wrapped in paper from the dresser and extended her arm stiffly toward Rosalie.

"What is it, Madam?" Rosalie asked, taking it from her hands.

"A painting. A present from Herr and Frau Bach. The frame is chipped and needs to be exchanged for another."

Frau Haydn sniffed again.

"But husband can take care of that himself."

She motioned toward the door. "Well, go on, then. I am quite capable of dressing myself and I do not need to be escorted to the breakfast room."

With a hasty curtsy, Rosalie backed away toward the door.

"It is ridiculous. The maids see more of the man than do I, his wife!" The words made Rosalie squirm as she hastened out of the room without a sound.

On Gutenbergstrasse, a few miles south of Nauener Tor, the city gate used by craftsmen and merchants, stood Herr Ritter's shop. Neither Haydn nor Johann had ever seen a more charming establishment.

The half-timbered house with its beige plaster looked like a cream-filled torte fashioned by a Viennese confectioner. A small, green sign with snow piled atop it announced the establishment of ***Ritter, Goldsmith and Jeweler***. To the left was a silversmith's workshop; to the right, a woodworker.

A wooden door, between two mullioned windows, stood a few inches ajar. Haydn came to a halt before it.

"This is Herr Ritter's establishment?" He turned toward the imperial ambassador's valet, needing reassurance of the fact despite the sign.

Boris nodded. "There is but one jeweler by that name in all of Potsdam," he replied. "And this is he." He raised the brass knocker and let it fall back against the door.

"Yes?" A young man clothed in a suit of muted gray stood at the door, summoned by the loud clang of the knocker. He stared at the Kapellmeister and his brother, his eyes barely glancing at the valet.

" Herr Ritter?" Haydn enquired.

"It is not him." Boris's voice, low and bewildered, reached the Kapellmeister's ears just as the young man began to speak.

"That is my name. What can I do for you?" The young man's gaze shifted toward the Kapellmeister's brother. "We do not open until an hour and a half later."

"We have come from Count Seckendorff's household," Johann began.

The young man seemed taken aback. "But His Lordship has no orders outstanding. It has been a month or more since his man picked up his last order."

"His man?" Haydn's head veered toward Boris.

"Not him," Ritter said. "I have never seen him. The man who usually came was older, not quite as tall. The Count's secretary, I suppose, judging by his ink-stained fingers. But as I said before, His Lordship has placed no new orders."

"And I take it you have never visited His Lordship's residence?" It was quite clear the jeweler had not. The Kapellmeister was asking the question merely as a matter of form.

The young man shrugged. "His Lordship preferred to come here himself. Or send his man. But why do you ask all these questions?"

"His Lordship is dead," Haydn replied. "Brutally murdered."

"Dead," Ritter repeated, but Haydn was still speaking.

"We were told you were the last man to see him alive."

"Who could have told you such a thing?" Ritter seemed more bewildered than outraged. "I have already told you it has been over a month since His Lordship conducted any business with us."

Haydn's gaze drifted toward Johann. Had someone impersonated the jeweler, then? To what end?

"Have you an older brother?" It was Boris who blurted out the question. "A man by the name of Ritter came frequently to see my master. He came last night as well."

"And it is on that account that you come to my door?" Ritter countered with an amused smile. "Why, there must be many men named Ritter in this city."

"He said he was a jeweler," Boris said. "There is only one by that name in Potsdam."

Ritter's head snapped up at that. "Then he lied." The jeweler's nostrils flared, and he stepped forward, fists clenched. "Is that not evident? My father and I are respectable men. Why do you come here seeking to besmirch our reputation?"

Haydn sighed. He held up a conciliatory hand. "It is only the truth we seek, Herr Ritter. As yet the Amtsrichter knows nothing of this matter. There may be no need to involve him at all—if you will but consent to help us."

The jeweler hesitated, his hand still on the doorknob. Once, he glanced over his shoulder into the shop within.

"Come in, then. I have nothing to hide from the magistrate. But to be questioned on a matter of murder would destroy our reputation."

The interior of the goldsmith's establishment was dimly lit. On the right, a door behind the counter led to the workshop beyond. Ritter passed through and held it open for his visitors.

An incessant clanging intermingled with the busy hum of men working in the warm, close atmosphere of the narrow workroom. Haydn stepped inside and surveyed its confines.

A large man in a black waistcoat sat with his back to them, beating a block of gold into a fine sheet. An emaciated worker pored over the design he was etching on a ring. A third carefully mounted pearls onto the tiny, teardrop-shaped surfaces of a gold necklace.

Haydn turned toward Boris, but the valet shook his head.

"None of the men here have had any dealings with the Count," Ritter said. "And my father, as you can see, is old and crippled." He pointed toward a white-haired man sitting by the stove in a rolling chair. "He goes nowhere."

Old Ritter gazed curiously at them but made no effort to maneuver his rolling chair toward them.

"These men come from His Lordship's residence, Father," his son called out the explanation.

Old Ritter gave them a cordial nod. "It has been a while since His Lordship placed any orders," he remarked.

"So your son was telling us," Haydn said with a smile. He turned to young Ritter, about to address him when Johann voiced the question in his mind.

"What was it His Lordship ordered?"

"He was fond of collecting sheaths," the jeweler replied.

"They are displayed in his bedchamber," Boris said. "All made after his own design."

"His own design?" Haydn repeated with a frown. Was there anything about the sheaths themselves that had necessitated such secrecy? His Lordship had never sent his valet to the jeweler's to collect his orders nor, it would seem, asked that the jeweler have them delivered to him.

Yet his journal had recorded the numerous visits made by a jeweler named Ritter.

And what did any of this have to do with the Grand Master's stolen diamond and Count Seckendorff's own brutal death?

"His Lordship brought us his designs, and then sent his man to collect both the designs and the sheaths. As though he feared we would steal his designs or fashion a similar sheath for someone else," Ritter said with an amused shrug.

"His Lordship's designs must have been most unusual." Johann's tone was light; the smile on his features calculated to draw out the jeweler.

Ritter's shoulders lifted again in a barely perceptible shrug. "In all truth, they were not very different from the kind of thing we usually make. Jewel-encrusted and ornate. But each had a secret compartment. Large enough to conceal a document. And every sheath seemed to be made for a knife with a broad, flat blade."

"A secret compartment?" Haydn's tone was contemplative. "And you say they were always picked up by a man with ink-stained fingers?" He was beginning to have a faint conception of what His Lordship might have been engaged in.

"What did this man look like?" he heard Johann ask the jeweler. But in Ritter's reply he heard nothing he did not expect to hear.

———✧———

"What is that?" Greta's voice rang out as soon as Rosalie set foot inside the servants' hall.

"Ah!" Rosalie gasped silently, nearly jumping at the sound. Her fingers tightened around the packet Frau Haydn had given her. She hadn't realized anyone was in the room when she opened the door.

Now, twisting her head around, Rosalie saw Greta sitting by the window.

"It's a painting," she replied, having recovered her wits. She set the parcel on the table and recounted her conversation with the Kapellmeister's wife.

She had barely finished when Greta nodded. "I remember now. Frau Bach was most insistent that it be delivered to Herr Haydn alone." Her plump, dimpled palm closed over the packet.

She drew it toward herself and began untying the string.

"I can't imagine why," she said as she finally withdrew the small frame from its wrapping and held it out in front of her. "It's a pretty enough painting, but nothing out of the ordinary."

Rosalie glanced at the picture with its muted, watery shades of grays, blues, and greens of the Katholische Kirche St. Anna. It looked more like a quick sketch executed in preparation for a larger work.

About a half-inch of paper all around remained white, as though the brush had run out of paint and the artist had simply neglected to lift some more. The edges were soft and ragged. Still, it made quite a quaint scene.

The signature scrawled on the bottom right caught her eye.

"Look!" She pointed to the "*J.S. Bach*" inscribed at the corner. "This must be her son's work. I suppose he seeks a commission from His Serene Highness."

Greta stared critically at the work. "A painting in oil might have been more likely to do the trick, then. I doubt that will do it. And just look at that frame! I have never seen anything so badly chipped. Frau Bach said it was, but just look at that."

She jabbed her finger at the top right corner. The gilt on the decorative flutes running around the frame was peeling off and a large piece of the wood had chipped off, exposing an unsightly patch of the rough, ringed layers of the yellowish sapwood.

Rosalie stared at the frame. It was in very poor shape.

"I suppose we could try to find another frame. Herr Haydn won't have the time for it." She looked across the table at Greta. "And there's nothing much for us to do here in any case."

Chapter Nineteen

THE church bells were pealing the ninth hour by the time Haydn and Johann entered Sanssouci. The entire walk had been conducted in silence, the Kapellmeister having been preoccupied with a single question.

How much of what he had gleaned so far should he reveal to the Empress? The bits and pieces they had uncovered of the imperial ambassador's doings formed a disturbing picture in his own mind. But whether they would convince Her Majesty he knew not.

By the time a footman directed them into the corridor that ran alongside the chambers assigned to the King's guests, Haydn had made his decision. He would do no more than suggest that the diamond he had retrieved be evaluated. What other way was there to prove His Lordship's innocence?

As to who had killed His Lordship. . . Haydn pressed his lips together. Given the circumstances, perhaps the magistrate had been right to be suspicious. Who could forget, the Count had been murdered barely hours after the Austrians' arrival?

With his eyes fixed upon the checkered floor, the Kapellmeister advanced briskly along the hallway when a deep, throaty voice stayed his pace.

"Looking for someone, Herr Haydn?"

"Master Johann," the voice continued as the Kapellmeister, brought to an abrupt halt, glanced up. Archduchess Maria Amalia surveyed him with a smile that spread slowly over her features.

Haydn bowed his head, ignoring the footman who stood a little too close to the Archduchess's slender person. How she conducted herself, he reminded himself, was no concern of his. "We were in search of the Empress, Your Imperial Highness."

The Archduchess's long neck swiveled to the left. "I don't believe Mother is in." She turned back to him. "What did you wish to see her about?"

Haydn hesitated, unwilling to disclose very much in the presence of the King's footman. He was still attempting to frame an appropriate response when Johann spoke up.

"Some new facts concerning the imperial ambassador have come to light, Your Imperial Highness," he said with a smile. "We merely wish to acquaint Her Majesty with them. They may help to bring His Lordship's killer to justice."

The Archduchess regarded them for a moment, her head tilted to one side. "What facts, if I may ask?"

"His Lordship was met by a man on the night of his death, Your Imperial Highness." Haydn chose his words with care. The footman was still standing near, detained by the Archduchess's fingers pressing lightly upon his wrist.

"If this stranger's identity can be ascertained, perhaps we may know more about how His Lordship came to be killed."

No need to mention Ritter at all, he thought. After all, it had not been the jeweler who had visited the Count on His Lordship's last night in this world. That much had been established.

The footman coughed. The Archduchess turned to him in surprise. "What is it, Karl?"

The servant, a tall, blond boy barely twenty years old, cleared his throat. "I believe Her Majesty wished to see the Chinese Teahouse again. It is in the palace garden. I would be glad to accompany you, *meine Herren.*"

"Excellent!" Johann beamed, forcing Haydn to clench his lips to prevent them from stretching into a smile. His younger brother seemed quite oblivious to the way the Archduchess's mouth had turned down at the corners.

The Kapellmeister half expected her to protest the arrangement, but she uttered not a single word. No doubt the Crown Prince of Prussia could be persuaded to comfort Her Imperial Highness, he told himself.

His Royal Highness, for all that he was a married man, would at least be a more suitable companion than the young Karl.

"A picture frame?" Frau Göss pursed her lips and frowned down at her knitting. Her needles clicked for a few moments while Rosalie and Greta waited patiently. "His Lordship might have something in his study. But if not"—she glanced up—"Herr Gosset, the frame-maker on Gutenbergstrasse, might be able to furnish you with something suitable."

"Gutenbergstrasse?" Rosalie repeated. The name sounded familiar. Wasn't that where the Kapellmeister had gone this morning?

Her pulse quickened. If it were, perhaps she and Greta could take the jeweler's bloodstained blue cloak and make some enquiries of their own. The Kapellmeister, she had noticed, had omitted to take the garment with him.

"Yes." Frau Göss's attention had returned to her knitting. "It is not far from here. And the frame-maker's establishment is but a few doors down from the jeweler Boris took your master to see."

"*Ach so.*" Rosalie tugged at Greta's arm and pulled her out of the room. "Come, let us be off." She waited until the door had clicked shut behind them before explaining her plan.

"All right," Greta said. "But we may not even have to go if we can find something in His Lordship's study."

But there were no empty picture frames in the study. The maids combed through the two drawers in the Count's desk, finding nothing save for several scores of music. "By Herr Bach," Rosalie said as she lifted them out of the drawer.

"And these," she said, indicating a set of bound scores in a cramped hand, "look like scales."

She had never learned to read music, but the notes ascending up the staves and then coming down again were depressingly familiar.

Sanyi.

Her younger brother's name floated into her mind, followed by a strange sensation as though a cloak of sadness had descended upon her. The papers in her hand blurred, her vision obscured by a mist of unshed tears.

"Look at this!" Greta's voice recalled her to the present.

Rosalie blinked. "What?" she said, raising her eyes.

Greta was holding up a thick sheet of paper with two small openings cut into it. A small square and a tiny rectangle. A triangular flap projected out from either corner of the sheet. As Greta tugged gently on the flaps, the square grew larger and the rectangle got smaller and smaller until it disappeared altogether.

"It looks like those things that artists use, doesn't it?" Rosalie said. She and Greta had seen one of the Esterházy artists use just such a device on one of his painting sessions. He had held it up at arm's length, squinting through the opening with one eye.

"It helps me catch the best view," he had explained when he caught them staring at him. He had shown them how the opening in his view-catcher encapsulated a small section of a panoramic landscape. "In this way, I can tell whether a scene will make a good picture. And when I look through the opening as I paint, I can quite easily see where each tree, shrub, or statue must go on the canvas."

"I wonder why His Lordship had a view-catcher in his possession." Greta pulled at the flaps again, making the square opening disappear this time.

Rosalie shrugged. "Perhaps he took an interest in painting."

"Then, where are his paintbrushes and paints?" Greta thrust her hand in the direction of the desk. Two ebony flutes lay upon the surface and the drawers were filled with scores. But there were no signs of any painting implements.

"It could be something else altogether," Rosalie replied. But she couldn't for the life of her imagine what other purpose the paper with its twin openings could serve. She rummaged around some more, sifting through the contents of both drawers.

"And there are no picture frames either." The corners of Greta's mouth turned down and she let out a heavy sigh; the prospect of a long walk clearly most unappealing.

She returned the paper to the drawer on the left and pushed the compartment back into the desk. "I suppose it's off to Gutenbergstrasse for us, then. Where is that cloak?"

———※———

A walk of less than half a mile brought Haydn and Johann to the Chinese Teahouse. They were still a few feet from it when Karl, the footman, pointed toward it.

"There it is, *meine Herren*, the King's teahouse. Her Majesty, the Empress, should be within." He would have continued walking, but his feet ground to a halt at Haydn's hastily uttered: "That will not be necessary."

The lad's head pivoted toward them and he stared, reluctant it appeared to be dismissed.

"We are mere musicians," Haydn assured him with a smile. "There is no need to stand on ceremony with us, my boy." The Kapellmeister pressed a few thalers into the footman's hand, eager to be rid of him.

It would be the work of a fool to allow one of His Majesty's servants the opportunity to eavesdrop upon their conversation with the Empress. The King was known to surround himself with spies.

They waited while the footman disappeared from view before approaching the teahouse, snugly nestled within a frame of snow-laden trees. Not even in his Prince's gardens had Haydn seen anything more exotically beautiful. The mid-morning sun glinted off the gilded statues and columns that adorned its facade and shone brightly upon the golden figure and its snow-covered parasol perched atop the cupola.

Ragged white patches of snow lay within the folds of the roof that billowed over the entire structure.

Through the large clear glass panes on the window, they caught a glimpse of Prince Nikolaus pacing up and down the floor before the seated Empress.

"Ah, there you are," His Serene Highness greeted the brothers as they stepped into a room hung with brightly patterned Pekings in shades of crimson so vivid, Haydn flinched. Johann paled, reminded no doubt, just as his brother was, of the gory sight that had greeted them the morning before.

"Have you any news, Haydn?" The Empress turned eagerly toward him.

"There may be a man, Your Majesty, who, if we could but find him, might be able to tell us who killed His Lordship and why." He began to recount the details they had uncovered.

"A jeweler?" Her Majesty interrupted the narrative. Her fingers tightened around the gold knob of her ebony cane. "Seckendorff was closely associated with a jeweler, you say?"

"It is what he claimed to be, Your Majesty," Johann explained. "But we believe. . ." He glanced at his older brother.

It was Haydn who had deduced there was but one man acting as a liaison between Ritter the goldsmith and His Lordship. Given the facts —the ink-stained fingers, the faded blue cloak—what other conclusion made sense?

Neither the goldsmith nor His Lordship's valet had been able to furnish them with a proper description of the Count's mysterious associate. But the cloak he habitually wore and the state of his fingers had impressed themselves indelibly upon both their minds.

Haydn clenched and unclenched his fists, wishing he did not have to disclose the unsavory fact. But there was no getting around it. The Empress and His Serene Highness were regarding him expectantly.

"We believe the man was impersonating the jeweler for reasons of his own, Your Majesty. His Lordship appears to have been aware of the deception. He was well acquainted with the real Herr Ritter, being wont to frequent the man's shop."

The Empress frowned. "What need was there to involve a jeweler?" she murmured, her voice so low, it was clear she was speaking to herself.

"It was no doubt a ruse to conceal His Lordship's association with the imposter. A way of passing information without drawing untoward attention to their clandestine relationship."

He had gone as far as he reasonably could toward revealing his suspicions. But Her Majesty seemed quite incapable of grasping the implication of his words.

"His connection with a jeweler makes the entire situation more awkward than it already is," she said, addressing Prince Nikolaus. "You may depend upon it, Frederick will take advantage of the fact."

His Serene Highness nodded unhappily. "I trust no one has been made aware of the matter?" His foot tapped uneasily on the floor as he turned toward his Kapellmeister.

"No one, Your Serene Highness," Haydn assured him quietly. His Prince and his Empress both seemed more concerned with preserving His Lordship's reputation than with uncovering the truth.

It was all a question of statecraft and diplomacy, he supposed—matters so far beyond his ken he did not pretend to understand the tortuous decisions they entailed.

"I believe there is a way to irrefutably establish His Lordship's innocence as far as. . ." his voice faded, unwilling to voice the accusation. God alone knew who else was privy to their conversation. A careless word might result in disaster.

"Yes, yes, Haydn." His Serene Highness's tone was brusque. "But what exactly do you propose?"

The Kapellmeister elaborated his scheme. "And we have just the man to do it," Johann added. "Herr Ritter has agreed to examine the stone. But a word from Your Majesty is required to set the plot in motion."

The Empress propelled herself up from her seat, leaning heavily upon her cane. "You will have to profess an interest in the diamond, Esterházy. I imagine that will be the best way forward."

Chapter Twenty

THE cloak had been left in a closet that was concealed behind a painting in the entrance hall. Rosalie and Greta were about to retrieve it when they heard Boris's voice.

"What are you two doing over there?"

Rosalie felt Greta give a violent start behind her. She herself spun around, the cloak clutched to her chest.

She held the garment out. "We were going to return it to Herr Ritter," she said. "Herr Haydn forgot to take it with him this morning."

Boris came forward, limping slightly, and plucked the cloak out of her hands. "There is no need for that. It was not he who came the other night."

"You were mistaken, then?" Rosalie glanced at Greta. Hadn't she suspected as much? Someone had impersonated the poor jeweler.

Boris appeared not to have heard the question. He returned the cloak to the closet.

"Who was it, then, the other night—if it was not the jeweler?" Greta asked.

Boris turned around. "I couldn't say. He was such an ordinary man. I always knew it was him because of his cloak. And his fing—"

He stopped abruptly and his eyes widened.

"It was *not* him. It was *never* him."

"What—what is it?" Rosalie and Greta said at the same time, but Boris had already rushed out.

"Whatever did he mean by that?" Greta turned toward Rosalie, bewildered.

"That it was someone other than Herr Ritter who habitually visited His Lordship?" Rosalie ventured, her voice sounding uncertain. Surely the jeweler wasn't so unremarkable that Boris had repeatedly mistaken someone else for him?

———•◦◦•———

The Kapellmeister and his brother were already outside the palace gates when they heard the sound of footsteps hurrying after them.

"Herr Haydn! Master Johann!"

Herr Bach's portly form charged down the road.

"If I could have but a moment of your time," he huffed, slowing to a halt as he neared them.

"Yes, of course," Haydn promptly replied. It was an unforeseen interruption, but there was little to do but wait until Her Majesty sent word that Ritter's services were required at the palace. But what untoward event, he wondered, had brought the King's harpsichordist running out after him?

"You have received the vignette, I trust?" Herr Bach said.

"The vignette?" Haydn looked toward Johann, hoping his younger brother had some notion of what was meant. He himself was at a loss.

"Painted by your son, I presume," Johann ventured.

Herr Bach's eyes brightened. "Yes. You have received it, then? Bastian's vignette of the Katholische Kirche St. Anna? It is in watercolor." He looked expectantly at Haydn who stared blankly back at him.

The Kapellmeister could not recall receiving any such thing. And even if he had, what was so significant about the matter that Herr Bach must detain him over it?

"You have not. . . received it. . .?" Herr Bach's voice faltered. "It was but yesterday that my wife put it in Frau Haydn's hands."

"Then it is still with sister-in-law," Johann reassured Herr Bach. "She retired well before we did last night, did she not, brother?" A valiant attempt to save the Kapellmeister's face, but it did not prevent a bright flush of mortification from suffusing Haydn's cheeks.

How could he have spent an entire day without so much as a word to his wife? At no time yesterday had he remained long enough in her presence for her to even mention the painting.

"Er, yes, so she did."

"Ah!" The accordion-like furrows between Herr Bach's eyebrows dissipated, and his lips parted in a smile of relief.

"The frame is quite badly chipped, I fear," he continued. "It must be replaced. But my wife has informed Frau Haydn of all this."

"Of course. I will see to it," Haydn said in response to the eager gaze the keyboardist directed at him. As Herr Bach continued to gape at him, the Kapellmeister wondered what else he was required to do.

Display the vignette to every person of rank in an effort to procure commissions for young Sebastian?

"His Serene Highness, I am sure, will be interested in seeing the work," he offered, hoping Herr Bach would come out in the open with his request. Surely there was no need for such reticence with a fellow musician.

"The Empress, too, I imagine." Herr Bach beamed.

Haydn's eyes slid toward his brother and they exchanged a brief look of amusement. The keyboardist's ambitions ran high if he hoped to win a position for his son at the Hofburg. On the basis of a vignette, no less.

"Yes, I suppose so." Haydn's gaze returned to Herr Bach.

"Excellent, excellent!" Herr Bach rubbed his hands together happily. "I see we understand each other well. Might I ask a small favor as well?"

What! Haydn's eyebrows lifted despite himself. Had he not already acceded to one favor?

His eyes met Johann's again before he responded.

"By all means. What is it you require?"

"The church organ is badly in need of tuning." Herr Bach's eyes rested upon the brothers for a brief moment before he continued. "I mean the organ at the Katholische Kirche St. Anna."

At the site of the imperial ambassador's murder? Haydn's stomach turned, his memory still afflicted by the gory sight they had encountered the previous morning. The body, brutally stabbed, had been removed. The blood, no doubt, cleaned. Even so. . .

"I would go myself, but the King keeps me far too busy to attend to such things." Herr Bach motioned helplessly toward the palace.

"Very well," Haydn said. He was not altogether happy to assent. But it would have been churlish to refuse.

"Excellent!" Herr Bach proclaimed again. "I will leave you to it, then." He began his retreat toward the palace.

"And when are we to make time for these tasks?" Johann said softly to Haydn as they watched the keyboardist's slowly receding figure.

"I suppose we may as well take care of them now," Haydn replied. "There is little to do until Her Majesty sends for Ritter."

———◆———

Herr Gossett, the frame-maker, peered at the framed vignette Rosalie held out for him. "Yes, I see," he said. "It is very badly damaged."

He raised his bespectacled eyes toward them. "How did His Lordship manage to break off that corner?"

"His Lordship?" Rosalie and Greta cried, astonished. But the frame-maker's attention had already returned to the frame with its peeling gold leaf.

He rubbed a calloused, brown finger over the rough surface. "The frame is new. I made it no more than a month ago. To the most precise specifications. And we use nothing but the best quality wood, I can tell you that."

"It was not His Lordship who broke it," Rosalie said. "Why, it didn't even—"

"No, I suppose it would've been one of his maids. Clumsy creatures! A frame is as much a work of art as the painting it encases. But it is too much to expect a mere servant to understand that, I suppose."

Greta's nostrils flared. "Are you suggesting—*Aww!*" she cried as Rosalie pinched her arm.

Rosalie ignored her friend's indignant glare. "The frame and the painting were a gift from Herr Bach, His Majesty's harpsichordist, to Herr Haydn, Kapellmeister—"

"I do know who Herr Haydn is," the frame-maker replied without looking up.

"I can scarcely believe Master Sebastian would treat his frames so ill," he continued, picking up the frame and holding it up to the light. "And you say His Lordship made a gift of it to him."

Rosalie sighed. It was not what either she or Greta had said.

"How can you be so sure that this is the frame you made for His Lordship?" Greta sounded peevish.

Herr Gossett fortunately took no offense at her tone. "Look!" he said, turning the frame over. "These numbers inscribed into the wood tell me when the frame was made and for whom. This was made for His Lordship, as I said before, no more than a month ago.

"I fear nothing can be done to repair the damage." He returned the frame to Rosalie.

Rosalie sighed again. "Can you give us another?"

Herr Gossett pursed his lips. "His Lordship was most particular about his designs. But I suppose something similar can be found. Wait here!" He disappeared behind a door.

"What an irksome man!" Greta leaned over to whisper into Rosalie's ear. "Making such a fuss about an ordinary frame. And after all that, His Lordship gave it away."

Rosalie remained silent. Why had His Lordship ordered a frame made for himself only to give it away?

She had barely time to ponder the question when Herr Gossett bustled out the door with a frame, a mat board, and a thick piece of paper.

"I had nothing with a rabbet as large as His Lordship usually favored. But it was just as well." He set the frame on the table and held out the mat board and what looked like another view-catcher with oval-shaped openings.

"Master Sebastian should have come directly to me instead of trying to fit his painting into His Lordship's frame. He had to stuff a mat board and one of his view-catchers to make the vignette fit into the frame."

He tapped the new frame of light oak and beamed at them. "This one, by the greatest good fortune, is just the right size."

Maria Anna was in the orangerie when Haydn and Johann returned to Lindenstrasse. Her slender neck, visible through the tall glass windows, rose above a heap of soft cushions piled upon a couch of woven willow.

They opened the door and stepped in. She must have recognized their footsteps on the paved stone, for Haydn saw her shoulders stiffen. But she kept her head resolutely down. A few tendrils of hair, freed from the confines of their pins, curled down her nape.

Three steps behind her willow chair, he paused and cleared his throat. Still, she did not turn. Suppressing a sigh, the Kapellmeister turned helplessly toward his younger brother. They would get little out of his wife in her current state of ill-temper.

But Johann, ever willing to take up the gauntlet, called out to her in a cheerful tone.

"We saw Herr Bach at the palace, sister-in-law. You have met his wife, I take it."

Still looking straight ahead, Maria Anna harrumphed. "If it is the vignette husband is after, brother-in-law, you may inform him it is with the maids."

She glanced over her shoulder at last, steadfastly avoiding Haydn's eyes. "They see so much more of him than I do, I thought it best to let *them* have the task of giving it to him."

"Ah-hm. . ." Johann faltered, left speechless by her words. He was still struggling to frame a response when Maria Anna turned her face away. Her chin jutted out at the potted creeper, its profusion of branches overflowing its green pot, upon the willow table in front of her.

But Haydn would not allow himself to be silenced so easily.

"A man has died," he reminded his wife. "Brutally killed. And worse, accused of theft. The Empress—"

"*Accused of theft?*" Maria Anna's head pivoted sharply around. "Why should His Lordship be accused of theft, husband? What are you on about?"

Haydn clenched his teeth together, wishing he had refrained from speaking. But it was too late.

"The Prince of Condé's diamond was found along with His Lordship's person at the church," he said, hoping the explanation would suffice.

"Why would that mean His Lordship had stolen it?" Maria Anna wanted to know. "He didn't so much as glance at it when the Prince thrust it among us. I expect His Lordship had seen it a thousand times before, with the Prince so eager to dispose of it."

Then, His Lordship had been given a thousand opportunities to steal it, Haydn thought. *And had resisted them all.*

The Kapellmeister felt an enormous sense of relief. His wife's words could do nothing to exonerate His Lordship. But they had gone a long way toward easing his own anxiety. Whatever else the Count might have been guilty of, it was not theft.

Chapter Twenty-One

THE coffeehouse on the corner of Gutenbergstrasse and Jägerstrasse caught Rosalie's eye. A slender, cloaked figure sat at a table with her back to the window. Rosalie grasped Greta's wrist.

"Is that Elma?" Had her enciphered letter brought their friend to Potsdam? But before Greta could respond, the woman turned around. *Not Elma.* Rosalie's shoulders slumped.

"Let's go in, anyway." Greta pulled Rosalie toward the door. "I'm freezing. I could do with a cup of coffee."

But the coffee Frau Doebbert, a bony woman dressed in black, brought to them had the strangest taste. *Like burnt wood*, Rosalie thought as Greta spat hers back into the cup.

"What is this?" Greta sputtered.

Frau Doebbert sniffed. "It's the best I can do. The King frowns upon coffee-drinking. There's more coffee in that cup than you'll get anywhere else."

"And the rest of it?" Rosalie wrapped her hands around the steaming cup. It might taste awful, but it would at least serve to warm her frozen fingers.

"Chicory," Frau Doebbert replied. "It's the closest thing to coffee the likes of us can get. Is there anything else you want?"

"A hot buttered roll," Greta said. "I hope His Majesty doesn't disapprove of those as well."

The King evidently didn't object to his subjects enjoying good bread. The rolls, when Frau Doebbert brought them a plateful, were deliciously soft and warm and the butter almost as good as the kind served in His Serene Highness's kitchens.

Rosalie brought out the view-catcher Herr Gossett the frame-maker had discovered within the chipped frame they had sought to replace.

"I'm not so sure this is a view-catcher," she said to Greta, frowning down at the thing. What had seemed at first to be two oval openings was, in reality, a single opening shaped like an hourglass.

"Why?" Greta mumbled, her mouth full. "What else could it be?"

"I don't know. But I don't see how it could be a view-catcher. I have seen oval paintings. And square and rectangular paintings. But what artist has ever painted a picture in the shape of an hourglass?"

"Oh!" Greta's lips, still blue from the cold, stretched into a stunned oval. A view-catcher, they had both learned, was always the same shape as the painting it was meant for. It had to be, to serve its purpose.

"And it has His Lordship's crest on it." Rosalie pointed to the inked impression of a crown surmounted with six feathers and a flag with a leafy vine entwined into a figure eight. Underneath it was a set of numbers: *11.10.68.*

Greta tapped her nail against the figures. "A secret message, do you think?"

Rosalie chewed her lip. That it was some sort of enciphered message made sense. Numbers often were, Elma had taught them. "But why would His Lordship entrust it to Herr Bach?"

"Frau Bach seemed most eager to get rid of that painting, you know," Greta said. "And she was very insistent that Herr Haydn replace the frame. I thought it strange that she hadn't done it herself. But she must have wished him to discover that."

She tapped the device. "I'll wager anything it's a secret message for Herr Haydn?"

Or His Serene Highness. Or, the Empress herself.

Rosalie thrust her chair back. "Then, we had best deliver it to him at once."

It was from Frau Göss, the Hausmeister's wife, that Haydn learned the vignette had already been taken to a frame-maker.

"Just as well. It is one less thing for us to concern ourselves with," Johann said to the Kapellmeister as they passed through the gates of His Lordship's residence onto the street.

Haydn tucked the bloodstained cloak belonging to the Count's mysterious visitor under his arm and nodded. His brother's remark had been intended to ease his mind, he knew. But he would sooner have gone in search of a frame than return to the place of Count Seckendorff's murder.

Better still, he would have preferred to track down the Count's mysterious visitor. The little they had learned of the man had given him some idea of who it might be. It remained but to confirm the man's identity.

Piles of hardened snow formed an undulating row of tiny hillocks on either side of the broad avenue that was Lindenstrasse. The ground itself was treacherously icy beneath their feet.

"How badly out of tune could the organ be?" Haydn kept his eyes on his shoes, ready to brace himself should his footing slip. He gripped the bundled-up cloak firmly under his arm "It was just the other evening that Herr Bach was singing its praises to us."

Johann's head swung sharply toward him. "So he did," he agreed quietly. "Could it be," he continued a few minutes later, "that it is not well-tempered, making it impossible to play anything other than the near keys?"

"I suppose so," Haydn conceded. Far better to suppose that Herr Bach, like his father, was not content with confining himself solely to the keys of C, F, and G than to suspect the harpsichordist had sent them chasing after wild geese.

Although that possibility had insinuated itself into the Kapellmeister's mind. How could it not, given Herr Bach's employer? On the other hand, perhaps, Johann had surmised correctly.

What musician, after all, would not be frustrated by an inability to modulate to more distant keys? That a system of tuning should dictate what a man could or could not play was simply intolerable.

Another thought occurred to the Kapellmeister and he smiled. "The organ was made by Gottfried Silbermann, was it not? Perhaps Herr Bach's ear still hears the wolf fifth of Silbermann's tuning."

"Perhaps." Johann's mouth widened into a grin. The single disso-nant fifth on a Silbermann organ—an unfortunate consequence of his tuning method—became immediately apparent when the organist will-fully chose to play in A-flat major. An offense Herr Bach's father, Se-bastian Bach, had habitually committed at every public demonstration of the organ-maker's instruments.

The bells were ringing the quarter hour when they neared the church. As they passed through the gate—unlatched today and standing ajar —the deep, sonorous clanging seemed to make Haydn's very nerves pulsate in unison. I t was a deeply discomfiting sensation, as though at any moment his entire being might be torn open by the sound.

Or perhaps it was merely his own discomfort at returning to the scene of His Lordship's fatal encounter with death.

The church door stood open, too, and the pastor appeared miracu-lously at the threshold the moment Haydn and Johann stepped through the gate.

"Herr Bach will have sent you," the pastor greeted them once the clanging had ceased. "The organ—" he glanced over his shoulder.

"Does the organist prefer—"

Haydn had been about to ask whether the organist preferred the more common meantone system to that favored by the Bachs when he was interrupted.

"He is not with us," the pastor informed him, an apologetic smile on his weathered features.

"Not with us. . .?" Haydn faltered. Had the gentleman met his demise as well? But in that case, why did the pastor smile so serenely at them?

"On holiday," the pastor explained. "In Hamburg. But no doubt, your brother will assist you." The pastor's bright brown eyes turned to-ward Johann. Without waiting for a response, he went on: "The tuning knife is near the pipes."

He tossed a quick glance over his shoulder, then turned back.

"You will wish to get started, I suppose."

A few minutes at the manuals told Haydn all he needed to know. The clarity and beauty of the thirds indicated the organist's preference for meantone. "It seems to be sufficiently in tune," he said. "Perhaps, a few adjustments. . ."

"Then let us make them and leave," Johann suggested. "The organist clearly chooses not to play in more exotic keys."

The Kapellmeister felt a twinge of guilt at so deliberately misinterpreting Herr Bach's wishes. But to re-tune the instrument to the harpsichordist's satisfaction would require far more time than was at their disposal.

The pastor returned just as Haydn had finished adjusting the slide on the last pipe. He stood by the manuals at Johann's side, a small, erect figure clutching a picture frame to his chest.

"We have no money to pay you," he said when Haydn came down to the nave.

"We had no such expectation," Haydn tried to say, but his voice was drowned out by the pastor's reedy tenor.

"I must insist. It is but a small token of our appreciation." The pastor held the frame out.

"A vignette," Haydn said, examining the painting. "Of the imperial ambassador's palace."

The pastor gave them a delighted smile. "I thought you might like it. It is by Herr Bach's son." He pointed to the signature. "An excellent artist. He gives these away. But it will not be long, I'll warrant, before his works command the price they deserve."

"Indeed," Haydn said. The work was charming enough, but it did not stop him wondering whether it was the prospect of being paid in his son's work that had deterred Herr Bach from undertaking the task himself. Certainly no tuner worth his salt would have found it satisfactory recompense for his troubles.

<hr />

They were almost at Yorckstrasse when Haydn realized the bloodstained cloak he had been carrying had been left at the Katholische

Kirche St. Anna. But when the brothers returned to the church, the garment was nowhere to be found.

"It was draped over the balustrade." Haydn pointed to the wooden parapet at the outer edge of the choir loft. He anxiously scanned the church. A winding set of wooden steps, in the shadow of an enormous pillar, rose to the choir loft. It was there that the organ pipes were housed.

As his gaze traveled down the stairs, a flicker of movement caught his eye.

"There!" he shouted urgently, racing toward the pillar. He reached it just in time to see a man slipping through a small door beyond the stairs. He wrenched open the door and, reaching for the stranger's shoulder, swung him around.

A man of medium stature and years stared back at him. His hair, the same shade of brown as a mottled umber, was streaked with silver. But for the light of intelligence that brightened his dark eyes, there was nothing particularly remarkable about his face.

Nevertheless, he seemed familiar.

"You were at His Majesty's supper table the other night!" The words burst out of Haydn's mouth just as Johann's footsteps sounded behind him. The stranger's gaze traveled over Haydn's shoulder.

"Herr Eichel?" Johann asked before the man could utter a word. "That is your name, is it not?"

"It is His Majesty's principal secretary, Anton Eichel," he explained in response to Haydn's stare. "I recall him sitting next to Herr Quantz."

"I pray you let me go, gentleman," Eichel said, his voice muted. "I had nothing to do with His Lordship's death."

Haydn glanced down at the bloodstained cloak, crumpled into a heap in the principal secretary's arms. "You were with His Lordship when he died?" He inclined his chin toward the cloak. "That is yours, I presume." The ink-stained fingers told their own tale.

"It is," Eichel admitted. "But I did not visit him that night. I had ceased to do so some time back when it became clear we had been discovered."

Haydn frowned. "And yet your cloak was found within this very church, covering His Lordship's body."

"It is not safe for me to be here," Eichel muttered with a nervous glance over his shoulder.

"But your cloak?" Haydn persisted.

Eichel's eyes darted toward Johann. "I was not here, I swear it. It was only the next morning that I discovered my cloak lost"—he swallowed —"and I feared. . ."

"And it was at the same time that the Prince of Condé discovered his diamond gone?" Johann mused. "There must be some connection between the two incidents, brother?"

But the Kapellmeister barely heard his brother's words. Quite another question preoccupied him. "You acted as the go-between for the Count and His Majesty, did you not? The imperial ambassador was a traitor—"

"No, no!" Eichel countered sharply. "You misunderstand the matter completely. It is not what you think."

The sound of boots tapping on the marble floor within startled them. Eichel's eyes widened. The color drained from his face leaving it a sickly gray.

"I was His Lordship's informant," he whispered. "I can reveal more to you. Tonight. At the Chinese Teahouse. But, please, I must go now."

The sound of boots grew ever louder behind them. In the noise of their rhythmic clatter, the words that had formed in Haydn's mind dissipated. Before he knew it, Eichel was gone. A blur of brown that mingled with the furze that grew between the church and the alley behind it.

"Herr Haydn!" A curt voice invaded the Kapellmeister's senses. He pivoted around, nearly bumping into Johann.

A man dressed in the dark blue livery of the House of Hohenzollern stood a few paces behind the door. A footman judging by the white waistcoat and white facings on his coat, yet his manner seemed strangely authoritative.

His narrowed eyes, directed over Haydn's shoulder, lingered on the scene outside a moment longer than was entirely necessary.

Haydn had barely time to wonder what had caught the man's gaze when the servant's attention returned to him.

"Her Majesty, the Empress, and His Majesty, the King, request your presence at the palace, *Meine Herren.*"

Haydn acknowledged the summons with a small nod. Ritter the jeweler had been sent for, he supposed.

Chapter Twenty-Two

"THERE you are!" Frau Göss cried as soon as Rosalie and Greta burst in through the servants' entrance. "Herr Haydn and Master Johann were enquiring after you before they left. I told them—"

"*Left?*" The maids stopped and stared at each other in dismay.

"Where have they gone?" Rosalie asked.

"To the Katholische Kirche St. Anna."

"But that was some time back," Frau Göss hastily added as the maids began to turn toward the door. "I expect Herr Haydn and his brother will be at the palace now. His Majesty sent a servant to summon them."

Rosalie let out a deep breath. Was there any point hurrying to the palace? What good would it do if the Kapellmeister and his brother were preoccupied?

"What is it you wished to tell Herr Haydn?" Boris's voice startled her. How long had he been standing by the servants' hall door?

"The frame we were sent to replace—" She heard Greta blurting out and hastened to interrupt.

"Belonged to His Lordship. Oddly enough," Rosalie finished. She refrained from glancing at Greta. There was no need to mention the secret message. Such things were not meant to be the subject of common talk.

"But it was Frau Bach who gave the painting to Frau Haydn, was it not?" Frau Göss led the way into the servants' hall.

A gift from His Lordship for Master Sebastian's paintings, I shouldn't wonder," Boris said as he ushered Rosalie and Greta into the warm room. A fire was blazing within.

The sudden blast of its heat recalled Rosalie's senses to her fingers, numb from the cold.

"But why use the selfsame frame for a painting intended for Herr Haydn?" Frau Göss lowered herself into a chair and began pouring from a porcelain pot of freshly brewed coffee. "Especially when it was so badly damaged. I can hardly understand it."

The housekeeper pushed steaming cups of the brew toward Rosalie and Greta.

"Damaged?" Boris's spoon ceased to clink against the cup of coffee he had been stirring. "It was damaged when Frau Bach gave it to you?" He looked across the table at the maids.

"Quite badly chipped," Frau Göss said before the maids could reply. She poured cream into her coffee. "You should've seen it. The corner almost broken off."

Boris's gray-green eyes turned back toward Rosalie and Greta. "I thought one of you had dropped it, and so damaged it."

Greta had been about to take a sip of coffee, but at the valet's words, she plonked her cup down. "Why does everyone think it was us?" She looked annoyed. "Of course, it wasn't!"

"I myself would have been ashamed to make a gift of it in that condition," Frau Göss continued as though Greta had not spoken.

"Perhaps it wasn't a gift," Boris said, stirring his coffee again. "Perhaps it was intended as a message."

"A message?" Greta squeaked as Rosalie covered her mouth to prevent the coffee she had just sipped from squirting out of it. Their eyes collided with each other. How could Boris have known about the secret message hidden within the damaged picture frame?

Rosalie swallowed her coffee. "What kind of message?" Her voice as she uttered the words sounded hoarse.

Boris's spoon continued to clank against his cup. The sound seemed to drum incessantly into Rosalie's brain. Unable to stop herself, she reached over and placed her palm over his.

"What kind of message?" she asked again, a little louder this time.

Boris looked up, his face ashen. Rosalie could see the fine lines etched into the skin at the corners of his eyes.

"I fear whoever killed His Lordship wishes to do away with all his friends as well."

"Boris!" Frau Göss exclaimed.

"Herr Bach must fear it as well." Boris gripped his hands together. "He called upon His Lordship almost as frequently as the man who called himself Ritter. And where is Herr Ritter now?"

"The jeweler?" Rosalie asked, feeling confused. Hadn't Boris found him at his establishment this morning?

Boris shook his head. "No, the man who allowed me to think he was Ritter. The jeweler never set foot in this house."

"His Lordship's visitor lied about his name, then?" Greta hazarded the guess, looking just as bewildered as Rosalie.

"I cannot be certain he ever gave it. I thought his name was Ritter when he said he had come from the jeweler's establishment. He never once corrected me."

"But it was this man—this false Ritter—who came for His Lordship the other night, wasn't it Boris?" The pot of coffee in Frau Göss's hand hovered hesitantly over her cup.

"No, Frau Göss. It was someone who wanted us to think it was him."

"Because he came wrapped in the man's cloak?" Rosalie said, the words sounding like a question.

Not that it was unlikely that the killer had wished to conceal his own identity—and to implicate someone else for the murder.

But what had Boris seen to be so convinced that the man had deliberately impersonated His Lordship's visitor? She leaned forward.

"How can you be so sure it was someone else, Boris?"

"His fingers," Boris said slowly, a distant look in his eyes. "They were not ink-stained. His Lordship's visitor always had ink-stained fingers. Even the jeweler commented on it. I thought there was something different about the man that night. But I was in such a pother, I couldn't tell what.

"Then this morning I recalled his fingers—slender and white, with not the slightest trace of black on them."

His shoulders drooped. "I opened the door to a killer, Frau Göss," the valet said. "He must have murdered the man who assumed Ritter's name and then come for His Lordship. And now I suppose he means to kill Herr Bach and, who knows, the pastor of the Katholische Kirche St. Anna as well."

The footman, who had only given his name as Fonso, conveyed the Kapellmeister and his brother from the church to the entrance hall of Sanssouci. There, with an imperious flick of his wrist, he summoned another servant.

"Take these gentlemen within, and let His Majesty know they are here."

Then, with a curt bow in their direction, he was gone, leaving the Kapellmeister to wonder why they were being left in the hands of another servant.

But it was idle curiosity, nothing more. No doubt, Fonso had other more important duties to attend to.

The second footman showed them into a small antechamber adorned with gilded mirrors and painted panels and left them to await His Majesty's pleasure unaccompanied.

A few minutes passed, marked by the loud ticking of a clock.

Then Johann cleared his throat and looked cautiously around the room.

"If Eichel was the Count's informant," he began in a voice so low, Haydn had to strain his ears to hear him. Johann paused and searched the room again, although it was doubtful the white panels concealed any eavesdroppers.

"Then, His Lordship was not acting as a spy for the King," Haydn murmured, his voice equally low. "I had feared he might have been."

That His Lordship had been a spy was not in question. What other reason could there be for the elaborate ruse Anton Eichel had concocted for his meetings with the Count?

The King's secretary must have concealed the documents he filched from his master within the secret compartment of the sheaths made by Ritter. A clever means of delivering sensitive papers.

What role the Katholische Kirche St. Anna and its pastor had played, if any, Haydn still could not fathom. His brother's voice broke the silence that had fallen upon them.

"And the Austrians could have—" Johann seemed to be overcome by another fit of coughing.

"Had no hand in the incident," Haydn said softly. "Nor any reason for wishing it." To have ascertained that much was a relief.

The Kapellmeister had never suspected the Empress of any misdoings. To be underhanded was not Her Majesty's way. But to what lengths might not her son and co-regent go? Especially in the face of the Empress's determination to keep the imperial ambassador in his position.

When they had learned of His Lordship's intimate relationship with the King, Haydn had wondered—although he had not voiced the thought in so many words even to himself—whether the Emperor had harbored any particular reason for not wishing his mother to visit Prussia.

Certainly, there had been some reason for Princess Auersperg to be strongly against it. She had categorically denied speaking on behalf of the Emperor. Yet her very denial had seemed to suggest otherwise.

"Even so, the timing of his death seems suspicious, does it not?" Johann's quiet voice broke into the Kapellmeister's thoughts. "To be despatched on the very night of our arrival."

Haydn nodded. "Lured to his death, it would appear." What other reason could there be for the killer choosing to impersonate the Count's informant? And as for the hour of His Lordship's murder—

"Haydn." The sound of his name, booming out at him, was like the explosion of a gunshot in the Kapellmeister's ears.

His startled eyes flew to the door, colliding with the small, hunched form of the King standing a few paces behind it, a sardonic smile on his lopsided features.

"There you are! Well, don't just stand there, my good man. Come in. Haven't you kept us cooling our heels long enough?"

—————

Haydn stared at the King. How much had His Majesty overheard of their conversation? How much had he needed to hear? Eichel had said they had been discovered.

By whom? The King of Prussia?

Had His Lordship's murder, then, been intended as a message for the Empress? Aware of the King's pale blue eyes on his features, the Kapellmeister swallowed his suspicions.

"Ritter—?" he enquired, his voice coming out in a hoarse croak.

"Has already been sent for," the King replied brusquely. "He is within."

Haydn bowed his head and walked the few paces toward the threshold. He was about to cross it when the King's softly uttered words arrested his steps.

"I suppose this entire stunt was your idea, Haydn. What is it you hope to discover by it?"

"The truth, Your Majesty." Haydn held the King's gaze for a single moment, then stepped across the threshold into the Music Room.

Within the Prince of Condé's voice swelled in outrage. "Surely this is completely unnecessary, Esterházy!"

The Grand Master's peevish tenor rose as effortlessly as an opera singer's—up the rocaille trimmings of gilded stucco on the white wall panels toward the thick vines and curlicues on the ceiling.

"The diamond was never stolen. Merely misplaced." The Grand Master pushed himself upright against the marble fireplace that had hitherto served to prop up his elegant form. "Your Kapellmeister discovered it in my room.

"There he is. You may have him confirm the details yourself."

Haydn's feet ground to a halt. He glanced uneasily at his brother. They could hardly confess to the deception they had been called upon to perpetrate. But he would lay his life upon it, the diamond in the Grand Master's possession was not authentic. How could it be?

The King's pale aqua eyes, he noticed, had swiveled toward him, his royal lips twitching in a telltale smile. The Kapellmeister struggled to fashion a response. Even his brother seemed to be struck dumb.

His Serene Highness fortunately intervened. "Nevertheless, it is a precaution I wish to take before I venture an offer." He stood at the other end of the fireplace, his voice heavy with ill-concealed impatience.

How many times, Haydn wondered, had his employer been compelled to present the selfsame argument?

"A sensible precaution," the King said. "But entirely unnecessary." He strode toward the harpsichord where Ritter stood, a leather case clasped close to his chest. "I have no doubt our jeweler will find the Grand Master's diamond pure and unblemished."

His Majesty turned toward Haydn. His lips curved into a smile. "No doubt at all."

The certainty in the King's voice caused a faint quiver of disquiet to flare up in the pit of Haydn's stomach. How could the King be so sure of what the jeweler would find, unless. . .

He quelled his suspicions. They would know nothing until Ritter had concluded his examination.

"But I suppose"—His Majesty turned toward the Empress who sat motionless in the window bay—"there is no harm in getting confirmation of the fact."

"No, there is not." The Empress's voice was quiet. Her hands lay unmoving upon her lap. The tight nod of her head, the only visible sign of tension in her appearance.

Chapter Twenty-Three

"How is it you wish to proceed, Herr Ritter?" Haydn had to grit his teeth to prevent his voice from betraying his qualms. He approached the harpsichord. "Have you everything you need?"

"Ehmm. . .yes. Yes." Ritter's head bobbed as he attempted to set his case upon the harpsichord. It slipped from his fingers, dropping onto the lid with a soft thud that seemed to startle him more than it did anyone else in the room.

What had so unnerved the young jeweler, Haydn wondered. The exalted company he found himself in? God forbid, there should be any other reason.

He watched as the jeweler fumbled with the brass fastener on his case. It flew open at last just as Haydn was about to offer his help. Ritter reached within, slowly drawing out a velvet-covered tray with lustrous gems of varying sizes.

How they would enable him to determine the authenticity of the Grand Master's diamond, the Kapellmeister failed to see. He pressed his lips together, his fingers clenching tightly into his palms.

Ritter withdrew an enamel disc with a golden-beaked white heron painted on its lustrous blue surface. "What is that?" Johann, who had come up behind Haydn, whispered into the Kapellmeister's ear.

"Something more useful than the gems he has brought with him, I hope," Haydn whispered back.

Ritter raised his head and cleared his throat.

"May I have a glass of cold water?"

"Nervous, are you?" His Majesty asked in a sardonic tone as Johann left the room to procure the water.

"Not at all," Ritter assured the King, his eyes wide and staring. Like a rabbit, Haydn thought, glancing up to find a fox in its path. Johann returned with the water. Ritter took a sip.

"And the diamond?" Ritter looked toward the fireplace. He turned hesitantly from the Prince of Condé to His Serene Highness. "May I have it?"

He extended his right hand.

With a snort of exasperation, the Prince of Condé, Grand Master of France, crossed the room. He extracted a velvet bag from his pocket and dropped it into the jeweler's outstretched palm. "I dare you to find the slightest flaw in that stone. It is the finest you ever saw."

Ritter made no reply, staring instead at the violet-hued stone that rolled out of the upturned bag onto his palm. He hefted it. "It appears heavy enough," he muttered to himself. Reaching for a stone from his velvet tray, he hefted both again. He repeated the motion with another stone from his tray.

Then, without warning, he dropped the Prince of Condé's diamond into the glass of water Johann had brought him.

"Hey! The Grand Master's sharp cry of indignation nearly pierced Haydn's eardrum, causing him to stagger back. He clawed at the edge of the harpsichord, seeking to steady himself, as the Grand Master bellowed on, oblivious, "What are you doing?"

Ritter smiled, appearing at ease for the first time. "Water will not damage the stone, Your Highness. I am merely testing its weight. Precious stones are heavier by far than glass or paste and tend to sink in water."

"And it is heavier than glass?" It was hardly a question. The Kapellmeister had seen the way the Grand Master's stone had sunk to the bottom of the glass of water.

"Just as we suspected," the King said. "I hope you are satisfied now, Esterházy. The thing is genuine."

Ritter coughed. "I will need to examine it further Your Majesty before I can assert that it is. . .

"That it is a diamond, I mean to say," Ritter went on hastily as the Prince of Condé glared at him. "Nearly every stone known to man is heavier than a bit of glass. But diamonds have special properties."

Haydn glanced at Johann. There was still a shred of hope, then. If the diamond proved to be genuine. . . He dismissed the thought, barely able to breathe.

Ritter fished the stone out of the glass of water, wiped it clean on a pristine white handkerchief, and then breathed upon one of its facets. A mist formed upon the blue surface but disappeared as quickly as it had formed.

Would to God, that meant nothing. But the jeweler took away that hope before it had even formed.

"Only a diamond can dissipate heat quite so quickly," Ritter explained. "It is quite impossible for it to remain fogged."

He held it up to the chandelier. "No blemishes visible that I can see. But, of course, it needs to be examined under greater magnification."

The jeweler picked up his enamel device and flicked his wrist. A lens mounted within a brass ring swung out. He held it over the diamond.

"As clear as day. And the facet lines are perfect."

Haydn's expectations had all but faded when Ritter raised his head. "May I have a newspaper?"

"Whatever for?" demanded the Prince of Condé.

"To see if I can still read the writing when I place the diamond over the sheet," Ritter explained.

He looked about him. "Any closely written sheet will do."

"There should be something in the antechamber," the King informed him drily. "Master Johann, if you would be so good—" With a quick nod, Johann left the room.

"Excellent!" Ritter said when Johann returned with a copy of the *Berlinische Monatsschrift*. The jeweler held the diamond over the newssheet and peered down at it.

"Can you read anything at all?" Johann asked.

Ritter was quiet. Haydn held his breath. Had a flaw been detected in the diamond at last?

Ritter shifted the diamond, peered this way and that. "No. Not a single word," he said.

"And what does that tell you?" The Empress spoke for the first time.

The jeweler turned toward the window bay. "That it is indeed a diamond, Your Majesty."

"You are quite certain," the Empress persisted.

The jeweler nodded. "Although there is one other test." He glanced around the room, but no one spoke. "If I could heat it briefly, then drop it into this glass of cold water—"

"No!" The word erupted out of the Prince of Condé's mouth before anyone could utter a sound. He glared at His Serene Highness, who stood by the fireplace. "I would rather live the rest of my days in debt than subject a precious heirloom to such a test. It is preposterous."

"A lesser substance might shatter under the strain, but a diamond—" Ritter began earnestly only to have the diamond plucked out of his startled hands.

"Preposterous," the Grand Master of France repeated and stormed toward the door.

The King's amused gaze followed him out of the room, then shifted to His Serene Highness. "Well, at least, you will not have to make the man an offer, Esterházy."

His thin lips curved into a wider smile. "I do hope the truth you have discovered is sufficiently to your liking, Haydn."

———•••———

With his blood-tainted cloak bundled into a small sack, Anton Eichel slipped out of the church grounds into Annaquartier, the alley behind the Katholische Kirche St. Anna. The narrow cobblestone path wound through the block of houses—also known as Annaquartier—where the majority of Potsdam's Catholic population resided.

Eichel had been troubled by the loss of his cloak. The news of His Lordship's murder had unsettled him even further. Then the Amtsrichter's report had fallen upon his desk. The reference to the cloak of faded blue had told Eichel all he needed to know.

He had been discovered.

But there would no formal reprisal for his sins. He would not be forever confined within the walls of Spandau, condemned for treason. No, a far worse fate awaited him.

To be charged with the murder of His Lordship, Count Seckendorff. He would hang, led to the gallows like a common criminal. The thought was insupportable, and his lips involuntarily tightened as he hurried through the warren of narrow cobblestone lanes that crisscrossed the area.

Not that anyone would think to pursue him here. But he needed most urgently to find a way to rid himself of the cloak—the place of its discovery and the blood on it spoke of his association with the Count. Without it, he could not be accused of murder.

He had, of course, erased all reference to the garment in the Amtsrichter's report before sending it along to the King. And he had repaired instantly to the Catholic Church, willing to confront the Austrian composer and his brother if necessary.

He turned into a narrow alley and slowed his pace, coming to a halt near a tall gray apartment. He reached for the cloak under his arm and grasped it in a crumpled heap before him. Heaps of rubbish littered the length of the alley. It would be easy enough to discard the incriminating garment here.

But what if some poor wretch scrounging around for scraps were to find the bloodstained garment? Would the creature feel compelled to raise the alarm and report the matter to the Amtsrichter? It seemed unlikely, and yet it was not an eventuality Eichel was willing to risk.

No, some other means had to be found. He paced the alley.

Never start an unjust war. His previous master King Frederick William's words rang in Eichel's ears.

The old King had been notoriously ill-tempered—a veritable grouch, in fact—and so frugal, he had been accused of miserliness. For all that, King Frederick William had taken Eichel in, responding to his widowed mother's petition that the King grant a dead soldier's young son the means to provide for himself.

Never start an unjust war.

But Prussia had waged many an unjust war since the old King had died. Years ago, King Frederick had marched into Silesia, confident the beleaguered Maria Theresa, newly ascended to the thrones of Austria and Hungary, would capitulate.

"A small compensation for my services in Your Majesty's hour of need," the young King had promised the even younger Queen.

Eichel had hesitated to remonstrate with his new master, then. But he had rejoiced to hear the Queen, a worthy opponent, scoff at the King's demands. The war had not been kind to her. But what she had lost in land, she had gained in esteem.

Still, it was one thing to start an unjust war. Quite another to insidiously tear another country apart. All in the name of religious tolerance. As though his master cared three damns for that.

In the matter of Poland, Eichel had found he could stay silent no longer. That the Count, a man from Austria, should encourage the King in his perfidy had galled the court secretary no end. He had sought out the Count.

But His Lordship had made a startling admission. "I seek his trust only that I may discover his secrets, Eichel. So far none have been yielded. Perhaps, with your aid. . ."

"Then Poland," Eichel had said.

"Can still be saved," the Count had assured him. "It is by keeping one's enemies close that one may thwart their worst ambitions."

Within the narrow alley, Eichel paced frenetically up and down. There was more at stake than just his life and reputation. But try as he might he could think of no solution.

He was almost ready to give up when he saw an old woman approaching from the opening at the other end of the alley. With her skirts hitched and a covered basket under her arm, she picked her way carefully through the icy cobbles.

She was less than half a yard away when she glanced up and peered at the dirty garment he still clasped to his chest. "Need a washerwoman, do you? A few pfennigs and that cloak will be as good as new, *mein*

Herr." She swiveled her basket around to the front, about to pluck the cloth that covered it when Eichel stopped her.

"I already employ one. I was merely searching for her house." But her question had given him a glimmer of hope.

His washerwoman would ask no questions if he were to hand the garment to her. And she was discreet enough to handle a few other tasks as well.

It was late afternoon when Rosalie and Greta walked into the Drei Könige Gasthaus on Bäckerstrasse, summoned by a note from Elma. The inn was empty just as Elma had promised it would be. But a fire blazed cheerfully within the brick fireplace, its golden-orange flames licking the logs of wood.

To the left of it, at a small square table covered in a white tablecloth sat their friend.

"I trust you come alone," Elma said, turning to greet them. The fire exuded an almost unbearable heat, but she made no motion to take off the crimson cloak wrapped around her.

Her question took Rosalie by surprise and she threw a quick glance over her shoulder. Not that anyone had accompanied them. Boris's offer to do so had been easily deflected. Besides, what reason did the Count's valet have for following them?

"Of course." It was Greta who responded to Elma's question.

She pulled out a spindle-back chair for herself and another for Rosalie. "We didn't think you'd be able to come."

"How could I not?" Elma replied with a smile. "But your letter caused me no end of concern. What trouble does Haydn find himself in? And Count Seckendorff—"

"His Lordship was murdered, Elma," Rosalie blurted out the words, only to clap her hands to her mouth at the sudden appearance of a woman. How could she have been so careless?

But it was only a waitress, bearing a pot of coffee, cups, and a plate of kuchen on a tray that she deftly lowered onto the table. To Rosalie's relief, the woman gave no sign of having heard anything out of the ordinary.

Elma reached for the pot. "Ah! One of the few places in Prussia where one may enjoy pure coffee." She smiled at the waitress.

When the woman had left, Greta leaned across the table.

"Herr Haydn and Master Johann found His Lordship's body in the Katholische Kirche," she said in a low voice.

Together, they recounted the details to Elma who sat, head bowed, listening quietly to them.

"His Majesty thinks Herr Haydn stole the Grand Master's diamond," Rosalie finished. "But it couldn't have been him. We know who it was." Rosalie took a bite of her kuchen, suddenly famished.

Elma's head jerked up. "What do you mean you know who it was?"

Rosalie swallowed hastily. "The man who stole Herr Ritter's cloak and came to see His Lordship that night. Who else could it have been? The cloak and the diamond were found along with the Count's body in the church the next morning."

Elma stared at the flames curling over the burnt logs in the fireplace. "Yes. Yes, I suppose that makes sense."

Greta leaned closer to Elma. "Herr Ritter and His Lordship were close friends."

She turned her head, quickly surveying the room. The inn was as devoid of people as it had been when they had first entered it. Even so, she lowered her voice when she spoke again.

"Boris, the Count's valet, says they were performing an important service for the Empress."

Elma's lovely blue eyes widened a fraction, eliciting a self-important nod from Greta. The maid cast another surreptitious glance around the room, then leaned forward to continue in an urgent whisper.

Whatever it was, it must have been dangerous. His Lordship has been killed. And Herr Ritter is nowhere to be found."

"Herr Ritter, the jeweler?" Elma seemed confused. "Was His Lordship really associated with a jeweler?"

"Not the jeweler," Rosalie explained. "The man—a secretary of some sort judging by his ink-stained fingers—who frequented His Lordship's residence. At all hours, Boris said. Boris thought he was Ritter the jeweler."

"An informant," Elma mused, her gaze resting on the fire. "An informant with ink-stained fingers. And the blue cloak the Count's killer wore belonged to this informant?"

"Yes." Rosalie searched Elma's features. They had provided little enough in the way of information. The details they had gathered so far were of the vaguest nature. But perhaps their friend could make sense of it all.

"He is nowhere to be found," Greta repeated. "The killer must have already disposed of Herr Ritter. Or the man succeeded in going into hiding. Boris thinks Herr Bach must be in danger, too."

"Herr Bach!" Elma's eyes widened. "Is he involved as well?"

"The killer must think so," Rosalie replied. "Herr Bach visited His Lordship as frequently as did the man who called himself Ritter. And then there is the secret message we discovered behind the painting Herr Bach gave Herr Haydn."

She wrote the numbers down for Elma: *11.10.68.*

Elma's eyes grew as large as saucers when she saw the figures. "Are you sure this is what you saw?"

Rosalie nodded. "But we don't know what it means," she said.

Elma's red lips curved into a smile. "Yes, but I do." She glanced up at them. "Never fear. We shall have this sorted out in no time at all. Count Botta will ensure no further harm comes to Herr Haydn."

Chapter Twenty-Four

ANTON Eichel, the Prussian King's principal court secretary, had just stepped into the palace entrance hall when he saw a sight that made him edge hurriedly back behind a marble column.

Why had Ritter the jeweler been summoned to court? To provide details of the man who frequented his workshop, purporting to be the imperial ambassador's personal secretary? A sudden palpitation in Eichel's chest made him wince.

It was not safe to remain in Prussia. Not safe at all. He leant back against the column, the marble feeling like ice against his clammy neck. But where was he to go?

To the Austrians? Why should Austria trust a Prussian? What reason had the King ever given the Habsburgs to trust anyone associated with the Prussian court? Still, Eichel had facilitated Count Seckendorff's work. Might that not allow him to throw himself at the Empress's mercy?

Eichel closed his eyes, forcing himself to take deep gulps of air. His lungs felt constricted as though iron hoops were bound around his chest, squeezing his ribcage in a hard vise.

"*Mein Herr*?" The words, softly uttered near Eichel's ear, caused him to stiffen against the column. His eyelids snapped open to encounter the mildly concerned face of a palace footman. "Is anything the matter?"

Eichel pushed himself away from the column. "Not at all. I am fine," he reassured the servant. Inclining his head in the direction of the departing Ritter, he went on: "Who requested the jeweler's presence?"

The footman paused, uncertain. His gaze wandered up in search of an answer. "It must have been Herr Haydn," he finally offered. "It was he who recovered the Grand Master's diamond—

"On the day it was stolen." Eichel recalled the commotion that morning—the very morning the imperial ambassador's corpse had been found within the Katholische Kirche St. Anna. It was Haydn who had made that discovery as well, was it not?

A memory surfaced. And dissipated before he could pursue it—chased away by the sound of the footman's voice.

"Oh, but the diamond was never stolen, *mein Herr*," the man informed Eichel. "The Grand Master merely misplaced it. Herr Haydn found the stone in His Highness's bedchamber."

"And entertained doubts as to its authenticity?" Eichel's eyebrows lifted despite himself. Why should the composer call into question the gem he himself had found? And what had taken him from the imperial ambassador's corpse to the Grand Master's bedchamber?

"The Grand Master wishes to sell his diamond," the footman suggested helpfully. As though a mere musician would seek to buy a priceless diamond!

Eichel motioned the man away and set off in the direction of the picture gallery. The large chamber assigned to him as the principal court secretary was at the other end of the gallery, right next to the court library.

As he walked, he mulled over what he had just heard. There was most likely a connection between the Grand Master's diamond, the imperial ambassador, and Haydn. But the only one that Eichel could think of would most certainly pose an insurmountable problem for the Austrians.

The long-forgotten memory that had surfaced at the mention of the diamond pressed into his consciousness again. A set of instructions he had been charged with. Eichel had not fully understood their significance at the time, but now he thought he knew.

He had offered to meet Haydn later that night. He hoped the Austrian composer would come. Eichel had determined to seek the Empress's mercy. But he would not be coming empty-handed.

With any luck, the principal court secretary would be able to help the Austrians clear the imperial ambassador's name. It was the least Eichel could do for a man he had come to regard as his friend.

—•••—

Within the Prussian King's Music Room silence reigned. Ritter the jeweler had departed, rewarded with a princely sum for his part in authenticating the Grand Master's diamond. Haydn had considered the idea that the jeweler had been bribed or compelled into his verdict.

But there had been no mistaking Ritter's elation at discovering a diamond of the first water. At each test the gem had surpassed, his blue eyes had widened in astonishment, alight with the passion of a man bedazzled.

No, the diamond, unfortunately, was genuine.

"I must commend you on your effort to clear the Count's name, Haydn." The King flicked open his ivory-inlaid snuff box. A strong whiff of cinnamon filled the air, inducing a violent fit of coughing in both the Empress and Prince Nikolaus. "Most valiantly done."

His Majesty took a pinch of the dark powder and inhaled deeply. The King's arm made a magnanimous sweep around the room, proffering his scented tobacco to his guests. But Haydn and Johann had never cared for the stuff, and the Prince was clearly in no mood for it.

"Are you willing to concede defeat, Your Majesty?" The King addressed his remarks to the Empress who sat by the window, a grave expression on her features. "Shall we conclude our agreement—"

"Your Majesty was gracious enough to grant us three days' time to consider your demands," the Empress reminded him, her voice low and musical. "We still have—"

"A single day. That is all. I will wait no longer than that."

The King swung sharply on his heels and marched out of the room.

"But what can be done in a single day, Your Majesty?" His Serene Highness, Prince Nikolaus Esterházy, burst out the moment the door clicked shut behind the King. "I see no hope of extricating ourselves from this predicament."

"I am quite convinced a replica does exist. It is merely a question of finding it," Haydn said at once. "The Grand Master left the supper table with a diamond in his coat pocket. He is most emphatic on the subject."

"That may be so." His Serene Highness conceded the point with ill-concealed impatience. "But how does that help us? The King will point out that the Count had an accomplice."

True enough. Haydn rubbed his chin. *The theft could not have been affected without one.*

"But why, then, would the accomplice proceed to pilfer the false diamond?" Johann's voice broke the silence that had fallen upon them. "Would that not give the game away?"

Haydn stared at his brother. "I must confess that point had not occurred to me. The only reason to reveal the theft would be to falsely implicate His Lordship." He turned toward the Empress.

"To jeopardize our alliance with the French, I suppose," His Serene Highness ventured. "Surely it was not merely to force Techsen and Troppau out of our hands?"

"I am sure the King has his sights set higher than those two duchies, Esterházy," the Empress informed him drily.

"Most likely, it was to force Austria into recalling His Lordship from his post," Haydn said. The nature of the Count's activities and the fact that he had been discovered suggested as such.

The Empress's eyes widened, but the Kapellmeister was too deep in thought to notice it.

"But in that case, what reason could there be for his murder?" the Kapellmeister continued with a thoughtful frown.

"Unless—"

The Empress rose. "I am in need of air, Esterházy. Take me outside."

Eichel stepped out of the picture gallery to the sounds of an ever-growing commotion. It appeared to be coming from the cluster of rooms beyond the chamber he occupied as principal secretary.

The noise was loud enough to arrest his motion, but Eichel noticed that the King's Italian greyhounds—sprawling lazily on their embroidered cushions—dozed on undisturbed. His own footsteps on the stone floor had merely caused one of the three dogs to open a single eyelid and glance reproachfully his way over a long, pointy snout.

Do make that infernal noise stop, Eichel, the creature seemed to be saying. *We are trying to nap!* In the principal court secretary's head, the greyhounds sounded just like their master, with a voice just as high-pitched and mannered as the King's.

He stood at the open door of his chamber, just able to make out the drunken voice of the cellist Mara raised in mingled rage with that of the harpsichordist, C.P.E. Bach.

Eichel sighed. He was tempted to ignore the clamor. But his underlings appeared to be having trouble getting rid of the musicians, and today of all days, the principal court secretary needed the area cleared as soon as possible.

He strode through his chamber into one of the inner rooms.

"What is the reason for this ungodly clamor?" he demanded brusquely. He glanced at Mara. The cellist's short spiky hair bristled in every direction as though the strands were pins in a pincushion. His wrinkled white shirt was half out of his breeches, giving him a disheveled appearance.

"We have not received our weekly allowance." It was Bach's exasperated voice that answered Eichel's question. "Yet again."

"That should be a simple enough matter to resolve." Eichel glanced at his harried-looking underling.

"It is Frau Mara who claims not to have received her allowance, Herr Eichel," the young man replied. "I was merely telling her husband here" —the secretary glared at the cellist—"that she will need to appear in person to collect her salary.

"I can hardly accept Herr Mara's signature on the document his wife must sign to confirm she has received her allowance."

Those were the rules, it was true. But to compel Mara to leave would take more effort than Eichel was willing to expend at the moment.

"Is Frau Mara unwell?" he asked.

"My wife is well enough," Mara grumbled. "But do you think any woman in her senses would want to be in the same room as those ungodly greyhounds?"

"They howl at anyone as the mood takes them," Eichel's underling muttered. "Frau Mara is hardly an exception. Why, just the other night they threw back their heads and bayed at Herr Eichel himself."

Eichel frowned. What was the young man wittering on about? The greyhounds had never barked at him. "The other night—?"

"Yes, after the supper His Majesty hosted for the Austrians. I had a question to ask of you, but you must have been in a hurry. The hounds seemed beside themselves with frenzy, straining against their leash as though they had a fox in their sights and wanted to tear the poor creature to pieces."

"Just the way they act in the presence of my poor wife," Mara said. "And you ask why she refuses to come in person. Bah!"

"Savage beings," Bach said. "Why, I have heard them. . ."

But Eichel, standing very still, paid the harpsichordist no heed. It would seem he had yet another piece of the puzzle to take to the Empress. The King's beloved greyhounds habitually disregarded Eichel. That they had not done so the other night could only mean—

"The money, Herr Eichel?" Bach's impatient voice butted into the principal court secretary's thoughts.

"Yes, what about our money?" Mara demanded.

"Yes, yes. Of course." Eichel motioned toward his underling. "Pay them whatever they are owed. I will make a note of the expense myself." He smiled at the young man who glanced up at him bewildered.

Recording payments was not the sort of menial task the principal court secretary normally took upon himself. But this afternoon—his last as a Prussian—he was willing to make an exception.

Chapter Twenty-Five

LEANING upon His Serene Highness's arm, Her Majesty made her slow progress down the series of low steps that cut a broad path between the terraced gardens of Sanssouci.

Haydn followed close behind with Johann, his hands as cold as ice despite the thick woolen gloves that encased them.

Why had Her Majesty so abruptly hustled them out into the frigid Prussian air?

The Kapellmeister's gaze swept over the snow-covered grounds—rolling down in broad white pleats to the icy courtyard below—and the brilliant azure dome of sky above that capped the entire scene.

For all its beauty, it felt oddly oppressive. Within Vienna's crowded, congested streets, a man could count himself entirely free. But here in the vast open spaces of the Prussian King's palace, there seemed no way of evading the King's hold.

They had descended halfway down the broad stairway when the Empress came to a halt. Releasing the Prince's arm, she ground her cane into the paved step. Her large form pivoted around until she faced Haydn and Johann.

"What is it you have discovered, Haydn?"

The question caught Haydn by surprise. Unsure how to respond, he looked toward Johann. But if his brother had a solution, he had no opportunity to offer it.

The Empress summoned their attention back to herself with a sharp rap of her cane. "Why should Prussia wish us to recall the imperial ambassador?"

There was nothing for it but to be blunt. "His Lordship's attempts to gather intelligence may have been discovered, Your Majesty," Haydn replied in as matter-of-fact a tone as he could muster. "It is what Anton Eichel, the court secretary, believes."

"On what grounds?" The Empress asked, her features frozen into an expressionless mask, her voice low and flat.

"What could Eichel possibly know of the matter?" His Serene Highness demanded at the same time, his brusque tones carrying over the Empress's voice.

"Herr Eichel was His Lordship's informant," Haydn addressed his employer. It was clear, neither His Serene Highness nor Her Majesty had been aware of the situation. "His Lordship must have intentionally kept Her Majesty in the dark. To protect Eichel's identity, no doubt."

"Eichel fears their activities have been discovered," Johann added. "But he did not say how he knew that to be the case."

"It will have been from the cabinet noir," the Empress murmured, speaking more to herself than to the brothers. "Seckendorff's letter must have been intercepted, and then sent to Eichel's desk. Small wonder, there have been no despatches for a month or more."

"I fear Herr Eichel's part in the undertaking may have been discovered as well." Haydn was careful to keep his voice low.

He surveyed the terraces flanking the stairway. Other than the snow-covered yews that lined the grounds and the fig trees, shielded from the harsh winter air by their green burlap wrappings, they appeared to be quite alone. "It was *his* cloak that covered His Lordship's dead body."

"But Herr Eichel himself was at the opera house at the time," Johann said. "His Lordship was not alone in mistaking the man who came to see him for his informant. His valet thought the same."

In hushed voices, he and Haydn recounted their encounter with the court secretary.

"That the court secretary might be falsely implicated in murder for his role in the affair seems likely enough," His Serene Highness said when Haydn had concluded. "But what reason could the Prussians concoct for the court secretary to kill the imperial ambassador?

"To say they were accomplices in the theft of the Grand Master's diamond merely serves to throw a poor light on the Prussian court. No." His Serene Highness shook his head. "That explanation does not suffice."

"Yet, whoever lured His Lordship out knew of his association with the court secretary," Haydn pointed out. He knew little enough of spies and intelligence-gathering. But the evidence seemed quite clear. He turned to the Empress, seeking her opinion.

"That is true enough," Her Majesty conceded thoughtfully. "But perhaps their association was mistaken to signify something quite different. That Seckendorff was betraying Austrian secrets to the Prussians."

"But that points the finger squarely back at us, Your Majesty!" Johann was aghast at the suggestion.

"Or to Poland," Her Majesty said. "What other reason could there be for killing Seckendorff in a church?"

In the five years he had been employed in King Frederick's cabinet noir, Peer had never had to contend with a visitor. He and young Ulrich worked alone, unsealing bags of mail, reading, copying, re-sealing. It was tedious work. But their days passed uneventfully enough.

But today just as Peer had sat down to his lunch of boiled cabbage soup, the door had been unceremoniously pushed open. The woman who entered—golden-haired, with striking blue eyes, and a crimson cloak—was the most beautiful he had ever seen.

So beautiful, indeed, that Ulrich's mouth had dropped open. A large piece of sausage had escaped his lips, falling onto the table much to Peer's amusement and Ulrich's consternation.

The woman's gaze passed coolly over Ulrich and rested upon Peer's older, sun-browned features.

"You seem intelligent enough. Can you find me this?" She thrust a paper at him.

Peer glanced down at the figures. He and Ulrich had been standing since the moment the woman entered the room. He wished he could resume his seat and return to his meal, but the woman who had invaded their tiny chamber in the Potsdam City Palace didn't seem the kind of person who could be easily denied or ignored.

The figures on the paper—*11. 10. 68*—referred to a letter, that much was clear. Sent two months ago on the eleventh day of October.

He met the woman's eyes. "It would be easier if I knew who had sent the letter. Easier still, if I knew to whom it had been sent. Numerous letters pass through our hands every day. Not every one of them is worth copying."

"It would have been sent from the imperial ambassador's residence. Most likely in his name. As to the recipient"—the woman's shoulders lifted in a delicate shrug—"The Empress Maria Theresa, I suppose. Or someone in the Hofburg."

Peer hesitated. With the exception of the King, his court secretaries, and some of the highest-ranking ministers, few knew of the existence of the cabinet noir. Certainly not many beyond a small circle of the King's most trusted advisors and staff had any idea where the chamber was even located.

Even so. . .

Before he could think of a way of phrasing the question, Ulrich took the matter out of his hands. "Who are you? And by whose authority do you come here?" he demanded, his tone rougher than it needed to be.

Poor Ulrich. As vain as a peacock and as unused to being slighted. By a woman no less. And his brusque tone was about to earn the boy another rebuke. The woman's face turned white, her nostrils flared.

Peer spoke up just as she was about to open her mouth. "The documents we obtain are treated with the utmost sensitivity. They are not to leave this room except by the order of His Majesty or one of the court secretaries."

The woman drew herself up. The hood covering her head fell back, revealing even more of her glossy golden locks. "I am Maria Wilhelmina von Auersperg. A friend of the King's, and I come upon important state business.

"Find the letter at once. Or the King shall hear of your insubordination."

"Yes, Your Highness." Peer had bowed his head hastily and retreated toward the battered pine press in which copies of diplomatic mail were stored. That had been a half hour ago. He had pulled out every single drawer, untied every bundle of correspondence, but had found nothing.

"The imperial ambassador sent nothing on the eleventh day of October, Your Highness." Most likely, whatever the ambassador had sent had not been worth copying. An appalling oversight, given the turn of events. But Peer was not going to admit to it.

"And I see no despatches to the Empress for that month either." He glanced over his shoulder. "Is it possible the date is wrong?"

"No," Maria Wilhelmina replied. She was quite sure it was not. Rosalie and Greta were incapable of dissimulation. Besides, how could they have lied about the information when they had no idea what it meant?

The letter, if it had been sent at all, must have been sent through alternative routes.

Or, perhaps it still remained in Potsdam. The only question was, *where*?

———✦———

Poland!

In the silence that followed the Empress's remark, only the soft rustle of wind whispering through the yew trees could be heard. A jumble of disparate thoughts tumbled through Haydn's brain. The imperial ambassador had been killed in a church. A Catholic church? But why should the Poles, a predominantly Catholic people, choose to defile a church of their own faith?

"I fear I am not as well informed as I ought to be of foreign affairs, Your Majesty," he said at last. "What does Poland have to do with His Lordship's murder?"

"The Polish Catholics have sought our aid in shaking the Russians off their back." It was Prince Nikolaus who replied. "Prussia has no interest in seeing the Polish Commonwealth survive and Russia seeks to control it. Austria is its only hope."

Ach so. Haydn nodded. "Then the ambassador's friendship with the principal secretary of the Prussian court might have been seen as a subversion of Austria's pledge of assistance?"

"But to desecrate a church?" Johann's voice rose as he glanced at his brother. "Surely that makes no sense?"

"They may have wished to stir up religious strife in Prussia," the Empress explained. "If Austria were to declare war against Russia on behalf of Poland, Prussia would immediately come to Russia's defense. But if the Prussians were engaged in keeping peace within their own borders, any help they could provide would be halfhearted at best."

"Then that must be why the King has been preparing for war," Haydn said, recalling Herr Bach's remarks at His Majesty's supper table. "According to Herr Bach, His Majesty spends far less on music than he was wont to."

"Can His Majesty not be persuaded to a more peaceful course?" Johann wanted to know.

His Serene Highness snorted. "That has never been the King's way. Besides, His Majesty wants nothing more than to carve up Poland. That would be the only way, in his opinion, to enforce peace. He sees the Poles as mere barbarians, unworthy of a nation of their own, incapable of managing their affairs."

"And somehow he has persuaded Catherine of Russia to his ideas." The Empress sighed. "I cannot fathom how. Russia's sole interest in controlling Poland is to gain access to the Black Sea. She must see her way to doing so, judging by the reports Seckendorff received.

"A great deal of effort has been expended in building up the Russian navy. Old ships have been repaired and new ones constructed. Worse still, the English have put at her disposal several experienced officers from the Royal Navy."

"She seems unstoppable," Haydn said, his mind still trying to come to grips with the intricacies of foreign relations. "If Russia, then, is willing to give up her chance to control Poland in its entirety, it must be because.

. .because. . ." He struggled to express his thoughts. What could Russia possibly fear?

Surely Prussia had more to lose if Poland ceased to exist as a buffer between itself and the far larger Russian empire.

"Because the King has somehow bamboozled Russia," His Serene Highness's voice—rough and irascible—broke into Haydn's thoughts. "What else could it be?"

The Kapellmeister had no answer to this. How could Russia have been persuaded to believe that owning a part of Poland was better than controlling all of it?

"But how—?" he was beginning to say when the Empress interrupted him.

"It serves no purpose to break our heads against the question, Haydn. We will never know how the deception was effected."

"Is it possible Herr Eichel had some knowledge of the matter?" Johann ventured.

"And shared what he knew with His Lordship?" Haydn gazed out into the distance, his eyes narrowed. A crease began to form between his eyebrows as another thought occurred to him. He turned toward Her Majesty. "Could that be the reason for His Lordship's death?"

The Empress stared, her eyes visibly widening as she regarded the Kapellmeister.

"If the information enabled us to drive a wedge between Russia and Prussia, then—" Her Majesty took a deep breath. "Then. . ."

"Then it would be worth killing for," His Serene Highness conceded. "His Majesty wants nothing more than the strip of Polish land that would unite West Prussia with East."

He turned away from the musicians."Could that have been what Seckendorff wished to communicate to us, Your Majesty?"

"It must have been," the Empress replied. "He said it was most urgent. But whatever it was, he has unfortunately taken it to the grave."

"As I imagine will Eichel. Unless we act quickly enough," His Serene Highness said softly with a hasty glance at their surroundings. The sun was setting low in the west, the sky a blaze of burnt orange. But for their presence, the grounds appeared to be deserted.

He returned his gaze to the Kapellmeister and his younger brother. "You are to question him on the matter when you meet him this evening, Haydn."

His Serene Highness rocked back on his heels. "Who knows we may still be able to persuade the King to allow Seckendorff to rest in peace, his reputation unstained by the vile accusations His Majesty has seen fit to hurl at him."

Chapter Twenty-Six

"WAS the diamond paste, as you had surmised?"
Maria Anna turned from the mirror, her brush still entangled in her curls, just as Haydn stepped into their bedchamber. Johann and he had decided to return to Lindenstrasse after the Empress had dismissed them.

Dusk had fallen. In a few short hours it would be time to meet Eichel. But until then, to loiter around within the King's palace would only invite suspicion.

Now, confronted with his wife's enquiring eyes, the Kapellmeister could only bite his lip ruefully and shake his head.

"Just as well, I suppose." Maria Anna turned back to the mirror and resumed brushing her hair.

"Why do you suppose that?" Haydn demanded, too astonished to prevent the words from tumbling out of his mouth. He sat down at the foot of the bed, the soft feather mattress sinking under his weight.

The proof of His Lordship's innocence had depended upon the gem being discounted as false. He saw no reason to rejoice in the fact that it was not.

In the mirror, Maria Anna's reflection eyed him askance. "You don't think the Grand Master would have raised the devil himself if he thought his precious diamond was paste?"

An unpleasant warmth made itself felt in the back of Haydn's neck. It rose up to his cheeks, making them browner than they already were. In his disappointment at the day's events, this aspect of the matter had escaped him.

"And what would you have had to say for yourself, then, husband?" Maria Anna spun around, brush in hand. "After all, it was you who discovered the diamond in the Grand Master's bedchamber."

It had, in truth, been Johann, not him. But Haydn saw no reason to correct his wife on that detail.

"I imagine I would at this very moment be desperately searching for the genuine item," he conceded with a sheepish smile.

"Or worse," Maria Anna countered. "What if the King, or someone else, were to say you had stolen it yourself? Do not tell me that could not happen."

A dark shadow seemed to loom across the room at his wife's words. He would not put it past the King to say just such a thing. But he saw no reason to alarm Maria Anna any further.

"Then let us be glad none of that has come to pass." His tone was mild as he met her eyes, wide with concern, in the mirror.

Her head moved in a barely perceptible nod, and she turned her attention to the creams and powders on her dressing table. "But you still think there was a second diamond?"

Against his will, she had coaxed the information out of himself and Johann earlier that day. But he was glad now to discuss the matter with her.

"How else could the original have been ferreted out?" He spread his hands wide. "Without the Grand Master raising the alarm at the supper table itself? It is not possible."

Then there was the white residue left on the gem. Clearly the diamond had been spirited out in a bowl of custard. And the killer had made no effort to wipe it off before placing it in His Lordship's pocket. Why else but to falsely implicate the imperial ambassador?

"Custard?" Maria Anna's voice intruded upon his thoughts. His wife seemed to have developed an unfortunate habit of reading his mind. Or had he spoken aloud?

"There were some remnants of it on the diamond," Haydn explained.

"I am not surprised at it," his wife replied, much to his astonishment. He gaped at her, too startled to comment.

"It slipped through the Crown Prince's fingers," Maria Anna continued, oblivious to Haydn's reaction, "straight into his custard bowl."

"The Crown Prince's bowl?" Haydn repeated. "You are quite sure?" He searched his recollection of the evening in question. Where had Maria Anna been sitting?

"I saw it with my own eyes, husband!" Maria Anna's lips pinched into a thin line of disapproval. "I have never seen a man more besotted. It was disgraceful."

"And then what happened?" Haydn regarded her closely.

Maria Anna snorted. "Why, I imagine he plucked it out of his custard. What else could he do?" She must have seen his eyes in the glass, for she closed her eyes, exasperated. "No, I did not see it. The Archduchess Amalia was in my way, rocking back and forth and giggling like a tipsy schoolgirl."

"You were sitting next to His Lordship, were you not?" The imperial ambassador had been flanked, he recalled, by his wife on one side, the Archduchess on the other.

"On his left." Maria Anna nodded. "Poor man! He was so afflicted by the gout, he ate very sparingly. He barely touched his chicken, and he turned down the custard."

"Turned down the custard!" Haydn sat upright.

"He was most adamant in his refusal. He waved the footman on when the man tried to give him a bowl of it."

If His Lordship had refused the custard, that meant—Maria Anna's question interrupted the thought in his mind.

"But what does it matter what His Lordship ate or did not that night, husband?" She turned around.

Haydn's eyes met hers. "It means that His Lordship could not have stolen the diamond. It was not he who exchanged a fake gem for the real thing that night."

That the exchange had been made at the supper table was not in doubt.

But it was only Maria Anna's word that proclaimed the imperial ambassador's innocence.

And the Crown Prince's guilt.

The Kapellmeister's fingers tightened around the tassels at the edge of the counterpane. They would need more than that to clear His Lordship's name.

———

"But sister-in-law has no reason to lie about what she saw," Johann said when Haydn informed him of the matter. "Why should she not be believed?"

"His Majesty might think she had concocted a lie for my sake." Haydn paced up and down the imperial ambassador's study.

Johann coughed. "I doubt anyone who knew her—or you, for that matter—would come to that conclusion, brother."

Haydn stopped pacing. Was his younger brother being facetious? It was quite unlike him, of course. He turned to meet his brother's eyes. But Johann merely stared back at him, an earnest expression on his features.

"And what of the Crown Prince's role in the entire affair? We can hardly accuse him of theft based solely upon Maria Anna's word."

Johann was silent. Haydn resumed his pacing. The brisk pace and steady rhythm usually helped him think, but he seemed to be wallowing in a fog this evening.

It could not have been worse had Maria Anna witnessed the King himself drop the diamond into his bowl of custard. Besides, if His Royal Highness had been in his cups. . .

He clenched his fists at his side, strode toward the window, and swung around.

"Could the Archduchess not confirm the facts?" Johann leaned his weight upon the imperial ambassador's green wingback chair. "I imagine the Empress will not object to questioning her own daughter," he went on when Haydn stopped mid-stride and stared at him.

The Kapellmeister sighed. "It is a possibility, I suppose," he conceded. "Although Archduchess Amalia seems so taken up with the Crown Prince, I cannot tell how willingly she will disclose the truth."

"If she even noticed it," he added after a moment's thought. "Still, it is worth a try."

———•••———

Below the terraced gardens of Sanssouci, within an alcove overlooking the great fountain, Maria Wilhelmina, Princess Auersperg, waited for her associate. In the gloom of dusk, there was little to be seen, and she could barely make out the water feature in front of her.

Not that there was anything particularly great about it. As a fountain it was a spectacular disaster. A mere pond, nothing more. Despite the King's best efforts, no water gushed out of its pipes to feed its vast basin.

Few people dared defy the King of Prussia.

But the laws of nature were a singular exception. The thought amused Maria Wilhelmina no end, and her lips curved into a smile.

She was still smiling when a rustling sound caught her ears. It came from the terraces situated above her. She ventured cautiously forth from the alcove, peering out into the shadowy dusk.

"There you are, at last," she cried, recognizing the person slowly descending the broad stairs that swept down from the palace past the terraces to the flat grassless expanse.

"Shh. . .h," her associate hissed. "I can't imagine why you wanted to see me. What's done is done. The Count is dead."

"And Haydn suspects the man who drew the Count out on the night of his death." Maria Wilhelmina couldn't resist the jab.

"I had nothing to do with that as you well know," the other replied sharply.

"Nor with the theft of the Grand Master of France's diamond? Haydn suspects the same person."

"Whatever he may suspect, he will find nothing."

Maria Wilhelmina considered the facts. "True enough," she conceded. "But that is not what I came for. Whose cloak did you borrow that night?"

Her associate frowned. "How did you know it was a cloak?"

Maria Wilhelmina's lips stretched into a dazzling smile. "I have my sources, my dear. Besides, you could hardly have gone in your current garb. I see you have found your way into the King's service." She allowed her eyes to rove down her companion's livery of Prussian blue.

"I saw no reason to continue wearing an ill-fitting olive-green coat and brown breeches. Although it was all I had to wear when I visited His Lordship. Not warm enough in this cold Prussian winter. Besides, the cloak served its purpose well. His Lordship's servant recognized it immediately, which brought his master out shortly after."

"And you led him to the church like a sacrificial lamb." Maria Wilhelmina gazed into her companion's remorseless eyes.

"He followed me willingly enough. That he died—" Her associate stood rigidly before her, hands clenched into tight fists. "It is regrettable, but what can one do?"

"Nothing," Maria Wilhelmina agreed. "But had you taken greater note of whose garment it was you borrowed, we would be closer to discovering his informant. It turns out—"

"My dear Princess, you're behind the times. We already know who his informant was. The news was obtained just this afternoon."

"I don't suppose you care to tell me who it is." A searing flame of anger suffused Maria Wilhelmina's cheeks. To be treated thus by this. . . this impudent creature. . . this youngling absorbed in an inspection of its fingernails.

"And what is being done about it?" Her voice rose, infuriated by her associate's utter disregard for her.

"Whatever needs to be done." Her companion looked up, lips widening into a smile. "Rest assured, Your Highness, the matter will be taken care of this very night."

In what manner, Maria Wilhelmina wanted to ask. But her companion would provide no satisfactory answers, she knew.

Chapter Twenty-Seven

*C*ould *Amalia be persuaded to tell the truth*?
The Empress did not know. The child was as stubborn as a mule. Her head sank back against her chair; her eyelids shut out the light.

"We can hardly accuse the Crown Prince of purloining the Grand Master's diamond, Haydn." Esterházy's voice, loud and blustering, hectored his Kapellmeister.

"It may not matter who took it as long as we can establish it was not His Lordship," Master Johann's mild voice interjected. "And sister-in-law's story—"

The Empress opened her eyes. "Is certainly one more piece of evidence in our favor," she said, ending the argument. She took a deep, labored breath. "I will question my daughter, although I fear nothing may come of it."

The air in the overheated room was close and stuffy. The Empress struggled to breathe, her chest heaving. Her fingers tightened around the ivory handle of her cane. "The windows," she gasped. "Open the windows."

"Your Majesty!" Esterházy threw open the windows, letting a blast of cold air in. "We should never have come to Prussia," he fussed. "The visit has offered nothing but trouble."

Her eyes closed, the Empress gulped in the icy air. It rushed into her lungs, soothed her face and neck. A semblance of calm returned, and with it a thought.

She turned toward Haydn. "The Archduchess is a heedless young woman. I cannot tell what she may have seen or not. But there is a better way yet."

"A better way, Your Majesty?" Esterházy was staring at her as though she had lost her mind.

The Empress nodded. "A much better way. If Haydn can persuade our new friend"—*Our new friend?* To her relief, the question on Haydn's face dissipated no sooner than it had appeared. She was loath to mention Anton Eichel by name—"to furnish the evidence."

Esterházy's eyebrows lifted, a question forming in the motion of his jaws and lips.

"The evidence pertaining to the manufacture of the false diamond," the Empress explained. "It must exist."

Ach so! Understanding illuminated the features of the men before her.

Esterházy's lips broadened into a smile. "It would be impossible to conceal." He turned toward his Kapellmeister. "It will strengthen our hand to have the information—along with whatever you can glean about the King's hand in Polish affairs."

The magnate paused, then went on:

"I trust you will be able to obtain it. I need hardly remind you, your own liberty is at stake."

Not words she herself would have uttered. But the Empress let them stand. Frederick had, after all, threatened Haydn. Perhaps the memory would lend the composer's efforts greater urgency.

She fastened her gaze upon him—the same steadfast blue eyes that years ago had melted the hearts of her generals. "We rely upon you, Haydn. And"—turning toward the Kapellmeister's brother—"you, Master Johann. The fate of the Polish Commonwealth hangs in the balance. And the good name of Austria along with it."

The remains of the evening meal had just been cleared from the servants' hall when the letter arrived. The faint hope Rosalie had that it might be from Gerhard evaporated when she saw the address written in firm, sloping lines across the cover.

"It looks like Elma's hand, doesn't it?" Greta peered over Rosalie's shoulder as she carefully inserted a penknife under the wafer and sliced the letter open.

"It *is* Elma's hand." Rosalie's gaze skimmed past the closely written contents to the name signed at the bottom. *"My dear friends,"* she began reading aloud. *"A few discreet enquiries have revealed that His Lordship had uncovered a most despicable crime. A plot to steal the Grand Master's blue diamond."*

Behind her, Greta gasped, her plump fingers pressing into Rosalie's shoulder blade. "Good God! That must have been why His Lordship was killed."

Rosalie cast her eyes down the page. "It must have been. Elma says His Lordship wrote a letter revealing the plan. Most likely to the King."

"So that was what the numbers referred to," Greta said. "A letter. 11.10.68. Clever of Elma to have figured that out."

"But it was never sent." Rosalie held Elma's note out toward Greta, her finger pointing to the relevant section. "Or so it appears."

They bent their heads over the page again and read the next bit.

Perhaps His Lordship wished to avert the plot himself rather than bring disgrace upon the thief, Elma had surmised. *At any event, I have reason to believe it remains in His Lordship's home. Most likely in his study.*

"And we are to sift through His Lordship's papers in the hopes of finding a letter." Greta sounded doubtful. "He was a diplomat. How many letters must he have written in the course of his life? It would be easier to find a needle in a haystack."

"We do have the date," Rosalie pointed out. "Besides, if it will help clear Herr Haydn's name—"

"I know. And bring His Lordship's killer to light. All in one stroke." Greta jabbed at the note. *For we can be sure they are one and the same,* Elma had written.

"Elma says it is all Count Botta needs. *Armed with the information, he can prevail upon His Majesty.*"

Greta sighed. "Very well. Ask Boris to unlock the study. We'll see what we can find."

But a thorough search of His Lordship's study revealed nothing more than sheets of flute exercises, a number of thick papers with holes of varying shapes and sizes cut out of them, and a small Bible.

"His Lordship was never one to keep copies of his own letters," Boris explained. He leant against the study door, his arms folded. "And as for the letters he received." The valet shrugged. "He destroyed them as soon as he had read them."

"What now?" Greta asked. "There's nothing Count Botta can do without the letter."

Rosalie bit her lip. To think they had been so close to resolving the matter. And that it would all be lost for want of a single letter.

"We ought to let Herr Haydn know. He may—" She hesitated. Elma had said nothing about informing the Kapellmeister. But surely she would not object to their doing so. "He may find a way to discover it."

Anton Eichel sat back in his chair and rubbed his eyes, red and weary from hours' of work. The candles in the wall sconces had already been snuffed out. Only one small candle flame tapered and flickered in the cold wind that rushed through the cracks in the window.

His affairs had been set in order. The documents he required to persuade Her Majesty, the Empress, to offer him protection had already been secreted out of the palace. To keep them on his person would have been foolhardy. And dangerous.

In a few minutes more, the principal court secretary would set out for the Chinese Teahouse. God be willing, Haydn was awaiting him there.

The sudden barking of the hounds outside his door aroused Eichel from his stupor. What were the dogs on about now? He glanced cautiously around. The warren of rooms beyond his, where the King's army of secretaries slaved from dawn till dusk, was in darkness. Eichel had dismissed them earlier than usual that evening.

The lights from the picture gallery cast a warm glow upon the marble floors of his chambers. He was about to push his chair back and walk toward the door when, just as abruptly, the hounds ceased their noise.

He threw his head back against his chair and closed his eyes again only to open them a second time.

"The chocolate you asked for, *mein Herr*." A gloved hand set down a porcelain cup and saucer on his table.

Eichel raised his eyes, puzzled. "But I never—" he began when he saw a glint of steel.

The tall footman held his gaze. "It would be as well to drink it, *mein Herr*."

Eichel hesitated. "What is it you want?"

He received no reply. Only a searing pain that flared in his ribs as a sharp point tore through his fine linen shirt and pierced his flesh.

The bells were clanging the quarter-hour when Haydn and Johann left the Empress's presence. The noise reverberated in Haydn's ears as his gaze fell on the large arched window set into the wall opposite them.

A transparent veil of darkness cloaked the palace grounds. The terraces with their yews and covered figs stretched beyond in varying shades of black.

"To the Chinese Teahouse?" Johann asked, his voice straining to be heard against the clamor of the church bells.

Haydn nodded. Their appointment with the principal court secretary had not been set for a particular hour. Eichel had simply promised to meet them at night. Whether he would keep his word, Haydn knew not. But a leisurely walk through the grounds might elicit less suspicion— especially if they were to chance upon Eichel himself.

They walked toward the entrance hall, silenced by the deep, resounding tolls of the bells. To Haydn's ears, each penetrating dong seemed to have the inevitability of a death knell.

Eichel is not safe.

Eichel is not safe.

Eichel is not—

Haydn's feet slowed to a halt at the double doors that led out into the terraced gardens. The bells ceased their *kling klang*, but his misgivings only intensified.

"We ought to go to his chamber," he said, pivoting around. But the light scuffle of his brother's footsteps behind him had stopped. And in the silence that followed, he sensed Johann's hesitation.

"The effort to implicate him in His Lordship's murder and so be rid of him has foundered." He looked over his shoulder. "Do you suppose there will be no further attempts on him?"

He heard the faint scraping of Johann's shoes upon the marble floor. "But our presence in his chamber will only serve to excite suspicion even further, brother."

Haydn clenched his fists, unable to refute his younger brother's remark. Yet a strange feeling within him urged him on. The lights in the picture gallery had been dimmed. Beyond, a faint light glowed in what he presumed to be Eichel's chamber.

"The other secretaries will have gone by now," he said. "The court library will be unoccupied as well. It adjoins Herr Eichel's chamber."

And the evidence His Serene Highness sought would be all the easier to obtain.

But he had no need to say it. Johann would understand.

"If anything were to happen to him afterward. . ." Haydn stopped, unable to continue. *How had it come to this? That reaching their intended purpose should matter more than a man's life?*

Out of the corner of his eye, he saw Johann's head dip in agreement.

"We would still have what we need," his brother said, his voice so quiet, the sound barely carried.

———————

Followed by Johann, Haydn hurried through the long, dimly lit picture gallery. Most of the candles in the brass sconces along the walls had burned out. The few that remained lightened the dark shadows with a faint, eerie glow.

The door to the principal court secretary's chamber was ajar. A small pool of light from within flooded the area between it and the picture gallery. In the grey shadows beyond, a hazy canine form shifted lazily on its cushion. Another lifted its head, then lay it down again.

But the royal hounds remained quiet, taking little interest in the proceedings.

"Surely that must mean nothing is amiss," Johann whispered into Haydn's ears. But the Kapellmeister's unease remained. "We shall see," he replied, careful to keep his voice down.

He raised his fist and knocked on the door. Then again, a little louder. No sound came from within. Not even the scraping of a chair. It was quiet. *Far too quiet*, he thought, when a soft, agonized moan came to his ears.

"We had best go in," Johann said, but Haydn had already burst in through the door.

The principal court secretary's head and torso were sprawled across his desk, his arms dangling by his side. *We are too late.* The words blazed across Haydn's mind as he stood rooted to the spot, unable to do more than stare at the ghastly sight before him.

A puddle of blood had collected in a ragged circle near the front leg of Eichel's chair. Within it lay a short ebony-handled dagger with a flat blade.

Another long-drawn moan drew the Kapellmeister's attention away from the dagger's sharp point to the man in the chair. "He may still be alive," he heard Johann say, his voice so faint it seemed to come from a great distance.

Haydn nodded. Was it possible Eichel could still be saved? He had not lost very much blood after all. He stepped gingerly around the chair to the other side of the desk. Eichel's features seemed pale and chalky.

Haydn gently touched his shoulder. "Herr Eichel?"

The principal court secretary's eyelid lifted a crack, revealing a glazed, stupefied blue iris. For the first time, Haydn noticed the near-empty porcelain coffee cup on the desk. Had Eichel been killed.

Or had he killed himself?

The principal court secretary's head rested on a sheet of paper. A note, judging by the few words Haydn could make out. A silver pen, its nib still wet and dark with the ink it had been dipped in, lay near the paper. His gaze returned to Eichel, whose eyes had closed again.

"Herr Eichel!" Haydn's voice was sharper this time. He felt the man's limp, clammy wrist and barely felt a pulse. "Herr Eichel! What have you done? Send for a physician, Johann." He raised his eyes. "If we are to save him—"

"Not me." Eichel's voice, weak and breathless, interrupted him. His eye opened again. "It was not me." His eyelid fell shut. "The dogs. . . dogs bark. . ."

"If the hounds had raised the alarm, surely someone would have heard." Johann, turning to leave, voiced the thought in Haydn's mind.

"It must have been someone the hounds were familiar with," Haydn replied. Although the possibility of an intruder could hardly be ruled out. The dogs had made not a sound when he and Johann had passed by. Would they have bestirred themselves had a stranger crept in?

"A woman. . . 'twas a woman. . ." Eichel's voice was so feeble, Haydn had to strain his ears to hear it. His breath rattled, his eyes opened wide. "Look for a woman, Herr Haydn."

The effort was clearly more than he could bear, for the principal court secretary's eyes closed as his head lolled into a final stupor.

Johann's hand closed upon Eichel's wrist.

"He is dead, I am afraid," he said after a pause.

Chapter Twenty-Eight

"You appear to have a singularly unfortunate habit of stumbling upon corpses, Haydn." Irritation laced the Prussian King's words.

Haydn had seen no choice but to interrupt His Majesty's evening concert with the news of Eichel's death. And His Majesty, clearly unused to having his concerts so disrupted, did not trouble to conceal his ire.

The King surveyed the scene, his head tilted to one side. Were it not for his large blue eyes and distinctive Roman nose, Haydn would have been hard put to recognize His Majesty.

Old Fritz, the soldier-king in his faded, snuff-stained uniform, had been replaced by a bewigged gentleman in a white silk suit richly embroidered with gold thread. His right hand rested on the ebony flute poking out of his coat pocket.

The King's gaze came to rest upon Haydn's features. "What was it that brought you to my principal court secretary's chambers, in any case? You have no business in this part of the palace. I trust you were not expecting to discover a dead body?"

Haydn swallowed. Even at Schönbrunn, he could hardly have found an excuse to venture near the chambers of the court clerks and secretaries. He *had* felt a vague premonition of danger. But only because he knew the principal court secretary to have put himself in a precarious position.

There was certainly no question of telling His Majesty that.

A voice at the door saved him from the necessity of a reply.

"Brother wished to borrow some of Herr Quantz's flute concertos from the court library," Johann explained, much to Haydn's relief. "We were given to understand that Herr Eichel dealt with such matters, and so decided to seek him out."

"Indeed."

"It was for the imperial ambassador's funeral," Haydn took up the thread Johann had offered him. "His Lordship was apparently quite fond of Herr Quantz's flute music.

A sour expression crossed the King's face but faded just as quickly when the Amtsrichter came into view behind Johann. "I made mention of it to Herr Haydn and Master Johann, Sire," the magistrate said. He took in the scene before him. "A fortuitous circumstance, it would appear.

"If only Herr Haydn and his brother had arrived a little sooner. They might have caught the killer in the act."

He walked into the room, tall and majestic in his dark blue officer's uniform with a silver sash around his waist.

"I trust nothing has been disturbed."

Haydn hesitated. Neither he nor Johann had touched a thing when they had first arrived. But when his brother had left to summon the magistrate, Haydn had picked up the porcelain cup on Eichel's desk and sniffed at it.

A strong whiff of coffee accompanied by the distinctly sweet-spicy, nauseating odor of laudanum had greeted his nostrils. He wondered whether to make mention of it but decided against it. Best to let the magistrate discover that detail for himself.

"I doubt Haydn would be quite so foolish a second time," the King remarked drily. The magistrate looked up in surprise, but the King, fortunately, did not trouble to elucidate his words.

The Amtsrichter returned to his work. His fur-lined Hessians tapped out a sharp staccato on the marble floor as he stepped around the area, taking in the scene. The principal court secretary slouched over his desk; the pool of blood near the front left leg of the chair; and the ebony-hilted dagger.

"He was stabbed, I take it."

"Is that not plain to see, my dear Amtsrichter?" the King replied. "The presence of the dagger clearly tells the tale."

"It does indeed, Your Majesty." The magistrate looked abashed. He scratched his chin and stared at the small puddle of blood near the chair leg. Haydn held his breath. Had the magistrate found the evidence quite as baffling as he himself had?

But the King directed the magistrate's attention away. "Strange that the dagger should have been left behind. What do you make of that, Herr Amtsrichter? As I recall, no weapon was found near the imperial ambassador's body."

"No, Your Majesty." The magistrate shook his head. "There was not. There is never any reason to leave a weapon behind. It is only when a man takes—" His eyes widened. "Takes his own life," he finished slowly, his voice hushed.

"But Herr Eichel said he was killed by a woman," Johann said.

"He was alive when you found him?" The magistrate's shrewd blue eyes rested on Johann's face, studying his features.

"He was close to death," Haydn replied for his brother. "But his reference to a woman was quite clear."

"Eichel was no weakling," the King countered testily as the magistrate began to hoist Eichel's lifeless torso up. "What woman could have overpowered him? Besides, who can tell what his mind was on, so close to death? He may have been suggesting that it was a woman who had brought him to this pass. It is what women do, as most men know to their cost."

The Amtsrichter succeeded in lifting Eichel's dead form, revealing the deep gash within his chest. "No woman could have inflicted a wound so deep or with such force," he said, breathless from the effort. His eyes fell on the note that had lain beneath Eichel's head.

He picked it up, held it out at arm's length, and squinted at it for what seemed like an eternity. He looked up at last.

"It appears you were mistaken, Herr Haydn."

The Amtsrichter handed the note to the King, who quickly perused it. "*I die by the very hand that killed His Lordship. May the Lord forgive me.*" His Majesty raised his eyes. "It seems clear enough."

He turned toward the Amtsrichter.

"You appear to have solved two murders in one stroke. I congratulate you." Turning to Haydn, he continued, "You will be good enough to inform the Queen of Hungary that her ambassador's murder has been resolved."

His Majesty was about to leave when the Amtsrichter mused out aloud: "It only surprises me that he bled so little."

It was the chance Haydn had been waiting for.

———

"Perhaps, it was not the dagger that killed him."

The King's cold blue eyes turned toward the Kapellmeister. "What else could it have been?"

Haydn took a deep breath and sought Johann's eyes. His brother, he hoped, would take his cue and bolster his arguments.

"Your Majesty, I still believe Herr Eichel was killed by someone other than himself. As to the murder of His Lordship. It could not have been Herr Eichel. He expresses no remorse for the deed—

"*May the Lord forgive me,*" the Amtsrichter interjected in a murmur.

"The desperate cry of a man about to die." Haydn paused, his gaze shifting toward the magistrate. Surely that much was clear? He was gratified to see the Amtsrichter's hesitant nod of agreement.

Haydn's eyes swiveled back toward the King.

"Besides, what reason could Eichel have had for murdering His Lordship? He provides no explanation for the deed."

"He was a loyal Prussian," the King responded coldly. "It was my father who gave him his first position. No doubt, he discovered the imperial ambassador was embarked upon a course detrimental to Prussia's interests."

"As a loyal Prussian, would he not have brought such a discovery to Your Majesty's attention?" Johann asked. "If he felt no remorse, why should he kill himself?"

The King was silent.

"Nor does he acknowledge that it was his own hand that committed either deed," Haydn pointed out. "The note he was undoubtedly forced to write is quite clear on the subject. Whoever murdered His Lordship also took Herr Eichel's life."

"But no woman could have overpowered him, Herr Haydn," the Amtsrichter pointed out. "I doubt any man could have either. There are no signs of a struggle. Surely there would have been some commotion."

"Not unless he was sedated." Haydn gestured toward the porcelain coffee cup on the desk.

To his satisfaction, the Amtsrichter reached for the cup and bent his head cautiously toward its rim. He wrenched his head away almost immediately.

"Laudanum. I'll wager there's enough here to kill a man, Your Majesty!"

The King's lips were pinched close. His fingers, white at the knuckles, wrapped themselves around his flute.

"Very well, then. You will be so good as to open an investigation and find me the person who did it, Herr Amtsrichter."

Several minutes after the King had departed, the magistrate was still poring over the note the principal court secretary had left behind.

He raised his eyes at last. "Is it possible Herr Eichel drugged himself with laudanum and then proceeded to stab himself?"

Haydn frowned, the question irritating him more than he cared to admit. The principal court secretary had not killed himself. But to explain how he came by that knowledge would only reveal Eichel's treason.

"But what reason could he have had to resort to *two* different means of killing himself?" Johann asked. "If he meant to drug himself, why use the dagger? If he meant to stab himself, why bother with the poison."

He waited a moment for a response. When none came, he continued: "The laudanum was administered in a cup of coffee. Does it not seem more likely that Herr Eichel's killer wished to keep him conscious long enough to write the missive he left behind?"

The Amtsrichter bowed his head, appearing to consider this.

"The wound from the dagger," Johann pressed his point. "Was it deep enough to kill?"

"I'll wager it was not," Haydn said. "Although, I suppose only a barber-surgeon will be able to confirm our suspicions."

The Amtsrichter made no response to this. Finally, he raised his head. "Why then does he ask for forgiveness? *May the Lord forgive me*," he read from the note.

Haydn sighed. Surely the circumstances of Eichel's death provided all the explanation needed?

"His killer must have induced him to write the words. Does it not seem significant, Herr Amtsrichter, that the principal court secretary takes care not to name the deed for which he seeks forgiveness? That he never claims as his own the hand that has murdered two men?"

The Amtsrichter inclined his head, the slightness of the movement indicating his continued skepticism on the matter. Seeing it, Haydn felt another stab of irritation.

"But to seek forgiveness— ?" The magistrate persisted. "Would even the threat of a knife held at his throat cause him to lie? In the hour of his death?"

"Herr Eichel was on the verge of death with no opportunity to confess his sins," Johann reminded the Amtsrichter.

The explanation appeared to strike a chord within the magistrate. His eyes opened wider, each blue orb visible in its entirety.

"And no possibility of receiving his last rites," Johann pressed on. "What man could die sanguine in such a case?"

This time the magistrate's nod was a little more emphatic. "That still leaves the question of who killed him."

Haydn pursed his lips. Had the man no idea how to do his job?

"It may be well to start with whoever brought—or was ordered to bring—him a cup of laudanum-laced coffee," he said in the most matter-of-fact tone he could muster.

The Kapellmeister himself was certain it was a woman. Not that he saw any reason to repeat his contention. He had no more persuasive evidence than before that it was so.

Besides, they had at least managed to counter the notion that Eichel's death had been caused by his own hand. It was sufficient for the moment.

Chapter Twenty-Nine

ROSALIE and Greta hurried down a broad, gloomy avenue that led toward Sanssouci Palace. The ground beneath their feet was icy; the night bitterly cold. But it was not the chill wind curling around her throat that caused a shiver of apprehension to run down Rosalie's spine.

Somehow, the task of finding Herr Haydn and Master Johann seemed more daunting than it should have. She reached out to clasp Greta's hand, taking comfort in the warmth of her friend's soft, plump palm.

Were the Kapellmeister and his brother within the palace that loomed large before them? Or somewhere on the vast grounds that surrounded it? Would it take long to find them?

"This place gives me the creeps," Greta whispered. Her head turned slowly to scan their surroundings. The trees cast deep black shadows along the dimly lit, grey ground. They seemed to be alone, and yet Rosalie could have sworn a thousand eyes were upon her.

All a figment of her imagination, no doubt, she scolded herself.

"It is just the dark," Rosalie said aloud, trying to reassure them both. "Come, let's see if we can find a footman to help us."

There would be one at the entrance, no doubt.

They were almost at the broad flight of stairs when a slim form emerged silently from the dark grounds and began racing up the steps.

"Hoy!" Rosalie called.

The figure paused and turned around. A slender lad, not much taller than herself. In the livery of the Prussian King; but the uniform hung loose upon his slight frame.

"Can you tell us where we may find Herr Haydn?"

The boy regarded her, his expression vacant. Rosalie sighed. Would she have to explain who the Kapellmeister was to this uninformed lad?

"Is he not at home—wherever that may be?" The boy gazed insolently down at them.

"If he were, would we be here?" Greta's tone was acerbic.

"He must be with the Empress, then. Or someplace else. How should I know?" The lad wrinkled his nose—dusted with freckles, Rosalie noticed.

Her brow furrowed as she continued to gaze at him. There was something about the eyes, something about the manner—

"Ask one of the servants within," the boy commanded sharply and turned on his heels.

"Ask one of the servants!" Greta repeated. "And what was *he*, may I ask?"

"Not a palace footman, I'll wager," Rosalie said.

"But he was wearing—"

"Yes, I know. But didn't you notice, it was the same cocksure lad who accosted us in the Haarhof in Vienna? When we thought Potsdam was in Poland."

"Are you sure?" Greta's voice rose, puzzled. "But what could a ragamuffin such as he be doing here?"

Rosalie shook her head. "I wish I knew. But I'm sure it is him. Although why he should have followed us to Potsdam. . .?" She left the question unvoiced, shaking her head again.

Had the boy's presence anything to do with the imperial ambassador's murder? Or the predicament Herr Haydn found himself in? The young ruffian had insinuated himself, unbidden, into their conversation outside His Serene Highness's wine cellar.

And when they had mentioned Potsdam, his impudent grin had subsided.

"We had best go find Herr Haydn," she said.

Perhaps once they were within the palace, they would see where the little urchin had gone. And what he was up to.

The principal court secretary had not rung for coffee. Nor, apparently, had any of the footmen delivered a cup to his chamber.

"There was no reason to," the steward informed the Amtsrichter. He stood, hands clasped, by the kitchen door and gazed earnestly at the men before him.

The magistrate had divulged nothing more than the mere fact of Eichel's unfortunate demise. That his questions about the principal court secretary's coffee—*When had it been brought in? By whom?*—had taken the steward by surprise was plainly evident.

The steward's eyes rested on the Amtsrichter's stern features, awaiting some sort of explanation. When none came, he continued: "Herr Eichel has never taken coffee after the mid-day meal, *meine Herren*."

The magistrate harrumphed. He glanced over his shoulders, his lips gathered into a pucker of frustration.

"It appears to have been a ghost who handed Herr Eichel that fatal cup of coffee."

Haydn pursed his lips too, a small gesture of sympathy. "Perhaps it is just as well," he said.

"Just as well?" The magistrate regarded him as though he were mad.

"Brother means," Johann said, "that it is just as well the palace servants seem not to have been. . ." he paused, eyes drifting up in search of a suitable expression.

"Unduly influenced," he finished, drawing out the words.

"*Unduly influenced*?" the Amtsrichter repeated. Then his expression cleared. "*Ach so!*"

Haydn nodded. One could hardly expect the King and his associates to have been foolish enough to involve any of the palace servants. That the servants would be questioned was inevitable. And the slightest hint of any connection with the crime would have compelled the magistrate to investigate their master.

Even so, there may have been other means of delivering the coffee to Eichel's chambers.

"Did any of the other secretaries ring for coffee?" The question had no sooner entered Haydn's mind than his younger brother voiced it.

"Not this evening." The steward shook his head. "They were dismissed earlier than usual."

"By Herr Eichel?" Haydn enquired, although the question hardly needed to be asked. Who else could it be? And the steward's emphatic nod confirmed it.

Clearly Eichel had planned to keep his appointment with them. Had he perhaps intended to share intelligence of value to Austria? Had someone divined that might be the case?

If so, it could only have been at the church. *When they had been so abruptly interrupted.*

"Is there a footman by the name of Fonso?"

The words were out of Haydn's mouth as soon as the name entered his mind.

"Fonso?" The steward stared. "No, *mein Herr.*"

"It was the name given by the servant who summoned us from the Katholische Kirche St. Anna this afternoon," Haydn explained to the magistrate as they strode back to the principal court secretary's chamber.

"The organ was in need of tuning," Johann added before the magistrate could ask what had caused them to return to the site of the imperial ambassador's murder.

"And this Fonso's manner seemed oddly imperious for a servant," Haydn went on. Had the footman detected Eichel's presence at the church?

"Then, most likely, it was he who killed Herr Eichel." The magistrate grasped eagerly at the detail. "And His Lordship, too—if we are to believe the note."

Haydn dipped his head in agreement, his hands behind his back. Although he refrained from pointing out that Fonso was almost certainly someone associated with the palace. How else had he known to summon Haydn and Johann to the palace that afternoon?

"At someone else's behest, no doubt." It was as far as Haydn was willing to go to remind the magistrate of Eichel's last words.

The principal court secretary had named a woman as his killer—and Fonso, a burly man, could hardly be mistaken for one. The Kapellmeister cast a surreptitious glance at the magistrate.

But the Amtsrichter made no reply, his nod so half-hearted, it was clear he remained unconvinced.

They were almost at Eichel's chamber now. A modestly dressed man stood by the doorway. "It is Geller, one of the under-secretaries," the Amtsrichter said. "He will—"

A furious barking erupted from the picture gallery, drowning out the magistrate's words.

Johann looked around, startled. "What could have so aroused those hounds?" he cried. "They took no notice of us when we came."

"It is a woman, I'll warrant." Geller's voice sounded hoarse from the effort of making himself heard above the greyhounds' snarls.

"They take great exception to any female," the under-secretary continued as they passed through the doorway of Eichel's chamber. "Even the few His Majesty appreciates."

The noise of the hounds' baying subsided as the door closed behind them.

"That is all they bark at, women?" Haydn enquired. Eichel had made mention of the dogs, had he not?

The corners of Geller's mouth drew down and his shoulders lifted in an apologetic shrug.

"Clearly a woman is involved, then." Johann was quick to seize upon the fact. "The principal court secretary said something about the dogs barking." He met the magistrate's gaze. "Before he enjoined us to look for a woman."

"But no woman. . ." The magistrate's eyes closed wearily. He stood with one hand on his hip, his frustration beginning to emerge in a forceful exhalation.

Geller coughed. "The hounds have been known to bark at Herr Eichel, himself."

The words caught the attention of the Kapellmeister and his brother.

"It was just the one time," Geller explained. "On the night of your arrival with the Empress, Herr Haydn. Herr Eichel was on his way out after supper—"

A loud rat-a-tat on the door cut him off mid-sentence.

———◆———

"Herr Haydn." The door opened a crack and Rosalie's head peeked in. "We were told—" Her gaze fell on the principal court secretary's body still sprawled upon his desk. The color drained from her face.

"It is a matter of some urgency," she managed to say, her eyes riveted in horror upon the dead man. Behind her, Greta's eyes were as round as saucers.

"Let us speak outside." Haydn hastened toward the door. Neither girl had, in all likelihood, ever seen a corpse.

"What is it?" he asked when Johann had emerged from within and closed the door behind himself. Had Maria Anna sent them, he wondered.

———◆———

Rosalie hesitated. There was no one besides themselves in the small passage. But a Prussian official and a servant of the Prussian court stood no more than a few paces away. They could at any moment be interrupted.

"It may be best to step outside," she said, unable to keep her eyes from darting to the door leading to the chamber beyond. "It concerns His Lordship."

The Kapellmeister must have agreed, for he began to make his way toward the picture gallery.

"Not that way!" Greta's voice was sharp. "The dogs."

Master Johann winced.

"Yes. yes, of course," he hastened to say. He pointed over their shoulders. "I believe there is another door over there. It will take us out to the grounds."

An icy blast of air hit them as soon as Master Johann opened the door. Rosalie pulled her cape tightly around herself. If only they could have stayed within. Shivering, she stepped gingerly out into the cold.

"We know why His Lordship was killed," Greta burst out, apparently unable to contain herself any longer.

Rosalie sighed. It was not the way she would've broached the subject. "It seems he had discovered a plot to steal a valuable diamond."

The Kapellmeister frowned. "The Grand Master's diamond?"

What else could it be? It had been the only diamond stolen thus far. Although, he was not sure the maids were even aware of its existence.

Rosalie bobbed her head. "Yes, and His Lordship wrote a letter about it," Greta said. "Only we can't find it. It isn't in his study. And—"

The Kapellmeister held out his palm, stemming the tide of Greta's response. "From the beginning, if you please. How did you even come by this information?"

"It was from the painting Frau Bach gave Frau Haydn," Rosalie explained. She told him about the hourglass-shaped view-catcher they had found behind the painting.

"A view-catcher?" The Kapellmeister repeated, but when she withdrew it from her pocket, his eyes widened in startled recognition.

———◆———

"A *mask!*"

It took Haydn an effort to keep his voice down. The discovery of such a thing on their persons would immediately denounce them as spies. He plucked it warily from Rosalie's fingers and studied it intently.

What had Herr Bach—or his son, for that matter—been doing with such a thing? The opening, placed upon a sheet of paper, was used to write out a secret message. Once the mask was lifted, the message was concealed by incorporating its words into a more innocuous text.

But the intended recipient of the secret communication could only read it if he had the selfsame mask. Had the Bachs attempted to use him to smuggle their mask out of Prussia? His skin prickled at the thought, a lightning-flash of anger and stupefaction blazing through him simultaneously.

He lifted his head and turned toward Johann. "What could it possibly mean?"

"That we were entirely right about His Lordship's work," Johann said quietly. He tipped his chin at the mask. "I assume *that* was his since the frame belonged to His Lordship as well."

"There were view-catchers just like that one in His Lordship's study," Rosalie said.

"But none quite so oddly shaped," Greta added. "We thought it was most peculiar because His Lordship had no other painting supplies. No brushes. Or paints."

The tightness in Haydn's chest eased. He drew a deep breath. How had he not seen what the maids had? He had beheld the thick sheets of paper with their square and oval openings and thought nothing of them. That they might be Cardan grilles commonly used by diplomats and intelligencers to disguise their communications had not occurred to him at all.

But how had this one made its way into the Bachs' hands? He glanced down at the hourglass-shaped mask. The tiny numbers inscribed on it clearly referred to the letter it was meant to decode.

No doubt, His Lordship had taken care to devise more than one grille to ensure his despatches were secure.

"And this one must have been intended for the Empress as well," he murmured. The letter had either not reached Her Majesty. Or she had been unable to read it because the mask required to decipher its secret contents had been waylaid.

"The letter was not sent, you say?" He raised his eyes and regarded the maids closely. "How could you know that? And what can you know of its contents?" Had the imperial ambassador truly uncovered a plot to murder him? What else could the theft of the Grand Master's diamond refer to?

"It was Elma," Rosalie said as Greta handed him a sheet of paper. He perused it, and then held it out to Johann. But the substance of the letter made as little sense as the name of the person who had penned it.

Who was Elma? What could possibly have made her think he was in need of clearing his name? And to suggest that the King of Prussia would be the one to do it. . .

"Who is this woman?" His voice despite himself was rough with anger. Whom had the maids been consorting with? Had they not been told to keep their own counsel?

Chapter Thirty

ROSALIE gaped at the Kapellmeister. What need had he to feign ignorance of the woman he had once loved?

"It is the woman who came to Wallnerstrasse," Greta said.

The explanation meant nothing to the Kapellmeister.

"Which woman?" he responded. There had in truth been so many in the months since he had uncovered the operations of a vicious band of thieves in Vienna.

"The one who came on the day the Empress summoned you," Rosalie said. "It was but a few days before we left the city."

The collar of his shirt felt inexplicably tight around Haydn's throat, the linen chafing his skin. His eyes sought his younger brother's.

"The Pri—" He stopped himself uttering the title just in time. What had caused Princess Auersperg to become so friendly with his employer's servants? And what information had she managed to secrete from them?

"She calls herself Elma?" He could think of nothing else to say. Not that anyone appeared to have heard.

Johann was questioning the maids. His low voice and the maids' higher-pitched tones seemed to reach Haydn's ears from a great distance. Why had "Elma" sought out the maids? What had she wanted from them? Some words caught his attention.

"She feared the King of Prussia wished me harm?" Haydn's voice rose.

"She said you would not listen to her," Rosalie said.

"And she regretted not returning your affection for her all those years ago," Greta confided with a sage nod.

"*Not. . .*" Was the girl utterly mad? But his mind had more important matters to pursue. He ceased to listen and pored over the letter again. There was a mention of Count Botta. The Princess—masquerading, it would seem, as Elma—had made no secret of her association with the Prussian ambassador to Saxony.

His fingers nearly crushed the paper. *Good God!* The letter was as plain an admission as they would get that Maria Wilhelmina von Auersperg was allied with the enemy. Small wonder she had sought to prevent their departure to Potsdam.

Could it have been due to her that the imperial ambassador's work had been betrayed? The Empress, no doubt, had imparted some particulars of what she had gleaned from Count Seckendorff to Emperor Joseph. His Imperial Majesty must in turn have heedlessly let fall some of these details to his dead father's mistress.

Or had it been she who had impersonated Eichel to lure His Lordship to his death?

Geller's revelation had made it clear it was a woman who had stolen Eichel's cloak that fatal night. Why else had the dogs howled at the cloaked figure Geller had seen—and mistaken for his superior? They had never before barked at Eichel—or any other man.

But the Kapellmeister's own certainty would hardly suffice to convince anyone of the facts. His lips hardened into an unyielding line. Could the Princess be tricked into revealing herself?

"The Empress will need to be informed, brother." Johann's voice rose within Haydn's consciousness, drowning out his thoughts.

The Empress contemplated the contents of the letter Haydn had handed her. She had read it twice already, but she kept her head bent over it. The bright patterns of the soft Turkish rug beneath her feet were visible on either side of the edges of the thick paper.

A pair of black shoes with silver buckles was planted on the marble floor beyond. Haydn's sturdy calves, encased in white linen stockings, rose above them. Beside them, Master Johann's slim legs descended into a pair of narrow shoes.

Her Majesty sighed. She would not have thought Wilhelmina—Francis's pretty, charming Wilhelmina—had the least interest in affairs of state. Much less the capacity to understand such ponderous matters.

Clearly, she had underestimated the woman. A twinge of furious jealousy assailed her. She had not begrudged the woman her beauty. Nor had she begrudged her Francis's embraces. But had Wilhelmina also sought to influence Francis's mind on matters of state?

"The woman should've been consigned to a convent," Esterházy, seated beside her, groused. "I have said it often enough, although my words seem to have fallen on deaf ears."

"And what good would that have done?" The Empress could barely stifle her exasperation. As though one could wrest a married woman from her husband's arms!

She cast the letter aside and picked up the hourglass-shaped mask resting on the low mahogany table in front of her chaise. "I doubt Seckendorff discovered any plot to steal the Grand Master's diamond. Most likely that was a ploy the Princess used to dupe your maids into cooperating with her. Fortunately, she did not count on their loyalty to Haydn."

The composer cleared his throat. "I take it Your Majesty received no communication from His Lordship dated the eleventh day of October?"

Maria Theresa raised her eyes and regarded the Kapellmeister. "I have received nothing for a month or more. As I have already mentioned."

Haydn lowered his eyes. "Yes, Your Majesty."

"Have the maids been informed that they were duped?"

Haydn raised his eyes, large and brown with an expression of grave concern in them. So had her faithful Khevenhüller, God rest his soul, gazed at her years ago when she had sought his aid to save her throne and her empire.

"I thought it best not to, Your Majesty. Not until the Princess has taken the bait."

Haydn had been nothing if not resourceful. If the mention of Poland failed to reel Wilhelmina in, she knew not what would.

Overcome with gratitude, the Empress could do no more than nod. What she had done to deserve the Kapellmeister's utmost devotion, she did not know. Saved his life, apparently, when as a boy he had recklessly climbed the scaffolds at Schönbrunn. "The spanking you ordered, Your Majesty, cured me of my stupidity and, I am sure, saved me a fall that could have cost me my life."

But surely such a small favor could not suffice to earn so strong an allegiance.

She fingered Wilhelmina's letter. "I would not have considered the Princess to be the sort of woman who would readily don the garb of a man." In her mind's eye, she saw Wilhelmina's alabaster skin, her small waist flaring into softly rounded hips.

These were the very feminine attractions that her dead Francis had named. That the woman was his mistress had been no secret. Even then, the featherheaded, vapid Wilhelmina had reminded the Empress of her youngest child, Antoine. And like Antoine, Wilhelmina was not one to willingly disguise her femininity.

"An accomplice, then?" Master Johann suggested. In her presence, he was usually quiet. Speaking only to defend his brother, the Empress had observed.

"An accomplice who remains in Vienna." Esterházy leaned forward to murmur into her ear.

Maria Theresa sat as still as a statue, unwilling to acknowledge the magnate's remark. Unwilling even to think about whom it was he meant. It was not a betrayal she could contemplate with equanimity.

She turned her gaze toward Haydn and his brother. "We shall know more I suppose when you have confronted the Princess." She leaned upon her cane and struggled to her feet. "In the meantime, I will speak with Amalia."

It was what she had intended to do when the Kapellmeister and his brother had interrupted them.

The news was even better than Maria Wilhelmina von Auersperg had expected. Esterházy's maids had scoured the deceased imperial ambassador's study and discovered a letter written on the eleventh day of October, 1768.

"But it bears no reference to the Grand Master's diamond. Or even a theft of any kind," Rosalie had written. *"His Lordship merely talks about Poland and a prize of some sort. Are you quite sure you are not mistaken in the date, Elma? For it is not even addressed to the King, but to Her Majesty, the Empress."*

Maria Wilhelmina's face broke into a delighted smile. She tucked the message into her sleeve and approached the imperial ambassador's residence on Lindenstrasse. With any luck she would soon know the extent of Seckendorff's information.

Her smile widened. That none of it had yet been exposed to the Empress might serve her in good stead.

The night was bitterly cold and the dampness from the icy roads soaked in through her embroidered silk shoes and her silk stockings.

The Princess had been compelled to dismiss her carriage at Gutenbergstrasse. Elma, the impoverished governess, could hardly be seen to be traveling in a chaise. But the discomfort was a small price to pay.

She swept up to the door and rapped her knuckles sharply on the wood panels.

"Where is it?" she demanded when Rosalie and Greta appeared at the door. "Where is the letter? It may be just what we need."

———•◦◦◦•———

Rosalie bit her lip uncertainly, her hand still on the door.

"I wish you had not come," she said, a nervous anxiety drawing her eyes to the floor above. Frau Haydn had retired to her bedchamber. But what if she were to come down, summoned by the sound of a strange woman's voice at the door?

The Kapellmeister had insinuated his wife was a jealous woman. There was no knowing what she might think.

"If Frau Haydn were to see you—"

"And what if she did?" Elma responded. She shrugged her slim shoulders.

"Do you suppose she would want to see a woman who might still be a rival for her husband's affections?" Greta demanded, her voice sharp with exasperation. "She might think you had come calling upon him."

Elma's mouth curved into a smile. Her tongue quickly flicked over her red lips. "Well then, let us make sure the good woman never sees me. Having me stand at the door won't help matters. Let me go to His Lordship's study."

Rosalie made no reply, merely opening the door a little wider. Elma stepped inside. "Where did you say that letter was?"

Rosalie glanced at Greta. It was the Kapellmeister who had, on the very day of His Lordship's death, conducted a cursory search of the study along with Master Johann; and the Kapellmeister who had found the letter. It had been the only piece of correspondence they had discovered in His Lordship's study that day.

"*I cannot think it is the one she means,*" the Kapellmeister had said. "*Although the date on the letter was the very same.*"

"*Could there not be other letters similarly concealed?*" Master Johann had suggested. "*Perhaps this Elma might be willing to take a look.*"

But Herr Haydn had not wished to be seen in need of Elma's help.

"*It is hardly seemly,*" he had said, his cheeks flaming, "*given our former relationship. Have her verify the date, instead. It is the best way forward.*"

"We saw the letter hidden in one of His Lordship's books. It is still on the shelf," Rosalie now informed the governess.

A fleeting expression of fury marred Elma's beautiful features, but before she could say a word, Greta thrust her chin out defiantly. "We would've retrieved it had we thought it had any significance. But the letter was all about Poland. How was that relevant?"

"I won't know until I see it, will I?" Elma snapped. "Most likely, the letter was enciphered. His Lordship would hardly have written openly about the theft. Do you at least recall where you saw it?"

Rosalie bit her lip again. The Kapellmeister had been exceedingly vague about where the letter was. "It must have been one of the middle shelves, toward the end closest to the window.

Elma sighed heavily. "Very well. Take me to the study. If it is there, I shall find it."

—————•••—————

Maria Wilhelmina—Elma—stepped into the imperial ambassador's study, her slender fingers gripping the base of a gilded ormolu-and-bronze candelabra. The flames from three slender tapers cast a circle of light around her, illuminating the parquet floors of the room.

She glanced over her shoulder at the maids. "Close the door. And guard it, if you please." The corners of her mouth arched up into an amused smile. "There's no need for the Kapellmeister's poor wife to get her feathers all ruffled merely because I am here."

The woman was no beauty, so the Princess had heard. Small wonder the Kapellmeister had succumbed to her own charms. Had she not had more pressing matters at hand, she might have considered toying with the man.

Despite his pock-marked face, there was something about Haydn's broad shoulders and his strongly marked features that was oddly attractive. His restraint in her presence, moreover, was quite admirable. The Princess was accustomed to men fawning over her. But Haydn had betrayed nothing of what he felt.

She inhaled deeply, her hand gliding slowly down her bodice. To coax him into revealing his emotions would be quite the most irresistible challenge. . .

The door clicked shut behind her, recalling her mind to her task.

She stepped forward into the room, set the candelabra down on the massive desk at the front of the room, and surveyed the study.

The bookcases lined the rear. But there were three windows. Maria Wilhelmina sighed. That meant six shelves, crammed full with books, to search through. Anyone with the least bit of sense would have withdrawn the letter from its hiding place. But the maids. . .

She shook her head. What else could one expect from a couple of serving girls? She must count herself fortunate, she supposed, that they had even thought to mention it to her. Taking a deep breath, she strode toward the bookcase on the left.

There was no need to take the candles with her. The letter had been found within the pages of a book. A quick sifting through each book would reveal whether any concealed a letter or folded piece of paper. Who knew, but there might be more than one letter of significance to be found.

A quarter of an hour at the first shelf yielded nothing. Biting back her frustration, the Princess walked around to the second shelf. She had just withdrawn a book from it when a quiet voice behind her made her jump.

"Your Highness."

Chapter Thirty-One

"Or would you prefer the name, Elma."

Haydn entered the imperial ambassador's study with Johann, who closed the door behind them.

"That is the name by which His Serene Highness's maids know you, is it not?" Haydn came to a halt beside the desk.

The slender shoulders of the cloaked figure standing with her head bowed near the bookcase seemed to stiffen. Then she whipped around. A smile stole across her beautiful features.

"I see you have discovered my small ruse, Herr Haydn." She spread her hands out before her as her shoulders lifted, then fell. "Had you but heeded my words, it would not have been necessary."

The searing heat of anger flared up within Haydn at the brazen attitude that accompanied this remark. As though the determination to follow his conscience were deserving of the ill-veiled threat the Princess had issued the day she had invaded his Music Room. As though it justified the deception she had perpetrated on the maids.

As though it provided just cause for murder!

"When the Empress commanded me to accompany her to Prussia, I had no choice but to obey, Your Highness."

The Princess replaced the book in her hands upon the shelf and came forward, smiling. "And what of the Emperor? Are His Imperial Majesty's wishes of no consequence to you?"

"As I recall, you claimed not to speak on behalf of His Imperial Majesty," Haydn countered.

The Princess's face darkened. "I nevertheless had His Imperial Majesty's interests in mind. Not that I would expect a musician such as yourself to understand that, Herr Haydn."

"Are we to believe," Johann said softly, "that it is in the Emperor's interests to carve up Poland?"

The Princes snorted. "How could it not be when there is land to be gained? Do you suppose Austria should stand by while Russia and Prussia amass wealth and land? What would that do to our standing in the world?"

"Does Your Highness suppose that profiting from a greedy venture would gain us the world's applause?" Johann asked. The Empress's sentiments on the subject had been quite clear. "Would it not threaten the very alliance that Her Majesty seeks with France?"

The Princess's face turned white. "Poland is lost whether Her Majesty wishes it or not. The Emperor has long known it. The King of Prussia's plan will at least serve to curb Russia's power and enable us to retain ours."

Johann was on the verge of replying, but Haydn shook his head. Continuing the argument would serve no good purpose. The finer points of foreign policy were far beyond their ken. Best to leave them to the Empress and her son. Besides, there was a far more sinister matter to be considered.

"Would the Emperor be willing to countenance the murder of the imperial ambassador to gain his objective?" he enquired, pleased to see a furrow of displeasure appear on the Princess's brow. "I don't suppose His Imperial Majesty will condone Your Highness's hand in it. Most certainly, the Empress will not."

The Princess clenched her hands. "I had nothing to do with that," she hissed.

"It was a woman who lured Count Seckendorff to his death, Your Highness." Haydn's voice was hard. To toy with a man's life for political gain was despicable. The Empress, he was convinced, would rather have lost all she had than be party to so vile a deed.

"How can you possibly know that?"

"I have my ways."

"I doubt even Count Botta," Johann added, "could persuade the King of Prussia to overlook the murder of his own principal court secretary."

"What! I d-don't—"

"Anton Eichel, the principal court secretary, was killed just a few hours ago. But not before he named his killer." Haydn's gaze never wavered from the Princess's features. She had seemed genuinely taken aback at the news? Or was it more dissimulation?

The Princess's eyes blazed. "That is absurd. I know nothing of Eichel or his involvement. I was nowhere near the palace—"

"And the guards and footmen will attest to that?" Haydn kept his eyes on her.

The Princess's erect form seemed to collapse. "I was nowhere near Herr Eichel," she said quietly. "No matter what you may have heard."

The candle flames bent low and arched gracefully up in a sudden draft of wind. Shadows danced on the parquet floor. Haydn contemplated them in silence. The magistrate had been adamant no woman could have inflicted the wounds that Eichel and His Lordship had suffered.

Had the Princess had an accomplice, then? Fonso, perhaps?

He turned back to the Princess. "Whom had Your Highness gone to meet?"

"I cannot tell you." Her lips drew into a firm line. "I would not be believed."

"It was a footman, I suppose." The widening of her eyes told Haydn all he needed to know. He pressed his advantage. "What servant could be so powerful—so much in the King's favor—that Your Highness would not be believed? Surely he could be commanded to confirm the facts in your case."

"It was not—" The Princess cut herself off.

"Or did Your Highness meet the man merely to give him his orders?" Haydn was beginning to have his doubts about the Princess's involvement in the principal court secretary's murder, but he pressed on nonetheless. "To kill Herr Eichel?"

Princess Auersperg glared at him. "I had nothing to do with that. I have already told you so."

"And what of His Lordship's murder, Your Highness?" Johann interjected. "It may not have been Your Highness's hand that committed the deed, but—"

He was not allowed to finish. "How can that be laid at my door?" the Princess cried, balling her hands into tight fists. "I was not even in Potsdam at the time." She turned to Haydn. "I was at Count Botta's residence. Your maids directed a letter to me at his address."

The Kapellmeister opened his mouth, then closed it again. He had nothing to say. There was no questioning the Princess's sincerity this time. But Eichel had clearly named a woman. And the barking of the King's hounds could only signify the involvement of one.

Johann drew him aside. "It would be best to let Her Majesty and His Serene Highness deal with this, brother," he said in a low voice. "The Princess has not denied having a hand in this affair. But we will never get the precise details out of her."

Haydn nodded. "Have Boris bind her to a chair and lock the room. She is a wily woman, and I would not put it past her to trick the maids into letting her go." He turned back to the Princess.

"I trust Your Highness will forgive the impertinence, but I must insist you remain confined to this room. Her Majesty would never forgive me if I were to let you go without learning the full truth regarding His Lordship's brutal murder."

"We only wished him to be recalled," she burst out. "To be sufficiently embarrassed that the Empress would have no choice but to call him back to Vienna. What choice did we have? The Emperor's repeated requests fell on deaf ears.

"But we knew Her Majesty would never tolerate Seckendorff's continued presence in Potsdam if it appeared to threaten her precious alliance with the French. If it seemed to jeopardize Archduchess Maria Antonia's marriage."

"And I imagine the Emperor and King Frederick were in agreement on this point." It was not a question. The Kapellmeister had no doubt that was the case. Emperor Joseph had never made any bones about his admiration for the Prussian King. Nor his antipathy toward his own mother, the Empress.

Haydn strode out of the study, uninterested in the Princess's response —if she had one.

———

It took but a few minutes to summon Boris. If the Count's valet had any qualms about restraining a lady, he chose not to express them. He received his instructions with an impassive face and set about his task as methodically as an automaton.

Stout rope pinned the Princess's arms tightly to her sides and held her fast to her chair. Each slender ankle was secured to the chair leg beside it. A wad of linen was deftly inserted into her mouth with a silk sash wrapped around to keep it in place.

But when the study door had been closed shut and the key turned in its lock, Boris turned to regard the Kapellmeister and his brother.

"Was it she who killed my master?" He watched Haydn closely. "What had His Lordship ever done to harm her?"

Haydn hesitated. These were questions he had no answer to. He was not even certain the Princess's involvement extended as far as murder. The news of Eichel's death had struck her like a bolt of lightning. And if she had not killed Eichel. . .

"That she had some hand in it is evident," Johann responded before he could. "Her interests were aligned directly against His Lordship's. And against the Empress. She is a woman of great wile—"

"Have no fear, Master Johann. I am not likely to let her go," Boris said. "I only ask because— " He broke off with a frown. His fingers twisted around the doorknob of the study door.

Haydn waited, knowing better than to rush the man.

"The man who habitually called upon His Lordship—the man I took to be Herr Ritter—had long, ink-stained fingers. A man's fingers, brown and strong. But His Lordship's visitor on the night of his death had slender, white fingers, so delicate I hardly think they could have belonged to a man."

Haydn exchanged a glance with Johann. It was the first confirmation of Eichel's last words. "A woman's fingers?" he gently probed.

"I would not have been surprised to learn that they were," Boris replied.

"Can you remember anything at all of the face?" Johann asked.

To Haydn's disappointment, Boris shook his head ruefully.

Princess Auersperg had claimed to be in Saxony. If it had not been Her Highness who had impersonated Eichel that night, who else could it have been?

"The accomplice His Serene Highness mentioned," Johann murmured, reading Haydn's thoughts with no effort.

If there was one, then no doubt, she, like the Princess, had reached out to the maids as well.

"Send Rosalie and Greta here, if you please, Boris."

"Someone other than. . ." Rosalie couldn't bring herself to utter the woman's name.

She glanced at the study door, visible in the space between Herr Haydn's and Master Johann's bewigged heads. To think she and Greta had been so easily gulled.

". . . any other woman." Master Johann's voice broke in upon her thoughts.

Rosalie's eyes shifted toward his face. She responded with a forcible shake of her head. No woman—other than the treacherous Delilah confined within the study—had sought them out in Vienna.

"No," Greta said. "But—"

The slight hesitation in her friend's voice caught Rosalie's attention. She frowned. What had Greta thought of now?

"The ragamuffin." Greta's bright blue eyes, round as saucers, met hers. "The lad we encountered in the Haarhof. Remember?"

"What of him?" the Kapellmeister demanded, his voice sharp.

"He was loitering around in the alley near the wine cellar." Rosalie's head swiveled slowly to face Herr Haydn. "The day we learned we were to travel to Potsdam."

Whether the lad had anything to do with the strumpet who had called herself their friend, she knew not. At the time, she had thought nothing of the boy thrusting himself into their conversation. But now that she thought about it—

"He seemed unaccountably interested in our plans." The words burst out of her mouth as she recalled how the color had faded from his freckled cheeks the moment they had mentioned Potsdam. "He had overheard us talking, and the news that we were bound for Potsdam seemed to mean something to him."

"And he has followed us here, God knows why," Greta blurted out. "We saw him just a while ago at the palace. Dressed as one of the footmen. Although I'll wager he has no business there."

Rosalie sniffed. The urchin had barely shown signs of having recognized them. And as for his manner— "He seemed to not even count himself a servant."

"No?" The Kapellmeister said softly when she had recounted the details to him. But it was not a question.

Haydn's mind was churning. "And this was a boy, you are quite sure of that? Not a man?"

He merely wanted confirmation of the fact. Not that there was any mistaking Fonso for a boy, for all that he had an imperious manner.

He regarded the maids closely. But they shook their heads vigorously.

Haydn scratched his chin. Had the maids seen a lad? Or a woman disguised as one? But which—

"Could the Princess have had more than one accomplice?" Johann voiced the question in the Kapellmeister's mind. It seemed unlikely that the one His Serene Highness had pointed out to him as they waited outside Herr Boehmer's establishment in Vienna could have made the long journey to Potsdam in secret.

Besides, few married women enjoyed the freedoms the Princess had given herself. Her Highness's husband was no more than a cipher. But the same could not be said of—

". . .the one you saw remains in Vienna, does she not?" Johann's voice interrupted the Kapellmeister's musings just as an image darted through his brain.

"The boy had freckles, you say?"

"A small smattering around the nose." Greta nodded her head vigorously.

A wave of unease crashed over Haydn's being. He turned to his brother.

"We must go to the palace at once, Johann. Her Highness's accomplice is not in Vienna at all."

Chapter Thirty-Two

L EANING upon her ebony-handled cane, the Empress studied her daughter's bedchamber as closely as she had the Prussian King's treaties years ago. The windows were closed, the curtains drawn. Her Majesty's watchful eyes detected no sign of a male presence.

Had she imagined the figure—a blur of blue—that had disappeared within her daughter's door? Then again, Amalia had taken far longer than necessary to come to the door.

The Empress's gaze returned to her daughter's disheveled form—the hair carelessly brushed back, long gold-brown strands already escaping the confines of their pins. The turquoise silk bodice seemed slightly askew as did the frothy frills that made up the skirt. As though the girl had dressed herself in some haste.

The way a woman might after—the Empress closed her eyes with a shudder. God forbid, the child should have offered herself to some hot-blooded Prussian lad.

"What is it, Mother?" The girl's impatient tone aroused the Empress out of her brooding.

Esterházy lingered uncomfortably by the door.

The Empress left him there, hobbling toward a chaise in the middle of the room. "I wished to hear your impressions of the Crown Prince." She lowered herself into the white damask chaise. This was not the time to chastise her offspring for her indiscretions.

"Why?" Amalia's voice was rough. "Is Your Majesty having second thoughts about the Duke of Parma now? Frederick William is a married man, and quite unlikely to marry a Catholic, I imagine."

"I would never suggest a daughter of mine marry a man quite so determined in his philandering as the Crown Prince appears to be," the Empress retorted. "And I doubt a woman of your spirits would be content to play second fiddle to his mistresses."

The Archduchess barely refrained herself from rolling her eyes as she sank into a chaise facing her mother's. "What is it you want from me, then?"

Esterházy coughed. "Your Imperial Highness sat across from the Crown Prince at the supper the King hosted for us on the night of our arrival. Is that not so?" The magnate sounded as though he were addressing a truculent child.

Amalia's head jerked up toward him. "What of it? It is hardly a crime."

"Esterházy was merely observing that you were in the best position to observe the Crown Prince's actions that night."

Amalia shrugged. "I suppose so. What am I supposed to have observed? His appetite and how he chose to satisfy it?"

"He partook of the custard, did he not?" Esterházy ventured.

"As did we all," Amalia replied. "Except for Seckendorff. The man ate like a lovelorn maiden in the presence of her beau."

"Is that so?" The Empress gripped her cane. Haydn's wife had been right, then. Seckendorff had refused the custard.

"What does it matter, who ate what?" The Archduchess's gaze shifted from her mother toward Esterházy.

A moment's silence followed. Then the Archduchess's eyes returned toward her mother. Her lips widened into a sly smile.

Oh, I see! Is that how the Grand Master's diamond was ferreted out of the Marble Hall that night?"

The Empress stiffened. She had never revealed the details of the theft to Amalia. The theft itself had ostensibly taken place the next morning, and then the diamond fortuitously found. That was all anyone knew, beyond herself and Frederick and the small circle of people involved in clearing her ambassador's name.

An image from long ago of Amalia dressed as Apollo surfaced in her mind, fusing with the little Haydn had gleaned from Eichel's dying lips.

The Empress pointed her cane urgently at the closet. Before she could say anything, Haydn and his brother burst through the doorway.

"Your Majesty," the Kapellmeister huffed. "The Princess Auersperg's accomplice—"

"Is in this very room," the Empress said. She jabbed her cane in the direction of the closet again. "Search it!" she commanded, her voice hoarse. "You will find your evidence within, I'll wager."

In an untidy heap upon the closet floor, lay the garments the Kapellmeister had expected to find. The Prussian blue coat and breeches that formed the livery of the palace footmen, a shirt of white linen, wool underdrawers, a pair of white hose. And most telling of all, linen bandages.

"To flatten Her Imperial Highness's bosom," Haydn explained to his brother as he swept the heap off the floor. They returned to the Archduchess's bedchamber.

"I never thought to see any child of mine become a murderess." The Empress gripped the top of her cane with both hands, her face white with fury. "You have the blood of not one man but two on your hands. What were you thinking?"

The Archduchess glared back at mother from under lowered brows. "I had nothing to do with Seckendorff's murder."

The Empress lifted her cane and stamped it down upon the floor.

"No," Haydn quickly agreed before the Empress could rage on at her daughter. "Your Imperial Highness was merely tasked with luring His Lordship to the church, is that not so?"

"The blood smears on Eichel's cloak tell the entire tale," Johann explained to the Empress and His Serene Highness. "Whoever wore it used the cloak to cover His Lordship once he had been killed."

"He was not supposed to be killed," the Archduchess said. "Merely sufficiently embarrassed that Mother would be compelled to recall him from his post." She stared defiantly at her mother. "No one but you wanted Seckendorff appointed imperial ambassador to Prussia."

She took a deep breath. "And as for Eichel, the traitor got what he deserved."

"In your estimation, any enemy of Prussia is a traitor, I suppose." The Empress's voice was icy.

The Archduchess leaned forward, her face contorted into a sneer. "No, Mother. I regard any enemy of yours as my friend. I have done so since the moment I realized my happiness counted for nothing in your ambitions."

"That is not true." The Empress's bosom heaved, her breath coming in short gasps.

"Quick, open the windows, Haydn!" His Serene Highness commanded.

"Her Majesty has never had anything but your best interests at heart, Your Imperial Highness," he went on as Haydn unlatched the windows and thrust the sashes open.

The Archduchess ignored the magnate.

"At whose command did Your Imperial Highness seek His Lordship out?" Johann asked after a moment's silence had ensued. "The Crown Prince, I suppose," he continued, answering his own question since the Archduchess remained silent.

"It was the King," the Archduchess said. Her mouth twitched. "He knew—who knows how—that Seckendorff wished to meet with Mother. To convey some news of importance, apparently." The smile grew wider. "Whatever it is, it has gone with him to the grave now."

A flicker of a notion stirred in Haydn's mind. It was gone before he could capture it. But they had discovered the grille meant to decipher a letter His Lordship had never been able to send. The letter itself might not be so very elusive after all.

"But I never thought"—the Archduchess leaned back in her chaise and smiled at the Empress, who averted her eyes—"that you would so easily believe your darling Mimi had betrayed you. I was quite pre-pared to badger you into letting me accompany you here, Mother. But you made the offer yourself."

"It was Your Imperial Highness that we saw meeting with Princess Auersperg," Haydn said, not particularly surprised that was the case.

They had caught a glimpse of a skirt and a gloved hand, no more. On the basis of that and the crest on the carriage, His Serene Highness had been convinced it was the Archduchess Maria Christina. An erroneous conclusion, obviously.

"I knew Esterházy would carry the news to Mother like the good tat-tle-tale that he is."

"But how could Your Imperial Highness have known the Prince would see you?" Johann asked, surprised.

The Archduchess gave His Serene Highness a sidelong glance from under her long lashes. "The next time you choose to spy on the Prus-sian ambassador, it would be as well to take a *fiaker* instead of your own distinctive carriage, my dear Esterházy. You were nothing if not predictable."

Haydn glanced up in time to see a carmine flush suffuse the Prince's fleshy cheeks.

The Archduchess was right. In one of Vienna's numerous hackney cabs—*fiakers*—His Serene Highness's presence outside Count Botta's apartment would have remained undetected.

"You may not have stabbed Seckendorff yourself," the Empress broke the silence that had fallen upon them, "but you have his blood upon your hands, nevertheless. That you feel no remorse for it, troubles me."

Her Majesty propelled herself to her feet.

"You will sign a confession of your involvement and all you know of this matter and hand it to Esterházy here."

The Archduchess began to protest, but the Empress held up her cane.

"You will sign a confession or you will be charged as a criminal."

"We will use it if need be," Her Majesty said in a low voice to Haydn once they had retreated from the Archduchess's bedchamber, "to com-pel Frederick to withdraw his demands. It matters not whether any more evidence is found. The replica of the blue diamond that must exist, the details of its manufacture.

"These are not so important"—Her Majesty swiveled around on her cane to regard Haydn closely—"as the letter Seckendorff tried to have sent to me. If you can find it, Poland may still be saved."

———◆———

Her Highness, Princess Auersperg, was being conveyed—her hands and feet still bound—to the Karmalitenkloster in Döbling at the Empress's orders. Four guards from Her Majesty's retinue were to accompany the carriage on horseback to the convent three miles northwest of Vienna.

"A short period of confinement will, I hope, serve to clip her wings," the Empress had confided, as she issued her orders to the Kapellmeister.

Haydn and Johann had seen the party off themselves. And now as the Kapellmeister climbed the stairs to his bedchamber, the distant rumble of departing wheels and the thundering of horses' hooves still rang in his ears.

Stifling a yawn, he paused outside his chamber door and twisted the doorknob. A single candle burnt low in a leaf-shaped silver holder on the dresser. In the dim light, he made out Maria Anna's form—a small, huddled mound under the coverlets.

Noiselessly, he hung up his coat and wig and crept softly toward the bed, but he had barely reached it when Maria Anna sat up.

"Is that you, husband?"

Haydn sighed, cursing the sharpness of his wife's ears. Maria Anna slept so lightly, the least sound could awaken her.

"I did not mean to wake you," he apologized, quickly undressing.

"It is quite all right," she said. "I did not think you meant to return home tonight. Where have you been?"

The Kapellmeister chose not to take umbrage at the question. His wife had most likely not intended to insinuate that he habitually whiled away his nights in a tavern or in the company of loose women.

"At the palace," he said, recounting the events of the past hours.

For some time after he had finished, Maria Anna was quiet. Only the steady ticking of the clock filled the room. When she finally spoke, her words took Haydn by surprise.

"It must take great strength to withstand such animosity from one's own child. I could never bear it." Her voice choked.

Haydn glanced away, unable to agree. An ungrateful child, in his estimation, was better than no child at all. But perhaps his wife was right. The pain of such a rejection, no doubt, far surpassed the pain of being childless.

Not that he would ever know.

"What of the letter His Lordship is supposed to have written?" His wife's voice recalled his straying thoughts.

"I cannot think where His Lordship can have concealed it," Haydn said, glad to direct his mind elsewhere. "The grille that deciphers the note lay beneath the vignette Frau Bach gave you. It was most fortuitous that Rosalie and Greta preserved it."

"Frau Bach was most insistent that you have the frame changed. Such a to-do, I thought, and over nothing, it seemed." Maria Anna drew her legs up and clasped her arms around her knees.

Haydn frowned as a thought occurred to him. "You don't suppose—" He paused. "The frame was originally fashioned for His Lordship."

"That it found its way into the Bachs' hands must mean something," his wife said. "Why else would Frau Bach make such a pother about it being damaged? And she never sought to replace it herself, although I imagine her son has frames aplenty."

Maria Anna turned to him. "And didn't Herr Bach remind you about the frame as well?"

Haydn nodded. "So, he did."

The imperial ambassador had gathered a diverse ring of agents around himself. Had Herr Bach been one of His Lordship's instruments as well? The harpsichordist's name had, after all, been recorded in the black notebook Haydn had retrieved from His Lordship's valet.

"Is it true His Majesty King Frederick reads every letter sent out of Prussia?" Maria Anna wanted to know.

"I imagine they all do," Haydn said. How else was any intelligence to be obtained? Not that he thought his wife needed to concern herself with that. The Kapellmeister doubted anyone was interested in parsing the details, however involved, of a woman's domestic affairs.

He opened his mouth to say as much but was cut off by his wife.

"Well, then," Maria Anna proclaimed firmly, "it seems only likely that His Lordship must have devised some circuitous means of sending his despatches to prevent them falling into the wrong hands."

"His Lordship *was* wont to visit the Katholische Kirche St. Anna after Eichel made his visits," Haydn recalled. It was a detail that should have meant something, but his weary brain was unable to make the connection.

"Then the letter must be at the church."

Maria Anna's quietly uttered words sounded like a foghorn in Haydn's head. The noisy jangle of thoughts slowly dispersed.

The Kapellmeister's lips broke into a broad smile. "Not anymore. I believe Herr Bach contrived to find a way to deliver it into my hands."

He turned to face Maria Anna. "He sent us off to the church. To tune the organ, he said, although it seemed not to be very badly in need of it. Our payment—which the priest insisted upon giving us—was a vignette painted by Bastian."

"Set within a damaged frame?" Maria Anna asked.

"No. But I'll wager His Lordship's letter is within it."

"How did you think to look for it there, brother?"

Johann looked on as Haydn withdrew three closely written sheets from behind the framed vignette gifted to them by the pastor of the Katholische Kirche St. Anna.

"It was Maria Anna who made me think of it." Haydn recounted his conversation with her from the previous night. "She felt sure the presence of the mask within the vignette Frau Bach had given her could not have been a coincidence. It seems she was right."

The Kapellmeister paused as he carefully unfolded the sheets and examined the pages. The writing—sharp, angular strokes forming each letter—was clearly that of the imperial ambassador's. There was no mistaking it.

Johann nodded. "And if one vignette contained the mask, why should not the other conceal the letter itself?"

Haydn made a murmur of assent, his eyes drifting toward the top of the page.

The date, October 11, 1768, matched the numbers on the Cardan grille the maids had discovered. The contents seemed innocuous enough, referring only to what was commonly known about the Polish situation —the confederation at Bar, the civil unrest that continued, and Russia's aggression.

The grille would no doubt reveal the secret message concealed within.

The morning sun bathed the parlor in a pleasant glow and enveloped the Kapellmeister in a satisfying warmth. He refolded the pages and tucked the letter into the frame that had concealed it. Its discovery was no small accomplishment. Her Majesty would be pleased, he was sure of it.

He was about to suggest that they set out for the palace when Boris appeared at the parlor door.

"Herr Bach is here to see you, *meine Herren*."

The harpsichordist's short, portly form could be seen beyond the valet's tall, muscular frame.

Chapter Thirty-Three

"Herr Hadyn! Master Johann!" Herr Bach pushed past Boris into the parlor, bearing a thick, leatherbound volume in his hands. Smiling broadly, he thrust the tome into Haydn's astounded arms.

"A copy of my father's *Musikalisches Opfer*," the harpsichordist said. "You have heard of it, I am sure."

"It was written for your master, was it not?" Haydn said. Why had Herr Bach thought to bring him the entire score? Not that he had no interest in perusing it. But surely this was not the time for such matters?

"A series of contrapuntal variations upon the very theme His Majesty was kind enough to furnish my father. No Prussian orchestra has ever played it. But perhaps your musicians might wish to perform it."

The harpsichordist sank into a chaise, uninvited.

Haydn and Johann remained standing, but Herr Bach seemed not to notice.

"The work may be difficult. But I have provided meticulous notes on its performance. If you would do me the goodness to turn to the relevant pages, Herr Haydn. They are inserted after the trio sonata."

The Kapellmeister looked on astonished as the harpsichordist continued: "I will endeavor to explain any detail that is not sufficiently clear."

"Could we not discuss this at another time—?" Johann began only to be interrupted.

"There is no time like the present, Master Johann. And I think you will agree that the work is sufficiently important to merit your entire attention."

What was the harpsichordist on about? With a frown, Haydn leafed past the two ricercars, the ten canons, and the four movements of the trio sonata that formed the older Bach's *Musical Offering*.

What he saw nearly made him shut the leather covers of the book.

"But this is. . ." the Kapellmeister's voice faded to a whisper.

"The hand of His Majesty's chamberlain, Alfons von Katte. I trust it is legible."

"It could not be clearer." Haydn cast another surreptitious glance at the pages attached to the musical score. Judging by the neatly recorded entries and the accounting of thalers and pfennigs, these were pages torn from a ledger book.

The royal ledger book. The very evidence the Empress had hoped to obtain to clear the imperial ambassador's name.

How had the harpsichordist obtained these sheets? Haydn handed the volume to Johann.

Herr Bach shifted his bulk in his chaise. "A fine fellow, Alfons von Katte. Plays the flute quite well. It would not be too much of an exaggeration to say he is the King's right-hand man."

Alfons. Haydn repeated the name to himself. *Fonso?*

"He appears to be in charge of recording the King's personal finances," Johann commented, turning the pages.

"Among other things." The harpsichordist steepled his fingers together and gazed around the parlor. "It was Herr Eichel who suggested the *Musikalische Opfer* might be of interest to you. His death is a great loss. I did not think. . ." He swallowed hard.

"No," Haydn agreed. No one had thought Eichel might be a victim of murder. Although the principal court secretary must have had some inkling of it himself. Why else had he entrusted these documents to Herr Bach?

"I cannot recall ever having seen him, this Alfons von Katte," Haydn went on. "Was he at the supper His Majesty was gracious enough to host for us the night of our arrival."

"Not at the table, no." Herr Bach shook his head. "But our Fonso served as a footman that night. It was he who brought in the custard."

And took away the bowls, too, no doubt, Haydn thought. *With the Grand Master's diamond hidden within the Crown Prince's custard dish.*

The entire matter was becoming clear to him. Small wonder the King had surmised at once that it was custard that covered the diamond. Custard that the imperial ambassador had not touched. Custard that Fonso had deliberately omitted to wipe from the diamond when he had planted it in His Lordship's pockets.

And if Fonso dressed as a footman whenever he pleased, it must have been he who had served Eichel the poisoned coffee. And what of Crown Prince Frederick William? To what extent had His Royal Highness been involved in the affair?

"The Crown Prince, Herr Bach?" he heard Johann ask. "What think you of him?"

The harpsichordist shrugged. "He is a harmless enough fellow. Much given to drinking, carousing, and philandering. His Majesty, as you may have observed, never troubles to hide the contempt with which he regards him. Nor allows him an opinion in matters of state."

Then the Crown Prince's drunkenness had only played into the King's hands, Haydn mused. *Either that or the Crown Prince had sought to impress his uncle with the small role he had played in the affair.*

The men sat quietly in the room: Johann perusing the leather book, Herr Bach surveying the figure of a portly cherub with enormous eyes and an even bigger horn.

"Is there anything else of interest?" Haydn enquired after a few moments. He inclined his head toward the book.

"His Majesty appears to have held his chamberlain in high esteem," Johann said. "The man received an additional five thousand thalers in the middle of October."

"Salaries are paid from the palace account, not His Majesty's personal funds," Herr Bach explained.

"The additional amount *was* from the palace account," Johann confirmed. "But"—he raised his eyes—"its expenditure only a week later is recorded under His Majesty's personal expenses. *Five thousand thalers to Herr Boehmer, jeweler, paid by Herr Alfons von Katte.*"

"Curious," Haydn said. "Most curious."

"That is not all. The jeweler's receipt made out to von Katte has the words *vor der König* inscribed beside his name. Albeit in a different hand."

"*On behalf of the King*," Haydn repeated the words Johann had read. Nothing could be clearer. The payment had been made at His Majesty's orders. "It is the chamberlain's hand, I suppose."

"No!" Herr Bach leaned over to peer at the page. "It is Herr Eichel's hand. Under the chamberlain's orders, no doubt. Our Fonso is no fool. His Majesty has dismissed many a *friend* for financial irregularities."

"*Friend*?" Why should the King regard a mere chamberlain as a friend?

"The rumors about His Majesty are quite true, Herr Haydn. Especially when a man quite as good-looking as the chamberlain is concerned. He seemed to be falling out of favor in the days following His Lordship's arrival."

The harpsichordist smiled. "Fonso's jealousy at the time was plain to see. Apparently, he was on the verge of requesting his pension when his fortunes just as abruptly reversed."

About the time the imperial ambassador's activities had been discovered, Haydn had no doubt. A betrayal His Majesty must have taken to heart.

Small wonder, the imperial ambassador had been so viciously stabbed. Fonso's fury at being surpassed by a foreigner must have been further inflamed by his master's outrage at being made the ambassador's gull.

"Jealousy is a powerful force," Johann said softly.

"It is, indeed." Herr Bach rose to his feet. "The chamberlain owns a mansion on Pflugstrasse. Although most of his nights are spent in a room adjoining the King's own."

"If Alfons von Katte ordered a replica of the Grand Master's diamond, then the false gem must be at his house," Johann said after the harpsichordist had departed.

"Or in his room at the palace," Haydn replied. "But we can hardly break into his residence or into his bedchamber."

"What are we to do, then?"

Haydn sighed. There was not much that could be done. Other than to inform the Empress of their discoveries. He withdrew his silver timepiece from his coat pocket and glanced at it.

"We had best leave for the palace," he began to say when another knock on the door interrupted him.

The imperial ambassador's housekeeper—Frau Göss, if he remembered her name aright—entered the room with a pale, red-nosed woman with a cloth wrapped like a turban around her head.

"It is the washerwoman," the housekeeper announced.

For several minutes, Haydn could do no more than stare at the woman the housekeeper had brought in. Her faded blue skirt was hitched up, revealing her grubby stockings. An apron covered most of her brown bodice and a washcloth was tucked into her waistband. The top of a cloth-wrapped bundle was visible above the rim of the wicker basket strapped to her back.

His gaze reverted back to Frau Göss. "I know not whether we are in need of one," he said. "My wife may, perhaps. . ." His voice faded. Had Maria Anna called for a washerwoman? And expected him to deal with her?

He glanced at his brother, who shrugged his shoulders, equally perplexed.

"It is about Herr Eichel, the principal court secretary," Frau Göss explained. "Martha heard the news this morning, and. . ." She turned toward the washerwoman. "You had better explain it yourself. Herr Haydn has some experience in such matters."

The washerwoman wrung her hands and then plucked at her skirt. "Herr Eichel brought me a cloak to wash yesterday, *meine Herren*. It was covered in blood. It was not that which bothered me. Bloodied garments are easy enough to clean if you know what you're doing. But his manner—it was so agitated."

"I suppose it would have been," Haydn murmured. The principal court secretary must have gone to see his washerwoman shortly after their encounter with him at the church.

"He said if anything were to happen to him, I should know that he had been killed. And I should inform the authorities. But I know not how to do it?" The woman gazed haplessly at Frau Göss.

"Martha doesn't think the Amtsrichter will listen to a mere washerwoman. And I can't say I blame her. Who would believe that a man like Herr Eichel had chosen to confide his fears in his washerwoman?"

"The Amtsrichter will most likely think I killed the poor man myself. And as for the cloak, Herr Eichel warned me not to speak of it."

"Yes." Haydn stroked his chin, the vaguest of notions formulating in his mind. "Yes, I see the quandary this puts you in."

"Then you will approach the Amtsrichter?" Frau Göss asked eagerly. The notion began to clarify.

"That might be the best way," the Kapellmeister agreed. "And, Johann"—he turned to his younger brother—"Would you let Her Majesty know I have found a way to recover the counterfeit stone?

Chapter Thirty-Four

HERR Boehmer's establishment was on Am Schlosse—halfway between the Long Bridge over the River Havel and Alten Markt, where the Town Hall was situated. Although it was a few minutes out of his way, Haydn, nevertheless, decided to stop by the jeweler's first.

Herr Boehmer—a smiling, bald man with a tuft of white hair encircling the back of his skull, cousin to the Viennese Boehmer as well as the French Boehmer—recalled the commission from the King's chamberlain all too well.

"Yes, it was Herr von Katte who brought the order. An exact replica of the seven-sided blue diamond belonging to the Grand Master of France. It must have been on behalf of His Majesty, for the chamberlain used the royal seal to authorize it."

"A diamond such as that would cost far more than five thousand thalers, I imagine," Haydn said, naming the figure he had seen on the receipt.

"Infinitely more. I myself thought a sapphire or blue topaz, or even an amethyst, cut in a similar pattern would be a more fitting gem for the King. But His Majesty, for all his fondness of fine things, is cautious with his money. And for five thousand thalers. . ." Herr Boehmer spread his hands apart, palms facing up.

"It was fine work, nevertheless," Haydn said. It must have been for its owner not to have detected the deception.

He took his leave shortly after, armed with all the information he needed to persuade the Amtsrichter to his point of view.

"Financial irregularities?"

Seated across from Haydn at the long table in the main room of the town hall, the Amtsrichter laid out the papers the Kapellmeister had brought to his attention and studied them intently.

"That point to a theft being planned," Haydn said. "It is the only interpretation that makes any sense."

He thrust his forefinger at the figures Eichel had underscored on the receipts.

"That the chamberlain included a private purchase on the King's personal account is suspicious enough. But I have just spoken with Herr Boehmer myself, and he confirms the chamberlain used the royal seal to authorize his purchase."

"It was the washerwoman who brought the papers to you?" The rising cadence of the magistrate's voice suggested he had some difficulty swallowing the tale.

"She came to Frau Göss, her friend, who advised her to entrust the packet to my care. Herr Eichel had been in a state of great agitation yesterday, greatly in fear for his life and babbling, or so it seemed to the poor woman, about a theft."

"I see."

The magistrate's tone, bland and uninflected, gave Haydn little indication of how his conjectures were being received. Laying his arms upon the table, the Kapellmeister went on undeterred.

"I myself would have given the story no credence were it not for the fact that Princess Auersperg said much the same thing."

The Kapellmeister saw no reason to mention that the Princess's remarks had been made not to him, but to Rosalie and Greta.

"Indeed." The Amtsrichter's interest appeared to have awakened.

"The death of both the imperial ambassador and Herr Eichel—by the same person, apparently—prompted the Princess to make some discreet enquiries of her own. She was adamant the imperial ambassador had uncovered a plot to purloin the Grand Master's diamond."

Haydn inclined his chin at the papers spread out before the Amtsrichter. "Indeed, His Majesty himself feared such an eventuality, given the Grand Master's careless handling of the diamond. His Highness passed it around the supper table as though it were no more than a trinket."

"It could quite easily have been swapped, I suppose," the Amtsrichter agreed.

"And Herr Eichel appears to have discovered proof of the imperial ambassador's suspicions."

A low rumble emanated from the magistrate's throat as he considered the matter.

"I hear the chamberlain was the King's favorite until. . ." Haydn allowed his voice to trail off.

"Until the imperial ambassador's arrival. That is right," the magistrate said. "To fall out of favor would have been one thing. To be forced to retire in disgrace, thanks to the offices of his rival, quite another.

"And His Lordship's suspicions coupled with the evidence Herr Eichel had uncovered would without a doubt have sufficed to cook the poor chamberlain's goose." The magistrate rubbed his hands together. "Yes. Yes, that is certainly a sufficiently strong motive for murder."

He raised his eyes. "And the replica, you say—"

"Is sure to be at the chamberlain's residence on Pflugstrasse. Herr Eichel would have discovered it, were it in the palace."

The magistrate rose. "It is all we will need to arrest Herr von Katte." He smiled. "Did I not tell you, Herr Haydn, that no woman could have committed those murders? You *will* admit I was right."

Haydn's own smile, as he bowed his head in apparent defeat, was sheepish.

Seated by the mullioned window of the Music Room on a chair upholstered in lime-green, the Empress heard Johann's report in lip-compressed silence. The letter he had given her was tucked within her sleeve. There would be time enough to read it later when her blood was not so close to boiling.

This, then, was the reason for the Prussian monster's invitation to her. To witness her own ambassador murdered. To see his reputation destroyed. And to have the despicable details of his apparent theft confirmed by Haydn, a man she trusted. The Kapellmeister had fortunately seen through the ruse.

But that was beside the point. That the monster had seen fit to humiliate her—and then to have the gall to demand Techsen and Troppau for his silence! The Empress clenched her jaw and ground her cane into the parquet floor.

"His death must be avenged." Whether she had spoken aloud or not, she knew not. Her dead husband seemed to be the only person to have heard.

"How? He is far more wily than you, my dear," her dead Franz whispered into her ear, but she turned resolutely from him. A view of the bare tree limbs outside and a few patches of clear azure sky met her eyes. On the other side of the window, Esterházy gazed mutely at her, waiting for her response.

Dear God, was she ever to be the only man in her retinue? Could no one ever take charge?

"And would you heed their advice, if they did?" her dead Francis asked. As though she had ever ignored good advice. But to capitulate had never been her way.

The door burst open, and the master of Sanssouci strode in garbed in an old woolen military coat of navy blue with a red collar and wide red cuffs and a faded, threadbare gold star upon his breast.

"The time has come Your Majesty." The Prussian King's large, protruding blue eyes gaped coldly at the Empress. "You have good tidings for me, I trust."

To the Empress's jaundiced eye, he resembled nothing more than a monkey, leaning upon his cane, his head thrust forward upon hunched shoulders.

"The minor points we have already agreed upon set in writing," the King said again. As though, even had she taken him seriously, a mere three days would have sufficed to send a letter to Vienna and receive one in return.

The Empress folded her hands in her lap and stared serenely ahead. "I have chosen not to discuss the matter with my son. I see no reason to accede to your demands."

The King seemed taken aback. "Was that wise? I hear the King of France has made no formal offer of marriage to Archduchess Maria Antonia. I doubt the unfortunate incident witnessed here would induce His Majesty to make good on any feeble promises he may have made."

"What unfortunate incident?" The Empress allowed her eyes to rest upon the King's grotesque features. "If you refer to the supposed theft of the Grand Master's diamond, you must know it never took place. The Grand Master himself has denied it."

It was the weakest card she had to play, but until Haydn arrived with the palace receipts he had obtained, it was all she had. *Other than her daughter's confession.* And she had no intention of using that, if she could help it. Were that made public, not even the Duke of Parma would wish to marry Amalia.

"I must also," she went on before her opponent could respond, "offer my condolences on the death of your principal court secretary, Anton Eichel. A good man. Employed by your father, Frederick William, I believe."

"Eichel was unfortunate enough to meet his demise, it is true."

"We have both lost good, loyal men. Count Seckendorff and Anton Eichel. Killed by the same person, I hear. Who could have wanted them both dead?" The Empress's voice hardened. "The monster must be found. And punished. That must be our foremost goal."

―――⋙●⋘―――

The King smiled. "The magistrate will leave no stone unturned as far as that is concerned. I can assure you of that. But"—he approached her chair—"I am not sure we should be so willing to blithely ignore all the facts."

The man who had ever been her nemesis tapped his cane on the floor, his smile broadening. "I have only to reveal to the Grand Master where his diamond was actually found to stir up quite the hornet's nest."

The Empress's gaze flashed toward Johann. Where was his brother with the evidence she needed?

"I believe we have some revelations of our own that the Grand Master is sure to find most interesting." It was a discreet blow, and she was just debating whether to put more weight behind it when a commotion beyond the door attracted their attention.

—————

"Your Majesties!" The Amtsrichter of Potsdam pushed past a footman to enter the Music Room. He graciously bowed in the direction of the Empress and then turned toward the King. "I regret to inform Your Majesty I have had to arrest the royal chamberlain, Alfons von Katte."

"Arrest the royal chamberlain?" The King thundered as the Empress leaned forward. "On what grounds, may I ask, Herr Amtsrichter?"

"On the charge of murder." It was Haydn who answered the question. The Kapellmeister stepped into the room as he resumed his explanation. "The chamberlain had boldly planned to carry off the Grand Master's diamond. Discovered by Count Seckendorff, Herr von Katte first killed His Lordship and then proceeded to murder Herr Eichel, who had also found damning evidence against the chamberlain."

"The jeweler Boehmer has confirmed that the chamberlain used the royal seal to authorize a replica of the diamond," the Amtsrichter added.

He held up a glittering, seven-sided, blue crystal. To the naked eye, it was no different from the diamond the Grand Master had exhibited at the supper table.

"My men found it in Herr von Katte's residence."

The Amtsrichter withdrew a sheaf of receipts from within his coat. "Worse still, it would appear, Herr von Katte attempted to implicate Your Majesty in the fabrication of the paste copy." He handed the papers to the King.

"His intent was quite clear, Your Majesty."

The King cast a cold eye over the papers, while the Amtsrichter looked on eagerly. "I must commend you on a job well done, Herr Amtsrichter." But the King's voice lacked any enthusiasm.

"I could not in truth have done it without Herr Haydn's help. His assistance has proved most invaluable."

"Indeed." The sour look on the King's face was one the Empress would never forget. Her mouth twitched. She allowed herself a smile.

Chapter Thirty-Five

THE gold the Kapellmeister had received from the King weighed heavily in his pocket. It felt like a bribe.

"I feel I have merely enabled the true perpetrator to evade justice," he whispered to his brother. "Alfons von Katte was but an instrument."

Johann cast an oblique glance at him as they followed the Empress and the Prince to the privacy of Her Majesty's room.

"You could have done no more than you have, brother. The receipts Herr Eichel unearthed told the tale to any who cared to hear. But we were hardly likely to gain a confession from the one man responsible."

"No, I suppose not," Haydn said. "But it was the sequence of events I concocted that allowed the truth to be so easily circumvented."

"Better to have some justice than to have no justice at all," his brother replied. "The royal chamberlain did stab both men. He was not entirely without culpability."

He closed the door behind them as they passed beyond it into Her Majesty's room.

———◆———

"I am glad this matter has been brought to a close."

The Empress turned to face Esterházy and his musicians.

"Not that I can be entirely happy about the royal chamberlain being made a scapegoat for his master's misdeeds. Although von Katte was hardly an innocent man."

Esterházy brought her a chair and she sank gratefully into it. With her cane, she reached toward the window and thrust the sash open. A blast of cold air rushed in. Her Majesty inhaled deeply and turned toward Haydn.

"But were it not for your efforts, I would not have been able to take a stand on Poland."

She would never consent to its partition, the Empress had informed the Prussian monster before she took her leave of him.

It was the least she could do, having failed to prevent the Polish crown from being snatched out of the hands of its rightful heirs, Augustus of Saxony's son Frederick Christian and his grandson Frederick Augustus. A failure that was as sackcloth to her skin.

Thanks to Russia's meddling, the Polish *szlachta* had instead elected Stanislaw Poniatowski. A man widely regarded as Russia's puppet, the former lover of the Empress of Russia.

"I do not control Russia," the Prussian King had snapped back. "The Tsarina leaves us no choice, as you well know."

"I feel certain Your Majesty can find a way," the Empress had said before she left the Music Room. "It cannot be in your interests, any more than it is in ours, to have Russia at your doorstep. And France will forever be in your debt."

A veiled threat to reveal Frederick's ploy to steal the Grand Master's diamond.

———

"His Lordship's letter," Haydn ventured, breaking into the Empress's reverie.

"I have yet to read it," Her Majesty replied. She withdrew it from her sleeve, laid it out upon the writing desk nearby, and placed the hourglass-shaped Cardan grille over it.

Several minutes elapsed. The Empress finished her perusal of the letter, leaned back in her chair, and gazed out the window.

"What does it say?" His Serene Highness finally asked.

The Empress drummed her fingers on the writing desk. "It is worse than I thought, Esterházy. Much worse. The incident at Bar. . . It was incited."

Haydn frowned. He had heard of Bar. It was a town in Southern Poland. The Catholic gentry had not long ago formed a confederation there to protest the Russian meddling in Polish affairs.

The Russians had not only forced the diet—under threat of arm— to agree to confer equal rights to Orthodox and Lutheran dissidents, but had gone so far as to arrest two elderly Bishops who had voiced a protest. King Stanislaw had succumbed quietly to these indignities.

"Incited?" Johann asked, with a quick glance at His Serene Highness, but the Prince appeared just as bewildered. "What does Your Majesty mean?" the magnate asked.

The Empress turned slowly around. "It was Frederick who insisted Russia force the issue of dissidents' rights, Esterházy. The monster was well aware of the consequences. That the Catholic *szlachta* would form a confederation."

"Any fool might have foreseen that, but—"

"The treaty, Esterházy. The treaty between Russia and Prussia allows for—*justifies*, to be precise—the use of military intervention should the Polish subjects form a confederation against Poniatowski."

"And the confederation at Bar is by its very nature against the Polish King." The Prince's lips tightened. "Although they only protest the King's inaction against a foreign threat."

Haydn listened attentively. Clearly, the Prussian King had done more than just take advantage of an unfortunate situation. He had catapulted it. But how could His Majesty have known he would profit from his actions?

"To what end?" he asked as the question formed in his mind, only to receive an uncomprehending stare from both the Empress and the Prince.

"Why should His Majesty wish to instigate Russia to invade Poland?" Johann clarified the Kapellmeister's question. "Surely he had as much to lose by it as anyone else?"

The Empress sighed. "The King, I fear, is quite the puppet-master. He knew Austria would have no choice but to intervene should Russia move into Poland. Frederick has quite deftly been playing our two countries against each other.

"Catherine has agreed to partition, thinking Austria will retaliate against her domination of Poland. But from the moment Stanislaw was elected, we were well aware Poland was to be a puppet republic.

"And Austria has been told that the only way to contain Russia is to partially slake her hunger for greater power by ceding a portion of Poland to her, while dividing the rest between Prussia and Austria."

"That would give Prussia control of West Prussia," the Prince explained.

"As well as the Vistula and the trade along it," the Empress added. "Poland will be devastated. Prussia will demand dues from anyone who seeks to move goods along the river. It is Poland's largest. There is no way to avoid that stretch of the Vistula and no way around it to the Baltic Sea."

"Can this intelligence not be. . ." Haydn hesitated, casting around for an appropriate expression. *"Released?"* he finally said. Surely if the Prussian King's hand in the civil unrest in Poland were divulged—however inadvertently—the rest of Europe would find itself compelled to take a stand.

But the Empress shook her head.

"Not without exposing Seckendorff's role in gathering it," Her Majesty said. "That would greatly hinder the freedom of future imperial ambassadors."

Her mouth puckered as she pondered the situation, then widened into a smile.

"But the information does give the Emperor a reason to reach out to Russia—if he will take it—and suggest to Catherine that controlling the entirety of Poland from without may be more profitable than owning a small parcel of its land."

She grasped her cane and stood up. "Who knows Poland may yet be saved."

The End

Author's Note: Freedom's Death Knell

POLAND, unfortunately, was never saved. On August 5, 1772—less than four years after the events of this story—Empress Maria Theresa reluctantly agreed to the first partition of Poland.

All of Europe was shocked. If a country was at war with its neighbors, and unfortunate enough to lose, territories might have to be ceded. It was in this way that Empress Maria Theresa had lost the rich Silesian territories to Prussia during the War of Austrian Succession.

But Poland had not been at war with either Russia or Prussia, the two kingdoms that had initially decided its fate before compelling Empress Maria Theresa to their view.

In order to quell the swelling tide of criticism, Catherine the Great and Frederick the Great painted an unflattering portrait of the Polish Commonwealth as undeveloped and uncivilized, its people backward to the point of being barbaric.

Poland, they argued, was in need of Enlightenment. And theirs was the hand to provide it.

Nothing, of course, could have been further from the truth. In reading Adam Zamoyski's excellent history of Poland, I have been struck by how closely the Polish constitution with its system of checks resembled the system of governance in the United States of America.

How, then, could a country so devoted to the concept of individual freedom have come to such a pass?

Since the twelfth century, Poland had elected its monarch. By the fifteenth century, its people had come to believe that the King ruled the country on behalf of and with the consent of his subjects. He did not have a Divine right to rule. Nor was his power arbitrary.

The King, however, did not have to be a Polish nobleman. He could be a foreigner. So, it was that Augustus the Strong of Saxony became King of Poland in 1697. Now, Augustus did not actually win the vote. It was Francois Louis de Bourbon, Prince of Condé, who won the election. But by the time the Prince arrived in Poland, his rival had already had himself crowned king.

If there was one thing the Poles believed in, it was that no one person had the right to tell others how to lead their lives. This translated into a strong antipathy toward government in all its forms. "All government," the Poles felt, according to Adam Zamoyski, "is undesirable, and strong government is strongly undesirable."

If the Poles had been against concentrating power in the hands of the King when he was elected from among the Polish nobles, one can imagine how greatly they would have objected to strengthening the hand of a foreign king who, in effect, could take over their country completely.

The resistance to fortifying the King's hand had the unfortunate effect of boosting the power of the wealthy magnates. Towns with their commercial interests were underrepresented in the *Sejm*—an assembly of Polish gentry called the *szlachta*—and peasants' rights were not represented at all.

But there was one other constitutional liberty that served to cause havoc in the Polish system. This was the *liberium veto*, or the ability of a single member of the *szlachta* to veto any legislation agreed upon by the majority.

The Poles quite rightly believed that subjecting a minority of people to the whims of the majority went against the principle of individual liberty. In practice, the *liberium veto* merely forced the majority to attend to dissenting views when considering any kind of legislation. A member who was being unnecessarily stubborn could safely be ignored.

But in theory, any individual *szlachta* had the power to derail meaningful legislation. And by the eighteenth century, foreign countries were bribing minor *szlachta* to do just this. Polish attempts to abolish the veto were, therefore, viewed with a jaundiced eye by its neighbors.

Poland's strength was further undermined by its *Sejm's* reluctance to maintain a standing army. The *szlachta* were reluctant to take on the considerable expense entailed. They also feared a standing army might be used by the King against his subjects.

Thus, when Russia sent in troops to Poland to force the *Sejm* to vote one way or the other, there were no Polish troops to defend the Commonwealth. Now, Russia's influence over Poland went back to the time of Augustus the Strong. Shortly after being elected King, Augustus the Strong foolishly agreed to join Tsar Peter I of Russia in waging war against the very young Charles XII of Sweden.

The young Swedish King proved far more indomitable than either Tsar Peter—later Peter the Great—or Augustus the Strong had given him credit for. Although Tsar Peter eventually managed to rout him, the attempt had left Augustus the Strong and Poland in a very weak position. At one time, Charles XII had even threatened to invade Poland unless its people promised to dethrone Augustus the Strong.

Augustus thus found himself beholden to the Tsar for keeping his throne. Later, when the Polish *Sejm* refused to budge on certain reforms he proposed, he was forced to accept the Tsar's help in negotiating a compromise.

The resulting Treaty of Warsaw greatly curtailed both Augustus's power and the size of the Polish army. A larger army was deemed unnecessary since Russia would undertake to protect its neighbor. Russia even suggested leaving some of its troops within the Commonwealth.

In 1762, even before Augustus the Strong's successor, Augustus III, was on his deathbed, Catherine the Great—a German princess from an obscure principality who unexpectedly propelled herself to the position of Tsarina of Russia—resolved to put her former lover, Stanislaw Poniatowski, on the Polish throne.

Poniatowski was a member of the wealthy Czartoryski family, who were greatly interested in constitutional reform and restoring Poland to her former greatness. Although he was not their first choice, having Poniatowski crowned King was but a minor hiccup in their plans. Poniatowski was not against any of the reforms they had in mind.

But both Catherine the Great and Frederick the Great—whose intervention years ago had resulted in the German princess marrying the nephew of Tsarina Elizabeth, Peter the Great's daughter—were adamantly against any move to strengthen Poland.

Who first proposed the idea of partition is not known. But Prussia gained the most valuable Polish lands in the first partition, including the tract of land that separated East from West Prussia and control over Poland's lifeline, the Vistula.

Two more partitions were to follow. In each case, Polish territories were swallowed by the three countries involved: Russia, Prussia, and Austria.

But there was worse. Russian troops forced Poles to convert to the Orthodox church, threatening to maim or kill children if their parents tried to resist. Meanwhile, stalwart, loyal Poles valiantly tried to save their country and ensure its survival.

The history of Poland and its struggles are quite remarkable. In addition to Adam Zamoyski's *Poland: A History*, I have relied upon Robert K. Massie's *Catherine the Great* and Tim Blanning's *Frederick the Great: King of Prussia* to understand the motivations of each party involved. Edward Crankshaw's biography of Maria Theresa helped to flesh out the Austrian perspective.

Stefan Zweig's *Marie Antoinette*, Alexander J. Mahan's *Maria Theresa*, and Justin C. Vovk's *In Destiny's Hands* provided insights into the Empress's relations with her children. Vovk's book, in particular, helped to flesh out Maria Amalia Duchess of Parma's character. My portrayal of her in this novel is based on accounts of her doings after her marriage to Ferdinand, Duke of Parma.

Finally, John Nagy's *Invisible Ink: Spycraft of the American Revolution* provided excellent information on the topics of cryptography and steganography.

Nagy describes Sir Henry Clinton's use of masks—Cardan grilles—during the American Revolutionary War. Clinton was Commander of the British armed forces in America. His letter to John Burgoyne and the hourglass-shaped mask he used to conceal a message within it are in the William L. Clements Library at the University of Michigan.

Readers wishing to know more about the political and social conditions prevalent in Haydn's Europe are directed to the Haydn Mystery web site and blog: **ntustin.com/blog**.

ABOUT THE AUTHOR

A former journalist, Nupur Tustin relies upon a Ph.D. in Communication and an M.A. in English to orchestrate fictional mayhem. The Haydn mysteries are a result of her life-long passion for classical music and its history. Childhood piano lessons and a 1903 Weber Upright share equal blame for her original compositions, available on ntustin.musicaneo.com.

Her writing includes work for Reuters and CNBC, short stories and freelance articles, and research published in peer-reviewed academic journals. She lives in Southern California with her husband, three rambunctious children, and a pit bull.

For details on the Haydn series and monthly blog posts on the great composer, visit the official Haydn Mystery web site: NTUSTIN.COM.

Get Three FREE Stories at NTUSTIN.COM

Subscribe to the Haydn Blog at ntustin.com/blog

Made in the USA
Columbia, SC
23 March 2020